*"Greiman's writing is warm, witty, and gently wise."*

***New York Times*** bestselling author
Betina Krahn

Proud and independent, Savaana Hearnes's extraordinary beauty and fiery Gypsy blood have enflamed the passions of many—but she will *never* be indebted to any man. When an unusual offer from a well-dressed noblewoman is too tempting to resist, however, she agrees to impersonate the newly-wed Lady Clarette Tilmont. But when dashing Sean Gallagher comes to call, all Savaana's carefully laid plans are shattered by desire.

The handsome, rugged Irishman is a welcome change from the aging servants who are watching Savaana's every move, and Sean is pleasantly surprised by the palpable heat of her passion—so uncommon for such a highborn lady! But Sean himself is not what he seems. He is guarding a secret as shocking as Savaana's own. And the mission he is sworn to complete will be compromised if he allows himself to be bewitched by a mysterious minx he burns to hold and to have.

## By Lois Greiman

# An Accidental
# Seduction

**AVON**
*An Imprint of HarperCollinsPublishers*

AVON BOOKS
*An Imprint of* HarperCollins*Publishers*
10 East 53rd Street
New York, New York 10022-5299

Copyright © 2010 by Lois Greiman
ISBN 978-0-06-184934-3
**www.avonromance.com**

First Avon Books paperback printing: October 2010

Avon Trademark Reg. U.S. Pat. Off. and in Other Countries, Marca Registrada, Hecho en U.S.A.
HarperCollins® is a registered trademark of HarperCollins Publishers.

Printed in the U.S.A.

10  9  8  7  6  5  4  3  2  1

# An Accidental
# Seduction

# Prologue

**C**arlotta's breath wedged tight in her throat. Desperate, terrified, she arched away from the bastard behind her. His blade felt sharp and cold against the pulsing vein in her neck. His stench filled her nostrils just as fear filled her soul.

She was caught. Helpless. So close to freedom, so close to hope. El Rey was nearby. Still bridled, he was the very embodiment of speed and strength as he stood in the inky blackness beyond the reach of the flickering torches. The darkness called to her, beckoned her with its promise of safety. Of solace. If only she had listened to her instincts, had left while there was still time. But too late now. Ramone Ortiz Delgado had returned just as he'd vowed he would.

"So I've found you." His words were a chuckled hiss against the loose web of her wild hair. He stood behind her, fingers clawing like talons on her bare arm, malice oozing from his detestable being. She could taste his evil, feel his despicable desires. "With no one near to hear you scream."

She closed her eyes. She had played out this nightmare a hundred times, had thought through every move. But all her well-laid plans were dissolving in the cold reality of her terror. Who was she to think she could escape him? She was alone in the world, poor, young, destitute. While Delgado was wealthy, powerful. All the things she was not. All the things she could never hope to be.

Yet she was Romany. That knowledge trickled slowly into her battered psyche.

She was Gypsy. A race as ancient as the sky, as unpredictable as the wind, unbowed by time and travail.

The thoughts sizzled silently through her frozen muscles, firing her memories, straightening her spine. Royal blood raced through her throbbing veins, the fierce pride of her elders blooming like a primrose in her quivering soul. Her people did not accept defeat. Did not lie down for the slaughter like a milk-fed lambkin.

Nay, she would fight till the death, she vowed, and with that influx of courage, she gritted her teeth and slammed her elbow into Delgado's ribs.

He grunted in pain, stumbling backward, and in that instant she lurched away. El Rey bent his great neck toward her, ears flickering. If she could but reach him . . .

In that instant, Delgado's fingers tangled in her hair. She screamed as she was ripped from her feet and spilled to the ground, but for a second she felt his grip loosen. Gathering every ounce of her strength, she curled into a ball, then tumbling full circle, sprang to her feet and leapt away, bright skirts flying, wild heart thundering.

El Rey waited, piebald hide gleaming in the firelight. Three more powerful strides and then she launched. Her hands landed atop his solid croup and she was astride him. But Delgado was as quick as a weasel and just as crafty. He snatched at her leg, trying to pull her down.

"Come, little slut," he snarled, and tore at her. "I'll have you now."

She rasped a denial, but her strength was ebbing, fleeing from her trembling arms. She felt herself slipping toward him and twisted her fingers into the gelding's tousled mane.

Delgado laughed, evil personified. "I'll have you," he snarled. "You and your pretty sister after you."

It was the thought of her family that drove strength back into Carlotta's limbs, that shot fire into her soul. Yanking her foot away, she kicked at his face. He jerked aside. Her bare heel slammed against his shoulder, driving him away. But his grip never faltered. Anger flared in his eyes. Promised retribution twisted his lips. His gritted teeth gleamed in the scattered light.

"For that you will not die quickly," he snarled.

She grappled for a better grip, grabbing for the pommel, and suddenly her fingers met steel. They skimmed the hilt of her dead father's sword. A thousand thoughts hurtled through her mind. Hope slashed through her, swung by desperation, honed by instinct. Yanking the blade from its scabbard, she swept it sideways in one desperate arc.

Delgado's eyes jerked wide. He clutched his throat with splayed fingers, gasping and staggering. His feet faltered. His breath rattled. He dropped to his knees, eyes staring, shocked that he could die. And then he fell, toppling forward into the dirt.

Silence ruled the night for all of three aching seconds.

Carlotta's heart raced like a galloping stallion in her chest.

And the crowd roared.

Savaana Alaina Hearnes glanced up, coming back to herself, out of the trance she created for each performance. Carlotta's indomitable persona was left behind, stowed away to wait in quiet suspension for the next show. As for Savaana, she smiled a little as she raised her left hand in greeting and scanned the audience. Perhaps she, like Carlotta, was searching for someone who had long ago abandoned her, someone with ginger hair and familiar mannerisms, but if that was the case, it was all subconscious now.

The anonymous crowd was spread across the westerly hill like scattered wildflowers, rising to its feet in one great wave of motion, clapping, yelling, tossing posies and love sonnets, some crying as they cheered. These Gajo were not afraid to show their emotion.

Tamas rose to his feet, unscathed, no longer the despicable Delgado, but the talented Rom she had traveled with for most of two years. He flashed his charismatic smile, thanked them in a voice completely unlike the accent he had adopted for their performance, and waved.

The applause grew louder, peppering its approval with the boos and hisses that assured them he had been convincing. He lifted a hand to Savaana, and she climbed to her feet upon El Rey's sturdy back. Her bare toes settled against the well-worn leather of the saddle as she acknowledged the crowd, throwing kisses from her fingertips.

Pandemonium ensued. Whistles and promises and proposals were flung generously into the evening. Daisies bound in scarlet ribbon sailed through the air, striking the big gelding's crest and flanks before falling to his heavy hooves. And now, with an almost inaudible signal from Savaana, El Rey lifted his feathered legs and pranced in a tight circle, heavy neck arched in response to the crowd's applause. His rider, slim as a willow switch and tough as whipcord, swayed with his rhythm, still waving, shifting smoothly on his broad, creased back. The crowd roared. She smiled, threw one last kiss, then directed her mount toward the dark comfort of woods.

Disappearing was the only way she knew to make the crowds disperse. She had learned that while still a girl.

Even then her act had been one of passion and hope. For more than a decade the crowds had cried for her tortured character, applauded her lusty courage, cheered her timeless revenge. Even as a scrawny, nervous child of twelve they had cheered for her.

Now she was neither scrawny nor nervous. Now she was Savaana Alaina, Gypsy maiden, wanderer, Rom.

She was also tired, she thought. Slipping from Rey's powerful back, she tucked the hem of her bright layered skirts into her belt for easier movement through the woods. It was the costume the Gajos expected to see her in, therefore it was the costume she wore. But it was entirely unlike the comfortable, earth-toned gowns she favored for everyday life.

Loosing the side reins that kept El Rey's head in check, she scratched the big gelding's bicolored ears. He canted his head toward her, half closing his eyes to her ministrations before following her to their encampment.

A trio of globed lanterns glowed from the bowing branches of a rowan tree, but no one was about. Everyone in the Dook Natsia clan worked, for they were not called the Magic Gypsies without reason. Indeed, each miraculous performance took a tremendous deal of effort. Every member of the troupe had appointed tasks, but there was little to do now except collect the coins given by the villagers. And that job fell to the smallest children.

Passing an ornately painted caravan that stood

unhooked beside the bustling stream, Savaana tapped its bowed ribs.

"Is all well, Grandfather?" The language she spoke was as ancient as her heritage. English was only used for the entertainment of the Gajos.

"Well enough for a gaffer," said a voice beside her, and she jumped as the old man stepped from the darkness.

Ever surprised that he could still startle her, she shook her head in mock disapproval. "Why are you not abed?" she asked, and loosing Rey's girth, pulled the saddle to the ground.

The old man laughed as he strode toward her, his back still straight, his figure as slim as a boy's. "You did not think a small thing like my impending death would cause me to miss your performance, did you, Printesa Dulce?"

"Don't say such things," she scolded, but he laughed.

"What things should I fear to say, Printesa? That I am about to die?" He had called her sweet princess for as long as she could recall, though in the truest sense of the word she was probably not even Rom. Just a child left in haste with the Gypsy wanderers.

"You're going to be playing your mandolin by the river's edge for another two decades at the least," she said.

"Whether I wish to or not?"

"Yes," she insisted, and he laughed at her resolve.

"I am not afraid of the great beyond. Only the puny

here," Grandfather said, and nodded toward the confines of the nearby caravan.

Despite Savaana's worry, she smiled at him. He had been her light in the darkness for as long as she could recall. The one person upon whom she relied.

Oh, there were others. There must have been, but those memories were little more than faint wisps of her imagination, like a scent of something from a distant place. Indeed, maybe they were not even that. Perhaps what she thought she remembered were only the stories Grandfather had told her. The stories of the red-haired woman who brought her to him. An enchanting creature with a voice like an angel. She'd been draped in diamonds, he said. But when pressed, he admitted that her clothes were ragged and her eyes haunted. Indeed, he had never seen the jewels she was said to wear. That was his brother's part of the tale. His brother whom they had buried more than a decade before. Sometimes the account included another child. A ginger-haired baby she had kept, while leaving Savaana in the care of strangers.

"The nights are becoming chill," she said now, and pushing the painful questions aside, allowed Rey to graze while she tugged the old man's collar around his scrawny neck. "You should be resting."

"I said *impending* death. Which means I am not yet ready to lie down and—" he began, but even as he said the words, he coughed, bending nearly double with the paroxysm.

Worry gnawed at her. She was not the poor ingenue portrayed by Carlotta's brave character, but that was all because of him. His generosity, his caring, his courage. "Get inside now," she said once the coughing had ceased. "I'll fetch your tonic."

His scowl had frightened more than one Gajo who had pursued her too boldly, but to her, he was simply the personification of love, despite his grumpy demeanor. "I need no damned tonic," he snarled.

"The physician said—"

"Physician!" He spat, and with his disgust, pride returned to his craggy features. "Charging you a king's ransom for naught but a thimbleful of spirits. We do not need him. He does not know the way of the Rom. A tincture of wild cherry bark stirred in a warm draught of brandy is what will put me on the mend. Not some bland Gajo syrup."

"The *physician* said," she repeated, emphasizing carefully, "that the tonic will help heal your lungs. And that you must stay warm and sleep inside."

He snorted, and she smiled.

"But I shall bring the tincture as well," she said, and kissed his weathered cheek.

He scowled at her, a bold meld of arrogance and love showing on his toughened features. "It is you who should sleep inside," he muttered. Her patent affection always embarrassed him. It was galling evidence that she had been badly spoiled long before her arrival in their camp, he had told his wife. But Florica had laughed and said he would die without the child's kisses.

Gently frayed memories brought tears to Savaana's eyes, but she did not let them fall. 'Twas the way of the earth to take back its own, and Grandmother had lived a full life.

"Don't be silly," she said, and smiled, though Grandfather's face looked more gaunt than ever. "You know I can't rest without the wind as my song and the stars as my blanket. 'Tis the way of the wild Rom, is it not?"

He made a harrumphing noise. "'Tis the wild Rom that worries me most." He scowled, watching her face. "I do not like the way Tamas looks at you. Like a wolf that has gone too long between meals."

She laughed, trying to make light of it, though in truth she knew enough of the handsome Rom to be cautious of him. "To bed with you now, old man. Let me worry about hungry wolves," she said, and after accompanying him to the caravan, led El Rey to the nearby stream.

But even as she did so, she felt someone watching her. There were eleven members in Dook Natsia. All of them were trusted friends, except Tamas, the man who so cleverly played Delgado to her Carlotta. Despite his marital status and four rambunctious children, he was interested in her. She had always known of his attraction, and perhaps that magnetism added a certain chemistry to their act. A lively element of life. Until recently. Recently his attention had become gratingly irritating.

El Rey lifted his head and glanced toward the east, seeming to sense a human presence. His long, ghostly white mane ruffled softly in the almost imperceptible breeze. He pricked his ears, then calmly lowered his head to drink.

But the presence didn't leave Savaana at peace. Who was it? Tattered memories stormed through her mind: a mother's whispered lullaby, a giant's snarling countenance, flight, harried and terrifying. But she was letting her imagination take control. The person who lurked nearby was most likely someone with whom she was well acquainted.

"Even the lichen know of your presence, Tamas." Savaana said the words in English, for in truth she did not like to think of him as Rom.

But he didn't answer. She gritted her teeth. Perhaps Grandfather was right. Perhaps Tamas was more dangerous than she knew. But what was she to do? Her act with him brought more coin than any of their other endeavors, including the wares their troupe sold during the day, and the tonic *was* expensive. "I believe I heard your wife calling," Savaana said. "Go to her. And cease lurking in the underbrush like some conniving weasel."

There was a moment of silence, and then a figure stepped from behind a broad oak.

"My name is Lady Tilmont," she said. "And I do not have a wife."

Savaana tightened her grip on Rey's leather lead and narrowed her eyes at the stranger. She was dressed in a dark gown atypical of England's frilly, pastel *ton*. Her face and upswept hair were shadowed beneath the curved brim of a dark bonnet. But her haughty tone evidenced her breeding and subsequent boredom.

"The village lies yonder," Savaana said, lifting a hand toward the east. "If you've got turned about."

The woman tilted her head at a cocky angle. "What I've got, Gypsy, is a proposition."

Savaana scowled. "If you'd like our troupe to perform for some future occasion, I'm not the one to whom you should speak. Grandfather makes those decisions."

"Does he make the decisions about your share of the funds as well?" she asked, and paced closer. Her posture was extremely correct, her body ultra stiff.

Savaana watched her, trying to see her face, for even in the deepening darkness there was something strangely familiar about her. Perhaps she was one of Tamas's many conquests, she thought. Regardless of class or financial disparity, women tended to make foolish mistakes regarding men like Tamas. She had learned that much long ago. "I do not believe my funds are any of your affair, madam," she said.

The woman pressed her gloved fingertips together. "There you are wrong."

"Oh?" Savaana feigned interest. She was, after all, no stranger to the stage. As for El Rey, he felt no need to be congenial, and nibbled at the thorny forage that grew alongside the ragged riverbank. "And what makes you think so?"

"A hundred pounds sterling."

Savaana lifted her hand to steady herself on Rey's prominent withers. A hundred pounds would be enough to pay for Grandfather's tonic for the rest of his life. Enough to allow them to return to the continent, where their income might be less but the climate was more favorable. "A hundred pounds?"

"So you're interested."

Savaana executed a casual shrug. A master performer. "That depends."

"On?"

She had been trained to haggle since her first memory, but there seemed little point in pretending with this woman. Tamas had most probably told her something of their financial circumstances. "On whose life would be forfeit," Savaana said, and the woman laughed.

The sound was low and husky, filled with steady confidence and a lifetime of condescendence. Savaana automatically stowed the haughty cadence in her memory banks, hoarding it for another time, another character she might someday be. For she didn't just *act,* she *became.* It was, her grandfather told her, what made the crowds continue to throng to see her. She was believable. And it was probably true, for while performing, she herself believed. Sometimes she was a princess. Sometimes she was a thief. Sometimes, in fact, she was both.

"I don't need you to kill anyone," the woman continued, and though most of her face was hidden from the scattered moonlight, her lips could be seen quite clearly. They were plump, full bottomed, and tight-pursed with disapproval. "But then you're a Gypsy, aren't you? So perhaps that wouldn't concern you."

Savaana smiled coolly. Sometimes it was difficult to find herself following a performance. Not now, however, not when faced with such blatant stupidity. True, she had been dealing with such preconceived foolishness for as long as she could recall, but the insults still burned, still seared her soul and made her realize she was not one of the pampered Gajo who desired but disdained her. She was Rom, by choice if not by blood.

Cueing El Rey to follow, she turned toward camp. Sometimes there was no need to respond to the irritating jibes, but a noise scratched from out of the woods to her left, and she found she could not quite ignore the woman's toxic barbs.

"Best wishes on your return to camp," she said, letting

her voice take on just a sliver of drama. "And do not worry about the wolves. Rarely do they attack before full dark."

Though Savaana didn't turn toward the other, she could feel the lady's immediate tension and grinned into the darkness as she stepped away. Revenge might be churlish and immature, but it was deliciously satisfying.

"Wolves?"

"'Tis only a small pack," she said. "By Romany standards."

Lady Tilmont hurried through the trees now, noisy in her haste, and Savaana all but laughed aloud.

"Holy hell." Her words were breathy as she scrambled along in Rey's broad wake. "Perhaps you expect an apology."

Savaana continued on, amused despite her anger.

"He beats me. My husband," Tilmont said. She had stopped dead in the faint trail behind Savaana. "I can't bear it anymore."

Savaana halted, then turned slowly to look at the woman. Silence ticked away. That sense of familiarity tickled her again, but she no longer cared. Tamas's castoffs were no concern of hers. "You lie," she said. Her voice was even and dramatic in the evening stillness, as if she had the Gypsy sight. As if she were gifted. She was not. "You lie," she repeated, "and not particularly well."

"What makes you think—" But Savaana interrupted. She could be polite when it suited her. Just now it did not.

"If he beat you, I believe you *would* want someone dead," she said, and tangling her fingers in Rey's mane, vaulted lightly to his back, but the woman had already scurried around in front, blocking their path.

"Very well, he doesn't beat me," she said, and managed to sound piqued by the fact.

With a little pressure against Rey's barrel, Savaana cued him from the trail, but Tilmont turned with him, blocking their way.

"He's possessed by the devil." Her words came out raspy and breathless.

Savaana raised a brow. "I am told that a bit of meadowsweet tea can be a tonic for madness," she said, and pressed Rey past the intruder, who was forced to step aside, talking as she did so.

"I did not say he was mad," she argued.

"The tonic is not meant for him."

The lady stopped in her tracks, but whether she understood the insult was unclear. "Did your grandfather teach you of herbs?" Her voice was challenging now.

Savaana didn't deign to turn her head. "You know nothing of my family."

The woman raised her voice. "He's failing, you know."

Savaana tightened her fingers in the piebald's mane. "He but needs rest."

"He needs medicine."

"Which I am giving him." She had almost reached the clearing where they'd camped.

"And you cannot afford."

Anger was growing now. Anger and worry. Savaana turned, glaring through the gathering darkness. "What is it you want?" she asked.

"I want freedom. I *need* freedom," Tilmont said, and strode rapidly through the underbrush toward her. "I have a child. A little boy." Her voice was thick with sudden tears. "I haven't seen him since I married. My husband will not permit it. I miss him terribly."

Savaana sat unmoving on El Rey, almost believing, then shook her head. "Amazing. Truly." She nudged the gelding back toward camp. "Even your first lie was better than that," she said, but Tilmont grabbed her, catching her bright skirts near the knee.

"Two hundred pounds," she said. Her haughty, upper-crust accent had slipped a notch, prompting a dozen unspoken questions. "And no one the wiser."

For a moment Savaana was almost breathless with the thought of that much coin, but nothing came without a price. That, too, she had learned as a child. "I fear meadowsweet may not turn the trick in your case. Best to try some poppy with chamomile," she said, and urged Rey forward.

But the woman held tight. "I'm not mad," she hissed,

and lifted her face toward the river of moonlight that flowed like white wine into the clearing.

Savaana's breath caught tight in her throat, for at that moment she recognized her. It was the face she saw in her mirror. And a dozen half-formed hopes bloomed to life in her soul.

# Chapter 1

"**M**y lady!" The aging maid's voice was muffled through the six-panel door of the bedchamber. A portal crafted of solid walnut, it would subdue all but the loudest noises from without. Or within.

Sitting before a low dresser with gracefully curved legs and a beveled looking glass, Clarette Stenejem studied her regal image. Known as Lady Tilmont since her wedding two months before, she turned her head slightly, examining her high, perfect cheekbones. She was a handsome woman. Her dark hair was tinted with fiery highlights and reached in seductive waves to the middle of her back. Her nose was straight, her eyes a genteel blue against her fair skin. Like a princess, really.

Noticing a slight blemish above her upper lip, she touched it with a pampered pinky finger and scowled. She was not one to suffer imperfections, not even in this backwater sty where she'd spent the past six days.

"My lady?" the maid called again from beyond the door.

Clarette sighed loudly. "What is it now, Margarite?"

"My lady, I do hate to disturb you, but—"

"Then do not," she said, and patted her knuckles against the underside of her jaw. The skin there was as firm as a fresh plum.

"But—"

"Be gone now."

"But your husband has arrived."

"What!" she gasped, and as she jerked toward the offending portal, her persona shattered. Lady Tilmont fled the scene, leaving a shocked Savaana Hearnes tumbling in her wake. Beneath her, the cushioned stool nearly clattered to the floor, but she caught it in one deft hand. Barely breathing, she straightened, found her equilibrium, and steadied her carefully cultivated tone. "What say you?"

"It's Lord Tilmont, my lady. I am told he has returned early from his travels. Gregors says to tell you that your husband has arrived."

"My husband!" Savaana rasped, then grappled with her tone, smoothing it carefully, though she'd been closeted in these same chambers for most of thirty-six hours and her nerves were beginning to fray like weathered hemp. "Surely you're mistaken. Lord Tilmont is not due to return for a fortnight at least." Or so his lady wife had said. After some insistence on Savaana's part, she'd also revealed a bit of her storied past and the fact that she was off to meet a lover. Off to conceive the child her husband seemed ill-suited to provide.

In the meanwhile she needed someone to take her place. Someone who looked like herself. And that Savaana surely did.

"Aye. I know 'tis true; my Lord was not due to arrive for some time," Margarite admitted. "But I am told he is in the parlor even now. Shall I tell him you'll be down to greet him or should he come up at his leisure?"

No! He shouldn't come up. Neither should she go down to greet him! This wasn't in the agreement. It would ruin everything, for thus far she'd discovered nothing of the baroness's past, and Tilmont's arrival would surely not help on that front. She was supposed to merely sit tight for a couple of weeks. At least that had been the baroness's well-paying plan. Now everything was out of control. Out of . . . But in that instant, Savaana remembered who she was. And who she was *supposed* to be. Lady Tilmont—cool, cultured, condescending.

"My lady?"

She drew a careful breath through her uplifted nose and delayed for several seconds before she found her tone. That perfect blend of breeding and superiority. "I'll need a moment."

"But Gregors—"

"Can keep his thoughts to himself," she said, and snapped a weak glance past the walnut secretary toward the high, latticed window that overlooked the balcony. It was open several inches, letting in a wash of rain-freshened air that called to her like a siren. But that was not her way. Not yet at any rate. She clenched her jaw, straightened her spine, and clasped her hands in front of her pink, beribboned gown.

"Shall I tell him—"

"Tell him whatever you wish," she said. "I shall be freshening up."

"Freshening . . ." Poor Margarite sounded all but aflutter. "Of course, my lady. Might you be wanting Emily to see to your coiffure?"

For a moment panic struck her anew. What the devil was a coiffure? She didn't believe she owned one. But she calmed herself in a moment. "What say you?"

"Your hair, my lady. Shall I send Emily in to assist you?"

Hair. Of course. "No. That won't be necessary. My coiffure is fine," she said, and turned a frantic circle, searching for a hat, because her coiffure was *not* fine. It was damned well out of control, flowing down her back like a dark wave gone wild. But she wasn't supposed to worry about such things. She had planned to simply keep out of sight for a fortnight, or so she had told Lady Tilmont, who didn't need to know about her suspicions, her hopes.

It should have been a simple task if she had been

afforded the opportunity to spend her days astride on the moors outside her windows. But it had been drizzling since she and Clarette had traded places in the dark of night, and she doubted the woman she impersonated was one to enjoy getting soaked to the skin.

"Are you certain, my lady? It wouldn't be no trouble. As you know, Emily has a rare—"

"Margarite!" Savaana pressed her fingertips together, closed her eyes and drew her misplaced persona about her like a mantle. "Is there something amiss with your hearing?"

"No, my lady."

"Excellent. Then tell Lord Tilmont I shall be down anon."

There was a pause followed by an almost audible head bob. "Yes, my lady," she said, and clattered rapidly away from the door.

Inside the bedchamber, Savaana drew a cleansing breath and caught a glimpse of herself in the mirror. Handsome. She was handsome, wealthy, and well bred, if a bit unassembled. Pacing to a small wooden chest atop the broad wardrobe, she shooed away the tabby cat that habitually slipped through the open window. Withdrawing two small pearls from the sparse array of jewelry, she attached the little bobs to her ears. They hurt like hell. She barely noticed. A row of rough cut stones haphazardly strung on a leather thong had been tossed on the chest's velvet bottom. A coarse gift from Lord Tilmont's lucrative coal mines? A sentimental bauble from some lusty but impoverished lover? It was impossible to know, and just now she had no time to debate.

In a moment she had located a chapeau. It was broad brimmed, embellished with enough feathers to set a peacock in full flight and as pink as a gardenia. She placed it on her head, tied it snugly under her chin, and faced the mirror again.

Handsome and well dressed.

When she finally deigned to step from the room, two maids stood by the railing not three feet away. They bobbed like ducklings in rough water.

For one frantic moment Savaana tried to recall their names, but reality struck her in a moment; it hardly mattered who they were for they were underlings, inconsequential servants hired for her alone. Thus, she raised her brows and gave them a baleful stare.

"Excuse me, mum." The girls, dressed in matching black and gray gowns with white ruffled aprons, bobbed again, arms folded beneath fresh linens. "Gregors said to see to your chambers whilst you was belowstairs."

"Did he?"

"Just a bit of spritzing," said one girl.

"And fresh sheets," said the other.

"Ahh . . ." She gave them a nod, making sure her chin never dipped below her Adam's apple. "Very well then, carry on. But be quick about it," she said, and made her stilted way down the curving stairs of the ancient estate. Had her feet kept abreast of her heart, she would have been on the ground level in a fraction of a second, but she was trained to perform, and perform she would.

At the bottom of the stairs her knees felt a bit unsteady, but she tightened her resolve and turned toward what she hoped was the parlor. The door stood ajar. Closing her eyes for an instant, she drew a deep breath and stepped inside.

"My lord . . ." she began, but the man who turned toward her from the mantle stole any additional words from her lips.

Tall and dark, he had a rogue's smile and an angel's eyes. He was dressed simply in leather breeches, scarred boots, and a nubby woolen vest over an open-necked tunic.

"I . . ." She blinked. "I didn't expect . . ."

"Lady Tilmont," he said, and bowed. His dark hair was wet and gleaming as it fell across his brow in a wayward wave. "'Tis sorry I am to inconvenience you on such a bonny day."

"Bonny . . ." Her mind was spinning like a whirligig as she tried to shoulder a wagonload of ungainly information. Her husband seemed to be Irish. A working man. And ungodly pretty! Perhaps he couldn't father the necessary heir, as his wife had said, but a woman would surely not be inclined to give up too easily.

"I would have been happy to be received in the entry," he added.

He had dimples deep enough to drown in, and the suggestion of stubble darkened a jaw as sharp and precise as an anvil.

"Or out of doors even."

"I—"

"My apologies, my lady," drawled Gregors from behind.

Savaana turned and blinked. Her butler was little more than a cadaver, his skin barely managing to cover the sharp edges of his bones.

He bowed, looking as if he might break as he did so. "I did not mean to mislead you, certainly."

Mislead her about what? she wondered frantically. But she lifted her chin and waited in silence, refusing to rush into the fray.

Gregors returned her stare with bored panache before speaking. "Halstead led me to believe Lord Tilmont had arrived."

Savaana's fingertips met in front of her silly gown as she waited to be enlightened. Explanations seemed to be forthcoming, and they'd damned well better hurry before she exploded into a thousand nervous shards. But it was the stranger who spoke first.

"You thought me nobility?" he asked the butler, and laughed. It was a ridiculously pleasant sound. Masculine, but lighthearted. Self-confident, but self-deprecating.

Gregors turned grimly toward him. "Apparently Halstead's eyesight is not what it might be. I assure you I shall correct him forthwith," he said, and turned toward Savaana. "I hope I did not cause you alarm, my lady."

"Alarm?" Lady Tilmont had warned her that the aging butler disliked her. He was also fiercely loyal to her husband and would surely be on guard for any shenanigans. Just now there was something in his frosty tone that demanded caution. Savaana straightened even more, emulating the rigid posture of the true lady of the house. "Why would I be alarmed by my husband's early return?"

He watched her, expression unreadable. "Why indeed?" he said finally, and turned stiffly away.

She watched him go, reminding herself to breathe.

"Me name is Sean."

Pulled from her reverie, she turned back toward the man who was *not* her husband.

"Sean Gallagher, me lady. Fresh from County Wicklow."

"Wicklow?" she said, and raising the brows she had only recently lowered, immersed herself in her role again. "Are you quite serious?"

His eyes twinkled like an ill-mannered leprechaun's. "County Wicklow. Aye, me lady."

She allowed a small smile. Perhaps because her own birthplace had not been named after a truncated candle. Perhaps simply because she was so immensely superior in every possible way. "And what brings you here, Wicklow?"

He paused a moment as if debating whether to correct her, seemed to decide against it, and spoke. "I'm a fair hand as a smithy."

"A smithy."

"Aye, shaping horseshoes, mending wheels. I can even draw out a decent knife if the spirit moves me," he said, and bending, pulled a dagger from the top of his tall boot. The hilt was etched with intricate knot work. "A body should never be without a fine blade."

She pursed her lips, waiting for him to continue. He didn't. "And?"

He blinked, grin never fading, though he looked soaked to the skin. His shirt was all but plastered to the high, tight muscles of his chest. And his breeches looked snug enough to have been born with him.

"I could be using a job, I could," he said, and watched her, green eyes sparkling with hope or mischief or some decadent blend of the two.

She watched him back. She was quite certain Lady Tilmont had never liked the Irish. They were an ungroomed lot, though honestly, this one's conformation could hardly be faulted.

He tilted his head a little as if waiting for her response. "I can even fashion a fair lock if you need something kept private," he said. "I've some skill in me hands."

She'd bet a small fortune he did that. But she didn't say as much. Ladies of quality kept their lascivious thoughts to themselves . . . until they were well out of sight. "And why, may I ask, are you speaking to me of this?"

He grinned. "I come by asking to speak to the lord of the manor, but I was told he was out and about." *About* sounded like *aboot* from his diabolically curved lips. "Thus I asked after the one what sees to the farm, but Mr. Underhill seems to have been stove up."

That's right. He had been wounded by a horse just the day before. When she first heard the news, her curiosity had galled her like acid before she remembered her role, at which time she told them to care for their own and rose, nose tilted, to her lofty room above stairs. She rather wished she were there now, staring at her handsome reflection in the gilded mirror above the dresser. But she was not. And why was that, exactly? Could it be that Gregors wanted her elsewhere? And if so, what were his reasons?

"Me lady?"

She drew herself regally back to the present. "Are you accustomed to managing a country estate . . ." She waved a dismissive hand toward the surrounding hills outside the rain-washed windows and made a mien of contempt.

" . . . such as this?" she asked. Off to her right she heard a rustle of noise from behind a wall. Spies perhaps. But why?

"Managing?" Gallagher's dark brows rose. "No, me lady. I've not an inkling how to keep such a grand place as this. I'm naught but a humble Irishman with a bit of skill, is all."

She found that her gaze had slipped to his aforementioned hands. They were long-fingered, smooth-skinned, and oddly tempting, but when she lifted her attention, she thought that a sharp sparkle of something new now showed in his gem-green eyes. Challenge perhaps. Or interest.

Humble, my shapely behind, she thought, and lifting her frothy, beribboned skirts in tandem with her chin, turned away. "Then I can see no use for you," she said, but before she had taken a trio of steps, Gregors reappeared.

"My lady." He bowed, his bony face unreadable. "I do not mean to overstep my bounds."

"Then don't," she suggested. Holy hell, she was mean, she thought in surprise. But what shocked her even more was the realization that she rather enjoyed the role. It was quite freeing. Being nice required a good deal more energy.

Gregors nodded, as if he acknowledged her order without caring a whit. "'Tis simply that Lord Tilmont insisted that the young gelding be fit for a saddle before his impending return."

*Young gelding. Young gelding. Young gelding.* Her mind spun. If she'd been told anything about this, she couldn't remember it, so she pursed her lips and waited impatiently as if she knew all but felt no compunction to respond.

Gregors cleared his throat with what she had thought of as Celtic stoicism until her very recent introduction to the all-but-giddy Sean Gallagher. "The Irish are said to have some expertise with the beasts of the field."

They were also said to have some expertise with women. She wondered if either was true. And why did Gregors care if this man stayed? By the look of the aging cadaver, he shouldn't care about anything but the condition of his coffin. Would that be too rude to say aloud? Even for Lady Tilmont?

"Well?" she said finally, and turned toward Gallagher.

He canted up one corner of his cocky mouth. "Well what, me lady?"

She let her brow crinkle with impatience. "Are you skilled with horses?"

"Horses, is it?" he asked, then shrugged, nonchalant, as if it were of no great importance if she turned him back out into the weather like a homeless hound. "Aye, me lady, skilled enough."

She watched him, wondering. What went on here? "Very well then. I shall consider the matter closed," she said, and turned away, dismissing all as she ascended the stairs. Her footsteps were silent on the plush runner, soundless as she turned the corner toward her chambers.

"Not a soul." The words were whispered from the hallway.

"You're certain?"

"I've got me eyes, don't I? And me other senses, too, come to that. If there was another in there with 'er I'd 'ave knowed it."

# Chapter 2

"**G**regors," Savaana said, then paused on the stairs, hand just so on the banister, poised for effect. The midnight blue riding habit she wore was a tad tight. She would have to forgo a few of Cook's delicacies if she hoped to continue to inhale while wearing this particular garment. Accustomed to vast amounts of exercise, she felt overstuffed and understimulated from the time she'd spent eating ultra rich foods in the solitude of someone else's stifling bedchamber.

"Yes, my lady." The old cadaver turned toward her, his face as expressionless as a rock, his tone absolutely without inflection. If he were, in fact, Celtic, he must have beaten his brogue into submission years before. Which seemed a shame, because Gallagher's musical lilt continued to sing in her memory, titillating her nerve endings, exciting her—

But what was she talking about? The baroness wasn't the sort to get either titillated or excited.

On the other hand, the Rom were just that sort,

especially when she'd been isolated in the airless confines of this mausoleum for three days. Three days, fifteen hours, and two minutes, to be precise. There was
an extremely accurate clock atop the mantel in her bedchamber. A clock she was rather likely to hurl into the
beveled looking glass if she spent one more second without feeling the wind on her face.

"I wish to ride," she said. Her tone was marvelously
restrained, not suggesting for a moment that she intended
to hurl things . . . things that very well might include his
bony person if he stood between herself and fresh air for
another moment. "See that a mount is prepared."

"Ride, my lady?" countered Gregors.

"Yes." She raised her brows in concert with her chin.
"If that meets with your approval." Holy hell, she was as
accomplished at sarcasm as she was at nasty. Who would
have suspected?

"Of course, my lady," he said.

She nodded once, then continued down the stairs. She
was the epitome of elegant grace. She was certain of it,
but his next words stopped her.

"I shall find you a companion posthaste," he said, tone
bored.

"A companion!" Her own attitude was harsh and
perfect.

"Surely my lady does not wish to ride alone."

That was exactly what she wished, but what the hell

was his snide expression all about? She raised her left brow an extra notch.

"I assure you, I am a better equestrian than any you shall find to accompany me."

"I am certain that is true, madam. But I made a vow to keep you safe until my lord's return."

She considered that for a moment, remembering that Clarette had been adamant that she arouse no suspicions. That she make certain her reputation remained unsullied and her identity unquestioned.

Savaana almost closed her eyes to her own folly. How foolish she had been to follow this goose on such a wild chase. Since her arrival at Knollcrest she'd found nothing to bolster her hopes regarding Lady Tilmont's true identity. "Very well," she said. "But if this companion of yours cannot keep up, she shall be left behind."

Gregors bowed again, looking as if he might shatter while doing so. "I shall surely relay that caveat, my lady."

"Do so," she said, and wondering about the meaning of caveat, glided back up the stairs to fetch a bonnet. In a matter of minutes she had secured a frilly straw hat upon her head and was heading resolutely toward the stables.

The sun had made a late afternoon appearance and shone crisp and bright on the saturated world. It made her feet itch to dance, but she kept her pace sedate, her demeanor refined until she reached the anonymity of the barn. She could not, however, keep a lively little ditty from trilling through her mind as she passed the lean-to that housed a smoking forge. Pacing briskly along, she sang a few bars under her breath as she stepped through the widespread doors of the barn. The air there smelled rich and earthy, soothing her frazzled nerves. She inhaled deeply, glanced about, then lifted her skirts and executed a skittering little jig to accompany her tune.

"Me lady."

Stifling a squawk, she swung about as someone stepped up behind her, but the villain was already laughing.

"I didn't mean to frighten you." Gallagher stood only a few feet away, eyes sparkling with mischief, one fist wrapped around a somewhat misshapen blade of twelve inches or so. "I apologize, I do."

Savaana pursed her lips and found Clarette's persona with surprising ease. What did that mean exactly? "Oh?" she said, and arched a brow. "And do you always cackle like a laying hen when you feel badly about your conduct?"

He chuckled again, reminding her that his laughter didn't sound so much like a cackle as a bubbling fount of earthly pleasures. He had rolled his sleeves up well-muscled arms, and a slight sheen of sweat glistened where his kindly shirt lay open at the neck. "Please," he said, wiping his brow with the back of a callused hand, "don't quit your singing on me own account."

She raised her chin. "I was not singing."

"I heard—"

"Incorrectly," she said. "For I do not sing."

"What of dancing? Did I imagine that light little jig as well?" he asked, and laughed as she deepened her scowl.

Dammit, she would have to be more careful about her conduct. "Tell me, Irishman, are you always so jolly as this?"

"Only when I've had meself a bit of sport with me hammering," he said, and slipped the incomplete knife into his boot. "A body should never be without a fine blade."

"So that's what makes you giddy? Hammering steel?" She employed her snootiest tone, but his forearms were corded with taut muscles; she felt a little giddy herself.

"Well, that, and accompanying a comely lass such as yourself."

"Accompanying . . ." she began, then understanding his meaning, deepened her scowl. "Surely you are not to be my companion."

"Think of me more as an escort." He bowed again, making the neck of his tunic droop enough to show the taut muscles of his dark-skinned chest. Her attention dipped there. "At your service, me lady." He straightened, and though she zipped her gaze instantly back to his face, his happy expression was already suggesting that he had noticed her wandering attention. For reasons entirely unknown to her, that obvious joy made her angry.

"As it turns out . . ." she said, "I do not require your services."

His lips hitched up a roguish notch, making her wonder if there was something amusing about her phraseology.

"Then you merely desire them?" he asked.

She frowned as she tugged on her gloves. The black kid leather felt soft and warm against her skin, too warm for this weather, but years of study had taught her that what the gentry wore had little to do with need and more to do with . . . madness. Besides, it would be best not to call attention to the calluses that ridged the underside of her palms. "Unlike Gregors . . ." she said, tugging the frilly sleeves of her blouse out from under her sturdy jacket, "I have not found the Irish to be particularly good with horses."

Something sparked in his eyes. Anger maybe. Good. 'Twas far preferred to his irritating good humor. "Perhaps you have tangled with the wrong Irishmen, then," he suggested.

She gave him an arch glance as she reached for a quirt that hung on the wall nearby. It was three feet long and crafted of fine braided leather. She rather liked the feel of it, and smiled as she tapped it against the heavy fabric of her skirt. "As it is, I do not 'tangle' with the Irish at all."

"Then perhaps 'tis time ye did," he said.

She straightened her back, haughty as hell, disapproval seeping from every pore. "Might you forget that I'm a married woman, Mr. Gallagher?"

"'Tis unlikely," he said, and there was something in his voice. Something almost calculating, that caused her to cant her head at him, to narrow her thoughts.

"And what exactly might you mean by that?"

"Me apologies," he said, and though he dropped his head in the semblance of chagrin, his eyes were steady when they reached hers again. "It but seems strange that such a bonny lass should spend her time alone on this estate so far from the company of others."

Bending an elbow, she flicked an invisible fleck of dust from her sleeve. "Perhaps the carefully bred don't become lonely so easily as the lower class," she said.

His eyes sparked again, but whether with anger or humor, she couldn't quite tell. Neither did she care, she thought, but it was not so easy to lie to herself as to others.

"And what of boredom, me lady? Do the carefully bred feel that?"

She tilted her head at him. In the past three days she'd been bored enough to chew off her own arm. But he was watching her, and perhaps it would not suit her elegant persona to admit as much. "I've but a desire to see how my lord's estate looks after the rain," she said, then pursed her lips and perused him for a silent moment. "If you've no objections."

Their gazes met and melded, and then he grinned. "No objections a'tall, me lady."

She placed a splayed hand to her chest with dramatic flare. "What a pleasant relief."

He laughed and gestured to a gelding tied to the nearby wall. He was as black as pitch. Tall and broad, he was deep through the heart girth and smooth through the forearm. Every elegant line flowed like river water into the next. He turned his broad head toward her, showing intellect and curiosity in his seal-brown eyes.

And suddenly it mattered little if she was Rom or royalty, for her heart was filled to brimming with something rather akin to love at first sight.

"Here then," Gallagher said, breaking the spell. "Allow me to move Indigo so that you may mount your own steed."

Tugging the gelding's lead from the ring through which it was tied, he led the black away, only to reveal a paunchy chestnut adorned with a lady's silly side-saddle. Little more than a spavined pony, the mare was barely fourteen hands at the withers. Never flicking an ear, she stood with one hip cocked and her bottom lip drooping.

Savaana stared at the aging hack for all of five

seconds, then turned toward her unwanted escort. "You jest." Her tone was perfectly level. Perfectly bored.

He raised a brow at her. "Me lady?"

Their gazes clashed. "Surely you do not expect me to ride that . . ." She lifted a dismissive hand toward the chestnut. " . . . thing."

Gallagher scowled as if confused, but even an inbred Irishman couldn't be as daft as all that. She was quite certain of it . . . until he spoke. "Mr. Gregors said to make certain you remained safe, and Daisy here will do just that."

She smiled, making sure the expression did nothing more than move her lips into a ghoulish configuration. "Did Mr. Gregors also say to make sure I do not move above a snail's pace?"

He shook his head once, looking befuddled. "I don't believe he made mention. But if that be your preference I shall surely—"

"Change the saddles, Lowwick," she ordered, though in truth she had never ridden aside as well bred ladies did.

"Me name's Sean, lassie. Sean—"

"I don't give a damn if you're the king's first cousin. Unless you've a penchant for riding aside, you'll change their tack about."

"The mare is a fine mount, me lady. A bit long in the tooth, mayhap, but well trained and responsive if you'll but—"

"Did I ask about the state of her teeth?"

He shook his head. "Nay, me lady, but I fear Gregors will be sore—"

She slapped the quirt against her skirt. "Remove the saddle or you'll have apt reason to fear."

There was something in his damned eyes again. If it was humor, she might well have to kill him. "Truly, my lady, I do not think—"

"And 'twould be a bad time for you to start now."

He stopped, almost looked as if he might laugh, then nodded sharply and turned on his heel.

Savaana tapped the toe of her tightly laced boot as she waited for him to do her bidding, but finally the saddles were changed about.

The dark gelding jigged a little as the girth was pulled tight.

"I would warn you that 'twas he what injured Mr. Underhill."

She ignored him. El Rey was a fine steed, broad and strong and able to carry their wagon as easily as she might lift a caper, but this animal was built for naught but speed.

"He's young and has not yet had much time under saddle," Gallagher added, but Savaana was far too excited to care about admonitions.

"Give me a leg up," she ordered.

He did so. Though it was a foolish way to ride, she

eased her knee over the curved pommels and settled into the smooth leather seat. The gelding reared a little as she turned him toward the door, but she reined him in, keeping him to a high-stepping trot as they left the yard.

A couple furlongs down the road, when the house was hidden from sight, Savaana loosened the reins a quarter of an inch and shifted her hips the slightest degree. Feeling a lively zephyr ruffle his forelock, the animal tossed his handsome head and settled into a well-collected canter. And though she knew better than to let him increase his tempo, she couldn't help herself.

The wind rushed at her face in happy waves as the gelding found his rolling rhythm. Behind an undulating stone fence, sheep grazed on a pastoral hillock, and beyond that a long sweep of green wended its way to a woods just turning to gold.

For a moment Savaana tried to resist her most primordial urges, tried to remember who she was supposed to be and keep the gelding to the well-packed road, but she could feel the power swelling like a dark tide inside him. Could feel the glory of him. And suddenly, though she tried to resist her true being, she was young and strong, and Rom. Tilting the black's nose to the right, she picked him up with her left heel against his heaving ribs and galloped toward the fence.

Maybe she heard the Irishman curse behind her. Maybe she even knew she should change her course, but she could not. As for the gelding, he never refused, never balked or swerved or questioned. Instead, he soared. Like a dove over open water, he flew, and then his forefeet touched down and they were racing uphill. The wind kissed Savaana's upturned face, the sun warmed her back, and gladness lit her soul.

Sheep scattered as they dashed among them. Water sprayed as they leaped through the stream. As for Savaana, she was no longer aware if she was being followed. No longer cared, for the gelding was picking up speed. She leaned into the wind, saw the log ahead, and pointed him toward its bowed center.

Power built in the fluid muscles beneath her, and then they were lifting into the air, soaring like unfettered eagles. But just as they were gliding over the top, a hare leapt from hiding and Indigo twisted wildly. Tilted from her foolish perch, Savaana saw the rocky ground hurtling toward her and threw herself free of the lone stirrup. Curling into a sphere, she hit the springy turf and rolled like a dislodged cricket ball out of harm's way.

As for the gelding, he found his balance with an adroitness born of a hundred years of regal breeding. Landing softly, he gathered his considerable strength, threw up his tail and bolted away.

Savaana watched him, all but breathless with elation.

"What an amazing *grast*," she breathed.

# Chapter 3

Sean reined the mare to a halt and leapt from the saddle, certain he would find the baroness broken on the far side of the log. But instead she was sitting at a crooked angle and beaming from ear to ear.

He slowed his pace, watching her, sure he was mistaken. But no. Though she had been dumped onto the damp grasses like a peck of moldy grain, she looked elated, which must mean that she'd been knocked senseless. And regardless of his own nefarious reasons for traveling to Knollcrest, his heart thumped with worry. Maybe it didn't entirely matter that she was the devil's spawn. She was, after all, an extraordinarily beautiful woman. His brother had been right about that much from the very beginning. Alastar hadn't said, however, that she was a conniving she-devil. That had been made clear later. But Sean was learning even more now. Such as the fact that she was fearless and strong and had a rare and shining smile that could light up the entirety of the Emerald Isle.

Sitting on the turf like a broken doll amidst a tumble of blue serge, she was grinning like a giddy schoolgirl.

"Holy hell . . ." she whispered. A few wild strands of glossy hair had blown against the heart-shaped beauty of her face. "He soars like an angel. Like a—" she began, then stopped abruptly and zipped her gaze to his as if suddenly finding her sanity.

He scowled from a few paces away, trying to sort out this odd turn of events. It had almost sounded as if she'd been speaking a different language moments before. But what was it? Surely not Romany, the language he'd heard spoken by the tinkers and entertainers he met during his travels. He wasn't the only one who made his living by hawking his metal wares, after all. Though he may have been one of only a few who did so while owning a thriving foundry. "Hit your head, did you, me lady?"

She stared at him, silent. Unwanted worry bubbled inside him, and he paced closer.

"Are you hurt? Are you broken?"

Something like annoyance crossed her recently animated features.

"Yes, of course I'm hurt," she said. "Anyone would be hurt." Her scowl deepened quizzically. "Wouldn't they?"

"I daresay." She seemed rather strange. Disoriented maybe, but she was sitting upright, looking him square in the eye, and though the foolish grin had disappeared, she still seemed all but euphoric. He frowned as he squatted before her. "I'll be surprised if a single bone in your body is unbroken. You tumbled like a wagon wheel."

She said nothing, just watched the gelding gallop into the distance for a moment.

He stared at her. "Where are you hurt exactly?"

"Oh." She pulled her gaze from the horizon. "It's my . . . shoulder," she said, and suddenly blushed, not as if she was the she-devil ascended from hell itself, but like a debutante, fresh-faced and pretty and somehow embarrassed that she had fallen from that high-headed fool of a horse. "Yes." She said the word with more conviction now and cradled her left arm with her opposite hand.

"Your shoulder?" He skimmed her body. Even crumpled as she was, it was not a difficult task. Her waist looked as firm and narrow as a well-hammered horseshoe, her bosom high and impressive. "Is that all?"

Her eyes glistened with challenge. "Isn't that enough?"

Her tone was somewhat aggravated. As if he thought her to blame for not managing to be incapacitated.

"Of course. Aye," he agreed, and remembered his brogue even as she began to rise. "No, me lady. Stay put," he said, and reached for her hale arm. "You mustn't damage yourself further."

For a moment he thought she would argue, but eventually she settled back down with a moan, belated though it was.

"Is something else amiss?" he asked.

"Perhaps," she said, then shifted her gaze resolutely from the horizon where the steed had disappeared in a flurry of hooves and a flip of his tail. She seemed to stifle a sigh.

Who was this woman? The haughty baroness in the gold gown he had seen in Tilmont's cameo, or the wild lass who soared over life-threatening jumps? "Mayhap you struck your head, too, lass. You seem a bit unsettled."

She turned toward him. "Are you saying I'm addled?" she asked, and something about the irritation in her tone made him want to laugh.

"I wouldn't think of it, me lady. Here, let me see to your comfort," he said, and grasping her right arm, gently eased her back against the log.

She winced.

"Me apologies. I thought it was the other shoulder," he said, and suddenly she looked increasingly peeved, eyeing him suspiciously as she settled back against the moldering bark of the fallen elm.

"Perhaps you could cease clucking around me like a worried hen and catch up the gelding before he finds himself trouble," she said.

"I don't think that will be the case," he argued. "And me task was to care for you, not some crazed beast what's a'feared of wild hares."

"He's not—" she began, then scowled and nodded. "Foolish animal," she agreed, but she was mooning after the black again, as if wishing she were still aboard.

Stranger and stranger. "Which shoulder was it?" he asked.

"What?"

"Shoulder. Which one?" he asked, and cradling her right arm near the elbow, set his other hand near her neck and rotated gently. The skin there was as smooth and soft as a kitten's underbelly.

He was no physician by any stretch, but he did have a younger brother, one who had sustained multiple injuries. Some of them relatively severe. All of them foolish.

"Does that hurt?" he asked.

She was staring at him. "No." Her tone was dreamy and mildly surprised. "It feels rather—" She stopped herself abruptly, and though he knew better, he couldn't quite help grinning a little.

It was then that she seemed to come to herself. "It's the other arm," she snapped.

"Oh, aye, of course. Me apologies," he said, and setting her right hand carefully in her bunched lap, he reached for the other, slowly now, as if she were a frightened gosling. "Shall we remove that glove?"

She was scowling a little, but distractedly, as if displeased by some internal debate. "My hand is fine."

"Let's just have a look at your wee fingers," he said, and gently stroked her wrist. It was narrow and oddly appealing, though he had no particular affinity for women's wrists. He was an ankle man himself. But just now he had other things on his mind. Other reasons for coming here, and they had nothing to do with either wrists *or* ankles. "Lady Tilmont," he mused. "The title does not seem to suit you exactly. What be your given name?"

"My given name is none of your affair," she said. "And my fingers are entirely uninjured."

"But perhaps you cannot tell," he argued, and gently began tugging the soft leather from her hand. "Once upon a day me brother fell from the roof of the henhouse. When he limped into the kitchen we thought sure he had broke his leg, but 'twas not the case a'tall." She had very pretty hands, pale and long fingered. The little shells of her nails were cropped short, and as he stroked her knuckles, she curled her digits inward like a purring kitten. But she pulled her gaze from his ministrations and pinned her attention on his face.

"Why was he there?"

He glanced up. Good God, she had eyes like a siren. As blue as the sea on a cloudless morning. As wide as forever and strangely innocent. And suddenly he couldn't remember what they had been talking about.

"Your pardon?" he said.

"Your brother." A scowl marred her perfect features, and though it was often there, it somehow seemed out of place on her guileless features just now. "Why was he atop the henhouse?" she asked.

He shook his head and eased his fingers over her

pinky, remembering his goal. "'Twas where the squirrel went. Or so he said."

She nodded as if she understood such logic, which was ridiculous, of course. She was nothing but a spoiled, grasping harridan. Out to get whatever she could. On the other hand, she had just launched eighty stones of heaving horseflesh over a stationary object as if she'd sprouted wings. For a spoiled, grasping harridan, she had a good deal of nerve. And ridiculously soft skin. Except for the row of calluses that crested the underside of her hand. Odd, that, he thought. Slipping his fingers beneath her wrist, he tried to ignore the feelings that shivered through his abdomen and lower.

"And what was truly wrong with him?" she asked.

"What's that?" He lifted his gaze to hers, reminding himself she was no one to be trifled with. Then again, wasn't that why he had come here? To trifle?

"You thought his leg was broken . . ." she prompted.

"Ahh, yes," he said, and gently massaged her index finger. The skin looked unbroken and hale. Hell, the skin looked gorgeous. "In truth, it was his thumb that had been damaged," he said, and trailing his fingers over the little hillocks of her knuckles, drew her hand up to his lips and kissed her digits.

She sucked air though her teeth and tried to jerk away, but he held on gently.

Perhaps he was moving too quickly, but he'd come

here with a mission in mind, and had no intention of staying longer than necessary. 'Twas revenge that kept him here and nothing else. "Did that hurt, me lady?"

"No. It felt—" she began, then raised her peaked chin, pursed her luscious lips, and tugged her hand firmly from his grip. "As I said at the outset, 'twas my shoulder. Not my hand."

"Ahh . . ." He grinned a little. His mother had been known to say he had a smile like a sainted bandit. Other women had found less innocuous comparisons. Most suggested he could not be completely trusted. And he supposed that was true. It had been Alastar who was the soft touch. His brother who had been naive and loving and kind. Helper of men, or so his unusual name implied. And it had suited him. It seemed the perfect name for a wise barrister in training. But no more. "Right you are, lassie. 'Twas your shoulder," he said, and gently eased his way up her elbow, flexing it lightly. "Does that hurt?"

"No."

He slipped his hand toward her upper arm. "That?"

"No."

He skimmed his fingers to her upper joint. Her lips had parted slightly. They were as pink as the inside of a conch. Soft, shiny, and pearlescent. "That?"

"N—" she began, then jerked her arm away. "Ouch."

He raised his brows at her sudden reaction. "That hurt?"

She was scowling at him. "I said ouch, did I not?"

"So ye did," he agreed, and almost laughed, because she looked far more peeved than pained. "It's your shoulder, then."

"That's what I said at the outset. Now, if you'll catch my mount, we can be on our way," she groused, and shifted as if to rise.

But he caught her hand. "Sure, you cannot mean to ride that wild beastie again."

"Of course—" she began, then touched her shoulder as if just remembering the pain there. "—not," she finished, and turning her gaze to the cock-hipped chestnut, seemed to stifle a shudder. "But even if I do mount that *thing*, you'll still have to fetch the gelding."

He glanced into the distance. Her hand felt warm in his. "The blighter looks to be long gone."

"He soars like a wild hart."

There was an odd look in her eye again. The kind he couldn't quite decipher. Surely it couldn't be admiration. The damned horse could have killed her.

"Like Pegasus," she whispered.

He frowned at her. "What's that?"

"When he—" she began, then stopped abruptly and raised her brows in imperial dislike. "You should have warned me of his propensity toward flightiness."

For a moment he almost argued, but she was not the only actor on this stage. "You are right, of course, me lady. I should indeed have been more cautious. One cannot be too careful with a beauty such as yours," he said, and raising her hand slowly to his lips, kissed the little dip in the center of her palm. "But I did not realize you were such a brave little soldier."

His ploy worked like magic, for he could sense her softening. Could feel her weakening. The problem was, his own loins were beginning to stir. But that was foolish. He was hardly some raw lad enthralled by every pair of pouty lips.

"And because of me shortcomings, I feel the need to set things right."

Her teeth shone between her plump, berry-bright lips, her eyes looked as soft as moonlight. "They feel pretty right," she murmured, and he almost laughed out loud.

How the mighty had already fallen. He smiled, giving her a little of that sainted bandit. "I feel it me duty to check your shoulder, me brave little Amazon."

"My shoulder?"

"The injured one," he said, and leaned forward, ready to kiss the skin just above her severe neckline, but in that moment she launched from her position on the ground and sent him sprawling like a spanked bairn.

"Fetch the gelding," she ordered. Her tone was rock solid, the softening maid long gone as she glared down at him. "And quit your foolery."

With the setting sun sinking red in the gentian sky

behind her, she looked as perfect as an Irish rose, as formidable as a Scottish thistle. And for a moment he almost forgot all. His brother's slide into dissipation. His father's death, his own vow to set things right. But he brought himself firmly back to reality. Back to anger. Back to revenge.

"I suppose worry over an injury seems foolish indeed to a warrior woman such as yourself," he said.

"I am *not* a warrior."

"Ahh, but they're you're wrong, lass. A brave little Amazonian is what you are."

Anger flashed in her eyes. "I am no such—"

"Indeed, I believe I'll call you Lady A."

"You'll call me Lady Tilmont. Or Clarette, if stringing two words together is too difficult for one of your limited resources," she insisted, and he almost laughed as he won another round.

"As you wish then, Clarette," he said, but as he rose, he stumbled on a tussock behind him and almost fell.

And in that moment she reached for him, hands strong and steady against his arm. "Are you well?"

"'Tis naught to worry upon," he said, and grinned a little at this odd turn of events. Had she softened so much already that she actually cared? He barely dared to hope. "I but landed wrong when you rose so abruptly."

She drew her hands away. "You're saying this is my fault?"

He almost laughed at the taut anger in her tone. "Not a'tall, lass," he said, and turned away with a carefully pronounced limp. "I shall be about fetching the gelding now."

She let him hobble off for several yards before stopping him. "Come back here."

He turned carefully, hiding his humor. To be honest, his ankle did hurt a bit. "You are in need of something afore I go, me lady?"

How could her scowl look so bonny? It made no sense. "At that rate it shall be morning before you catch up with the steed."

He glanced toward the sun. It was nearing the horizon. "I shall try to make haste, me lady."

She stared at him a moment, then gave an impatient huff and glanced toward the chestnut. "Take the mare."

He raised his brows in honest surprise. "And leave you here afoot? I could not."

"I'm quite sure you're wrong."

"I don't mean to argue, but—"

"Then don't."

He grinned a little at her tone. "But I vowed on me life to keep you safe."

"These fields are hardly filled with ravaging beasts."

"Perhaps not, but I cannot afford to lose this job."

She scowled at him. He waited, then turned slowly and took one limping step toward the horizon.

"We'll ride together."

He stopped, smiled into the distance, sobered carefully, and turned. "I couldn't ask you to—"

"And you didn't. Can you mount or do you require assistance?"

He didn't allow the surprise to show in his eyes. "I'm certain I can—" he began, then grimaced artfully as he stepped toward the mare.

"Stay where you are," she insisted.

"Truly, me lady—"

"Not another step," she ordered, and hurrying to where the mare grazed, led her to him. "Put your arm 'round my shoulder."

He refrained from raising his brows. He also refrained from kissing her. Suffering saints, he was the very picture of decorum. "I don't think it seemly for me to take such liberties, me lady."

She scowled, perhaps wondering about his previous behavior. But he could hardly be blamed for kissing her wrist. It was irresistible.

"Aye, well, I'm not thrilled about being stranded out here in the dark with an Irishman with too many hands."

He managed to remain absolutely sober. "I assure you, my lady, I have the usual number of hands. I was simply trying to—"

"Get on the horse," she ordered.

"Perhaps I should help you mount first, then climb up behind."

She gave him one raised brow. "I'll be sitting behind, Shortwick," she said. "Where I can keep an eye on you."

No fool, she. "Expecting me to swoon, are you, Lady A?"

"Only if I hit you on the head."

Containing his laughter was becoming more difficult. "I'd feel much safer if you were in front."

"You'd probably feel a lot of things," she countered briskly. "Now hurry or I shall leave you behind."

He glanced toward the farmstead. It was a good five miles to Knollcrest.

Daisy stood patiently as he mounted, and in a matter of moments he was aboard. He glanced down at the baroness. She looked peeved and a little thoughtful, but finally shifted the stirrup toward the animal's rump and put her foot in the U-shaped leather. He reached for her hand and she took it regretfully.

Helping her mount was simple enough, but not because she was particularly light. It was either because she was unusually strong or notably agile. He couldn't quite decide which, and it made him wonder, but in a second she was perched behind the saddle's high cantle.

Her breasts brushed his back. His penis shifted against the pommel.

"You'd best hold onto me," he said.

"I think I can stay aloft on this fiery steed," she said,

and in that moment he couldn't quite help but tap his heels against the chestnut's flanks.

Well trained and deceptively responsive after nearly two decades of life, Daisy leapt forward.

As for the baroness, she snagged his waist with sudden zeal. Her breasts pressed tight and firm to his back, and though it took some discipline, he refrained from closing his eyes to the euphoric feelings.

"If this little mare is too much for you, I could take the reins," she gritted, her lips near his ear.

He managed not to laugh as he slowed the chestnut to a more sedate pace. "You wish to change places, me lady?"

"Just try to control her," she ordered.

He glanced over his shoulder at her, trying to appear somber. "Certainly, me lady. Me apologies, Me Lady. But Daisy here is really quite a spirited steed."

His passenger snorted softly. Her huff of disbelief brushed the nape of his neck, doing foolishly erotic things to certain parts of his suddenly hard anatomy.

But he only shrugged, casual to a fault. "Believe what you will, lass, but not everything is as it appears," he said, and tried to ignore the discomfort of his ridiculous desire for her.

# Chapter 4

Savaana sat alone in Clarette's bedchamber, once again studying her reflection. Her persona was firmly back in place.

Perhaps it had not been particularly wise for her to ride on the previous night. But at least she'd learned that the Irishman was attracted to her. It was a good piece of information to possess, though she could hardly be surprised. She was, after all, a beautiful woman. As for Gallagher, he was not entirely lacking in charm. He was handsome enough, she supposed, and some might say his smile was . . . alluring.

But that meant nothing to her, she reminded herself quickly. After all, she was a married woman. Happily married. Her entire job was to remain here. To be faithful. To bear an heir. Hardly a difficult task. After all, she had plenty to eat. She had servants to attend to her every whim. She had warm fires on chilly nights.

And if she spent one more damned hour in this stifling house she was going to lose her mind!

Feeling her guise slip, Savaana jerked abruptly to her feet. She was at the door before she could stop her retreat. The carpet on the stairs was plush and silent beneath her slippers.

"Gregors!" she called from the stairs.

"Yes, my lady," he said, appearing from nowhere. She stifled a jerk. It was as if he lived underfoot, popping up out of midair.

"Fetch my cloak. I am going for a walk."

"In this chill weather, my lady?"

Yes! Yes! God yes! She wasn't accustomed to being trapped inside. She thrived in the open air, blossomed with activity. Tumbling, hiking, entertaining, but she revealed none of those things. Instead, she gave him her most withering look. "Might there be warmer weather available?" she asked, and half turned away.

"In hell," he said.

"What?" She pivoted back, wondering rather wildly if she'd heard him correctly.

"'Tis hard to tell," he said, bowing smoothly. "I shall see that Emily is ready with your cloak ever so quickly."

"Do that," she said, and though she couldn't help but wonder about the old cadaver's animosity toward the baroness, she was out of doors in a matter of minutes. The rain had begun anew before she returned from her ride on the previous day. Even so, she had insisted that the Irishman dismount and walk before they could be seen from Knollcrest's high windows.

The new day had brought intermittent sprinkles, but evening was setting in now, making everything still and secretive with the oncoming night. Hidden from the house by a small copse of rowan, she tilted her face toward the sky and stuck out her tongue, catching raindrops on its tip. They tasted like laughter, and she smiled as she wiped her chin.

"Is that you yourself, lass?"

She jumped as Gallagher stepped from the shadows near the barn. Behind him, the broad doors stood open.

"Must you always be lurking about?" she asked.

"Of course," he said, and even in the dim mist she could see his smile. For a man who slept in the stables, he seemed ungodly happy. "I'm an Irishman, trained to lurk for hundreds of years."

"Have you?" Inside the barn, it looked warm and cozy. Diffuse light glowed from the interior, gilding the scattered straw, the ruminating ewes, the one horned milk cow. The horses were stabled farther down. Savaana stepped toward the shelter, drawn against her will and better judgment.

"Pressed into secrecy from centuries of hiding from our betters," he added. Moving back, he swept his hand in front of him, inviting her to enter his domain.

"Your betters." She raised a brow and watched him from

the corner of her eye as she strode toward the byre. Sturdy pens filled with contented animals lined the wide aisle. "It's good to know you realize your place, Wickingham."

If her intentional slaughter of his name bothered him, he did not show it. "Indeed I do," he said. "'Tis well beneath the likes of you."

"Yes," she agreed, then faced him full on, wondering if there was double meaning to his words.

But his expression gave no clues. He was usually smiling, it seemed, and this moment was little different, unless there was an extra spark of mischief in his grin.

"You do remember that I'm a married woman, do you not, Wicknub?"

"Every waking moment, fair Clarette," he assured her, then: "How does your shoulder fare?"

"My shoulder?"

"The one you injured during our ride."

"Oh, yes." Holy hell, how hard could it be for her to remember she was supposed to be hurt? It wasn't as if the ridiculously alluring smile on his ridiculously handsome face was addling her thought processes, so it was probably the forced inactivity that was hampering her thinking apparatus. "Though in actuality I was fine during the 'ride.' 'Twas the fall that caused the problem."

"Had I been thinking proper, I would have leapt from old Daisy and raced to catch you before you hit the ground," he said.

"Yes. What were you thinking?" she asked, and wandered farther into the barn.

"I fear you may not wish to know," he said.

She turned to find his eyes, but if he was being suggestive, it didn't show on his face.

"Sorry I am that you were hurt," he said.

Some weak-kneed part of her was tempted to assure him it was not his fault, but she bullied that part into silence. "And what of your ankle? You seem to be quite yourself," she said, and wondered if his infirmary had been nothing but a ploy to gain him a seat on her mount.

"We Irish are remarkably fast healers. Survival of the fittest, I suppose, from living with our—"

"Betters," she said. "Yes I know."

He grinned. "Perhaps I could massage your shoulder for you."

"Still married," she said. "Remember?"

Crossing his arms against his tight chest, he settled his lean hips against the empty stall behind him. Indigo reached over the planks between them, tousling Gallagher's hair as he huffed into it.

"We are a far distance from a doctor," he said. "Surely even a married woman deserves a bit of attention when she's been hurt."

She wandered down the hard-packed aisle. A pair of speckled lambkins were nestled close to their mother's side, spiky, two-toned lashes closed over sleepy eyes. "I assure you I get plenty of attention."

"Oh? I was under the impression that your beloved husband was gone."

She eyed him askance. "I feel confident that he will return."

"Who would not?" he asked, and there was something in his tone that made her turn toward him.

He shrugged, still grinning. "I doubt you're unaware of your charms, me lady."

Dear God, he was a flirt. She straightened her back. "I'm not entirely stupid."

"Or modest."

It was her turn to shrug. "Seeming so would be a waste of my time."

"And your time is so valuable."

"What do you mean by that?"

"No offense, sure," he said. "You but seem restless this night."

She let her fingers trail along the top plank of the pigs' enclosure. A dozen spotted bodies were attached like living pods to their mother's underbelly. The piebald sow was smiling as she snored.

"Tell me, Lady A, why are you here?"

"I thought the answer to that was so obvious that even a candle would understand."

"A cand . . . ? Ahh, Wicklow," he said, and grinned.

"Well, perhaps I am even more daft than I appear."

"Doubtful," she said, and even *she* wasn't sure how she meant it. But he didn't seem to be insulted by any of the possibilities.

"Forgive me for me boldness, lass, but you do not seem the sort to be content on some country hillock, watching autumn chill to winter."

"You know very little of me," she said, and found that despite her considerable good sense, she wanted to tell him the truth about herself.

"I but wait with bated breath to learn more," he said.

She stared at him a moment, then shook her head. "Tell me, do your bumbling ploys work on the tittering maids of your homeland?"

He laughed. "Not near oft enough."

"And I can assure you they will not work on me."

"So attached to your husband, are you?" he asked, and crossing the aisle, tossed a bit of fodder to the soft-eyed milk cow.

"Till death do us part."

"And yet he is gone."

"But never replaced," she said.

"He must be quite a shining example of manhood to have won such loyalty."

"Perhaps I am just that sort," she said, and turning at the end of the barn, paced slowly toward him, still running her gloved fingers over the tops of the stalls.

"Loyal?" he asked.

"Yes." She stood within a few feet of him now, and regardless of her words of staunch faithfulness, she felt his allure like a warm wind on her face. Could feel it washing away her pretenses. Odd. It was not as if she had been cloistered before leaving her troupe. There had been more than a few men interested in her charms. Truth to tell, there had been more than a hundred. But they did not have his . . . something. And perhaps he could feel her own despicable yearning, for he faced her straight on, watching her, his mischievous angel eyes never wavering.

"So you are never tempted?"

She gave him the meanest of smiles and remembered her mission here. "Not by roughshod Irishmen from Wickham," she said, and let her attention drift to the dark gelding.

"By who, then?" he asked.

She let her gaze skim the animal's graceful neck. His mane gleamed in dark waves from his proud crest. His eyes were widespread and intelligent. What a splendid animal.

"None but my husband," she lied, and found Gallagher's eyes again.

"How very convenient."

"Much more than convenient," she said. Gripping a plank that ran perpendicular to the ceiling, she leaned back to arm's length and sighed toward the heavens as if she could not wait for her beloved's return. "He is everything—"

"Careful!" cried the Irishman, and leaping forward, snatched her hand from the stall just as the gelding's teeth snapped together.

Indigo backed away, shaking his heavy mane.

"Did he hurt you?" Gallagher asked, quieter now, but still holding her wrist.

Holy hell, that horse was a handful. It made her want nothing more than to hop aboard and let him run till they were breathless.

"Clarette?"

She dragged her gaze from the gelding's. "What?"

He turned her hand, gazing at it. "Are you unscathed?"

"Yes," she said, but suddenly the barn seemed strangely airless.

He took a step toward her. "You must be more careful."

If the cow's stall had not been behind her, she would have stepped back. Really, she would have. It wasn't as if she was mesmerized by his eyes, immobilized by his touch.

"You are certain you're unhurt?" he asked, and slipping her sleeve toward her elbow, bared her wrist.

"Of course," she breathed.

"It would be a shame to harm even an inch of such skin."

"Well, consider me shameless," she said, then sternly reprimanded herself for such a silly attempt at wit. She was a baroness, for God's sake. Or, barring that, she was Rom. Either one should be woman enough to withstand his pathetic advances. "I am unscathed."

He raised his gaze to hers for a moment. His thumb felt like magic as it worked a circle against the tender flesh of her inner wrist. "Tell me, lass, why do you take such risks?"

"Risks!" She tried to guffaw. It came out as nothing more than a soft puff of air, more like a sigh than a scoff. "Forgive me if I did not think the byre such a deadly place."

"I was thinking of yesterday," he said, "when you rode that black devil as if he were your pet pony."

"He's not a devil," she said.

"Nay?"

They were inches apart now, his eyes enthralling, his hands warm velvet against her skin.

"Just . . . just frustrated," she said.

The left corner of his scandalous lips canted up as his fingers trilled across her flesh. "Do we still speak of the gelding?"

She managed a nod, though it was a close thing.

"And why is he frustrated?"

"He doesn't like to be told what to do."

He moved half a step nearer. "And what of you, lass? Are you frustrated too?" He kissed her wrist. She tried to move away. Really she did, but he was some kind of weird magician when it came to skin.

"No."

"So you do not mind being told what to do?"

"No one tells me what to do."

"Then I shall ask nicely," he said, and taking the barest step toward her, slipped his arm beneath her cape, encircling her waist. "Might I kiss you?"

She opened her mouth to speak. It was possible she even intended to refuse. But no sound came out.

Perhaps he took her silence as agreement? Or perhaps her acquiescence wasn't required, for in that moment he leaned in.

She felt the breath leave her lungs. Felt his lips touch hers. Felt a thousand titillating sensations explode in her suddenly overheated body.

His hand moved up her back, pulling her against him as his thigh, as hard as chiseled granite, settled between hers.

She moaned. But whether she was a shameless baroness or a lusty Gypsy, she would never know, because in that instant he stepped abruptly away, shoving her into the empty stall behind her.

# Chapter 5

**F**ifty years later Sean would never be certain why he did what he did.

True, he heard Emily coming even before she opened her mouth to call for her mistress. And yes, he realized the scandal that would ensue if they were found in such a compromising situation. But wasn't that why he had come here in the first place? To cause scandal? To ruin her marriage? To ruin her *life*?

But in that fractured second when he heard the maid coming, he found he couldn't do it. Maybe, in the end, he was trying to protect the baroness despite everything he knew of her. But maybe it was something far more sinister; perhaps it was not enough to have her found in his embrace. Perhaps even then, with her lips soft and warm against his, he wanted to see her completely crushed. Or maybe he simply wanted the opportunity to bed her before the charade ended.

Whatever the reason, he shoved her, without a moment's hesitation, into the deepest shadows of the nearby stall just as Emily bustled in. A loose-knit shawl covered her head and shoulders. She'd dragged the edge forward to shield her eyes from the glare of the lantern.

"My . . . Oh . . . if it ain't the 'andsome Sean Gallagher 'isself. I didn't see you there," she said, and dropped the wrap from her strawberry curls.

With feigned nonchalance, Sean lifted a wooden bucket from a nearby peg and stepped more fully into the light. "I was just about to be finishing up chores. Is something amiss, lass?"

"Amiss? No. But something is a'missing," she said, and laughed at her own wit, plump cheeks dimpling. She was a pretty girl, but he had always preferred more worldly wise women, experienced ladies who had every intention of using him and tossing him aside. He didn't mind loving and leaving. Indeed, he was an expert at leaving, but quite ill-equipped at becoming jealous of his liaisons' rich husbands or subsequent lovers. Indeed, as far as he knew, he was entirely incapable of jealousy.

"You've lost something, then?" he asked.

"The lady of the 'ouse has gone roving again."

"You've misplaced the baroness?"

"'Twas not I who done the misplacing," she said, and lowering her voice, leaned closer to be heard. "And just betwixt you, me, and the slop bucket, I say 'tis no great loss if she don't never come toddling back."

Sean resisted a smile, refrained from skimming his

gaze to the stall behind him, and hoped to hell the object of their discussion wouldn't come barging out like a bull on a rampage at the maid's waspish slurs. The baroness didn't seem the type to suffer insults in silence.

"I take it you don't care for her," he said, and found that it gave him a certain amount of pleasure to know the woman who had ruined his family was just within hearing.

"I don't, and I'd tell 'er that to 'er face, given the chance. She ain't 'ad a good word to say since coming to Knoll-crest."

"And how long ago was that?"

"Ten and a half days," said the maid, and sniffed.

"You're counting?"

She canted her head at him in a sassy manner. "And not many more remaining, to my way of thinking."

"Oh?"

She shrugged, glanced outside as if to make sure they weren't overheard, then stepped closer and lowered her voice. "I 'eard she made a deal with the master."

"The baron?" he asked, sotto voce and honestly intrigued.

"Nay," she hissed, and catching his hand in an intimate grip, leaned closer still, the upper reaches of her round breasts just visible above her bodice. "The baron's old sire."

"What sort of deal?"

"I 'eard Gregors tell Margarite that if 'er ladyship

bears a rightful heir, she'll gain her 'usband's inheritance. And my lord'll be left 'igh and dry. Old Gregors is to keep an eye on 'er to see if she sidles up to another, if you take my meaning."

He was pretty sure he did.

She nodded sharply, important with her secret knowledge. "But the good baron will 'ave none of 'er even though 'e knows nothing of the arrangement."

But he *did* know. In fact, that very arrangement was the reason the baron had hired him to come to Knollcrest, but that wasn't the part of the story that particularly intrigued him. "So they've not . . . shared a bed?" For reasons entirely unknown to him, this unlikely news soared through his system like swallows in flight.

"Well, he left the very day he brought her to Knollcrest, didn't he?"

"But that doesn't necessarily mean—"

"My lord's too good for the likes of 'er," she said. "A thoughtful, kindly man. The very reverse of the lady, and 'andsome as the day is long."

Thoughtful and kindly? When Sean had met him, he'd been well on his way to gin poisoning. But not so far into his cups that he couldn't hire a passing stranger to seduce his wife and make sure his spying butler knew enough about it to report it to the man who held the purse strings. At the time, Sean had justified the idea in his own mind, for it coincided cozily with his own plans, but now he wondered about this baron. "So he didn't spend a single night here with her?" he asked, baffled by the idea.

She nodded again and looked a little peeved by his disbelief, but he couldn't help questioning further.

"And why would that be, do you think?"

Emily made a sound like a hissing snake and arched away from him, voice still hushed. "You've got a taste of her tongue, sure."

"She can be a bit harsh, perhaps, but—"

"A bit harsh? I seen adders with more 'uman kindness than she's got. Say . . ." she said and narrowed her eyes at him. "You ain't set your cap for 'er yourself, 'ave you?"

He raised his brows at the girl's absurdity. "I'm Irish, lass, not mad."

She stared at him a moment, then laughed. "And here I was a'thinking it was all one and the same."

"I'm wounded that—" he began, then paused to peer past her plump shoulder. "What's that, then?"

"What?" She jumped, making him suspect she wouldn't be *entirely* eager to share her feelings with Lady Tilmont.

"Someone seemed to be near the garden gate," he lied.

"It's not the baroness, sure," she said, and glowered into the darkness.

"I don't know who else it might have been."

"God save us," she said, and flipping her dampened

shawl back over her head, turned with a scowl. "Even a peahen has enough sense to come in out of this weather. I don't know why Gregors sent *me*. It ain't my job to . . ." Her voice dwindled as she stepped outside and hurried into the darkness.

Gallagher waited until the count of three, then snuffed out the lantern. In a moment he was back to the supposedly empty stall.

"Unless you're spending the night, lass, you'd best leave now," he said. "I don't—"

"What did she want?"

He jerked in surprise, finding her behind him. "How the devil did you get out there?"

"What did she say?"

He peered into the shadows of the stall. The side walls were constructed of solid planking. Designed to house amorous stallions, they were seven feet tall if they were an inch. He scowled.

"I don't believe she's overly fond of you."

She raised a brow. "It's going to be difficult to bear up under that devastating disappointment," she said, "but why don't you tell me her exact words nonetheless."

He was becoming accustomed to the darkness and could just make out the soft glow of her eyes. "If you don't care, why do you wish to know, lass?"

"Perhaps I'm as bored as you suspected. Tell me."

"She said you were to bear your husband's child," he said, and watched her. It was difficult to say for certain, but it almost seemed that she blushed.

"Doesn't that go without saying?" she asked.

"But your husband isn't here." The soft darkness and their close proximity made the situation seem hopelessly intimate. Without trying, he could remember the feel of her lips against his.

"Call me naive but I don't believe procreation is considered a full-time occupation," she said. "Surely you know that a man of my husband's stature has other duties to see to."

"Duties?" he said, and almost laughed out loud.

She turned angrily, but he caught her arm. "So he was called away on business?"

She hesitated only a moment. "Of course."

"After so short a time wed?"

She glanced away, lips pursed. And by the ragged light of the besieged moon, she looked as tempting as a siren. "My lord is ever mindful of our financial standing. For me and our progeny to be."

"Progeny?" he said, and now he did laugh.

She gritted her teeth.

"If I were your bridegroom I would be more mindful of you and less so of coin," he said, and reaching out, touched her face.

Her eyes lifted to his, and for one shattering second he thought she would kiss him, but in that instant Emily called again.

She pulled out of his grasp, then turning rapidly away, flitted through the doorway and into the shadows.


Her self-recriminations began immediately. Holy hell, what had she been thinking? A lady of breeding didn't hobnob with the help. Didn't spar with the underlings.

But she was no lady of breeding. She was—

She stopped herself immediately, remembering her mission despite the Irishman's hot allure.

She was Clarette Stenejem, Lady Tilmont. No one to be trifled with. And she should have stayed inside.

Lifting her skirts, she peered through the darkness toward the towering manse she had left less than a half hour before. At least she could have avoided the barn . . . or his *lair*, as she should call it. The man was as subtle as a cannon. She was a married woman and yet he tried to tempt her at every turn. She should send him packing, she thought, but glancing toward the byre, she remembered the cast of his crooked grin. Good God, it took her breath away. But maybe that was just the stench of the barnyard, she mused, and lifting her nose, proceeded toward the house.

"I cannot believe my eyes."

Savaana spun toward the cultured voice that issued

from the darkness. It was almost familiar, but not quite. "Who's there?"

The intruder stayed in the deepest of shadows. "Though the frilly costume of the simpering *ton* suits you. I would not have thought it so."

Her heart was thrumming in her chest but she kept her voice steady, buying time, trying to place his voice. "What is it you want?"

"I thought that much was obvious. Come along now," he said, but in that moment she raised her chin and buried herself fully in the sharp-edged persona of Lady Tilmont.

"I told Gregors we should get a hound to keep the vermin off the estate."

"Who—" he began, but then chuckled, low and deep as he stepped forward. "I always said you could play a part."

"One scream and my man will be on you," she warned, and backed away a cautious step.

"Your man!" Reaching out, he jerked her into the shadows, hands hard as steel on her arms. "Is that what you call him?"

"Let me go!"

"I saw you with him. Flirting like a whore."

"My lady!" Gallagher's voice resonated in the darkness. "Where are you?"

"Not a word," hissed her captor. His fingers tightened like talons. She dare not speak, but she dare not remain silent either.

"I'm here!" she yelled.

"Damn you! Play your games, then. Your grandfather will be the one to suffer for them," he said, and thrusting her roughly to the ground, disappeared like a wraith into the darkness.

"Me lady!" Gallagher's brogue broke the sharp silence.

"Here." Her voice was shaking, her elbows bruised where she had landed on them. She shifted now, ready to rise, but he was there, reaching for her. She let him help her, let him gather her gently against his chest.

"Lass, you're shaking. What happened?"

"I don't . . ." She shifted her gaze to the dark walnut trees that ringed the towering stone house. "I don't know. A man . . ." Her voice failed her.

"What man?"

"I've no idea."

"Lady Tilmont!" Gregors's cultured voice seemed strident and coarse after the Irishman's soothing brogue. In a moment he was there beside them, lantern swaying from his uplifted hand. Seeing them together in the darkness, he locked his attention on Savaana. "What goes on here?"

"Take her to the house," Gallagher said.

"See here—" Gregor began, but the other brooked no objections.

"Now!" he ordered, and turning, melted silently into the darkness.

# Chapter 6

Savaana moved straight and true down the stairway. Her nose was lifted at the perfect angle, her fingers skimmed the rail, her tread was light on the rose-hued carpet.

She was Lady Tilmont, wealthy, well-bred, refined. She was married now and 'twas her duty to care for this lowly estate, even if it was miles from civilization. Thus she wouldn't dwell on the attack, for it would do her no good. Perhaps the villain had been a wandering trades-man . . . with a highly refined accent. Or perhaps it had been the flirty Irishman himself. He had not, after all, shown up until after her attacker had disappeared. Of course, she had heard his voice calling from a distance while the other man was still clasping her arms, but that proved nothing. Not in her mind. Who knows what kind of shenanigans the Irishman might be able to conjure? He was a Celt, after all, and therefore suspect by nature.

Another possibility flitted fitfully through her mind,

but she swatted it down, kept it silent. For now. For a little longer.

An hour or so after the incident, Gallagher had come to the house to proclaim that he had seen no sign of an intruder. But then he wouldn't, would he? Not if he himself were the culprit. Maybe he only wished to scare her. To frighten her into his arms. But that would never work. She was no wilting lily, though she had been something of a *shaken* lily.

To battle her nerves, Margarite had suggested she partake of her favorite beverage. The Tuica seemed as strong as turpentine against her throat. She'd coughed a little but finished the plum brandy posthaste. After that she went to bed and slept until well after noon, breakfasting on poached eggs and muffins. But now she was ready to meet the world.

"Gregors." Her voice was strong and demanding. He appeared in a heartbeat, bowing stiffly. She looked sternly down her nose at him. "See that the wagon is made ready."

"The wagon, my lady?" Although his expression remained perfectly unchanged, she could hear the uncertainty in his voice, and in that instant she felt a tiny chink fall from her carefully polished armor.

Her mind spun for the correct word. Not caravan. Hack? Cart? Toboggan? . . . Oh hell! She was Lady Tilmont, she remembered, and raised her chin another notch. "Do you not speak the king's English, Gregors?"

Had she been asked, she would not have thought it possible for him to stiffen even more. She would have been wrong.

"Might you mean the cabriolet, my lady?"

Cabriolet. Well hell, of course that's what she meant. She gave a disdainful nod. "See that it's made ready," she repeated, and turned back up the stairs.

He cleared his throat. "'Tis a bit late in the day for a sojourn to London, is it not, baroness?"

She turned back, heart beating just a little too fast. Surely the hearts of well-bred ladies did not beat more than once or twice an hour. "Did you hear me say aught of London?"

"I but assumed."

She lifted her skirts in a regal hand and turned away. "Do not assume, Gregors."

"I've no wish to pry, my lady—"

"Then you should definitely refrain from doing that as well," she advised.

"But I feel it my duty to inform Mr. Gallagher where he will be taking you so as to prepare him for his days ahead."

"If you must know, I feel a need to do a bit of shopping. Therefore I will be traveling to Darlington."

"Darlington, my lady?" He raised his brows half a

centimeter. It was the equivalent of an open-mouthed stare in another. "To shop?"

She glared at him, though she knew her mistake. Darlington was not exactly known as a shopping mecca, but she had stuck her toe in the ground and she would remain there.

"As butler here you should already be aware that Knollcrest's larders are low on sugar."

He continued to stare.

She executed a delicate shudder. "Only a barbarian or a Celt would drink tea without sugar."

Still no expression, though she'd aimed the barb directly at his ancestry. Perhaps he wasn't Scottish after all. "Therefore . . ." she said, sounding vastly peeved. "I shall be traveling to Darlington to retrieve the necessary provisions."

He gave her the slightest inclination of his head. "As you will, of course, my lady, but surely Clare could make the—"

"Clare, " she began, "is the one who has failed to fill the larders adequately up till this point. I see no reason to believe she will improve her performance today. Thus I will be leaving within the hour." She turned again.

"As you will, my lady."

"And the Irishman will remain at Knollcrest."

"Your pardon, my lady?"

She didn't deign to glance at him. "If you are hard of

hearing, Gregors, perhaps you could find a replacement with sharper senses," she said, and glided back up the stairs.

"If only I were entirely deaf," he said.

She pivoted toward him, sure she'd heard wrong. "What say you?"

"He is the only one left," Gregors said. "Since Mr. Underhill's injury."

He was mocking her. She was sure of it, and though some traitorous part of her was tempted to laugh, she managed to say, "I'm certain you'll find someone," in a voice cold enough to freeze blood.

"May I inquire why you wish for Mr. Gallagher to remain behind?"

She studied him as if he were a descendent of some despicable insect. "If you must know, I do not entirely trust him." That much was true. It was also true that she didn't entirely trust herself. And how unlikely was that? "What of James?" She had seen the aging shepherd meandering through the flocks on more than one occasion. He was short and red-faced and not the least appealing. James would be perfect.

"His wife has begun her lying in."

"He's got a wife?"

He didn't tell her she was acting the idiot, but she was quite sure he thought it. "Yes, my lady. Hence the lying in."

"And she's giving birth?"

"I can think of no other reason for her confinement."

"Well . . ." She made an impatient gesture with one hand, but she was losing her haughty edge. Childbirth was not something with which she was entirely comfortable. Drina was Dook Natsia's midwife, and none usurped her authority. Nor had Savaana ever wished to. She was quite certain Lady Tilmont would feel the same. "That cannot take all day, surely."

For a moment she thought Gregors might actually laugh at her foolishness. In fact, it was a mystery to her how he could refrain. "I'm afraid it has been known to do just that, my lady."

She lowered her brows. "Very well, then, what of his eldest lad?"

"Enos . . . ?" He didn't so much as raise a brow. " . . . has yet to reach his ninth birthday."

"Emily?"

"Afraid of horses."

"Cook."

He gave her a single blink that spoke volumes. Good God, this man should be a mime. He could make a small fortune on the streets of Paris while being as irritating as he wished. "Perhaps you are unaware that before being convinced to come to Knollcrest, Monsieur LaFont was the chef for the Duke of Elbany."

She wasn't exactly sure what he was saying, but she

guessed it had something to do with the reason Cook would not be driving her to Darlington.

"Very well," she said, her tone pinched. "Then you shall have to take the ribbons yourself." She had heard that phrase on the bustling streets of London during one of her performances there and stashed it away for later use. But she couldn't have foreseen this little eventuality.

"My lady . . ." His stare was deadly even. "I do not venture out of doors."

Holy hell. She stared back. Was he serious? she wondered, and realized he didn't exactly seem the type to enjoy a good jest. "I beg your pardon."

"And you have it," he said stiffly, but Lady Tilmont did not back down so easily.

"Are you refusing to drive me to the village, Gregors?"

There was, perhaps, a pause for a fraction of a second. "Yes, I believe I am."

Even a lady knew when she was beaten, or at least she had to assume so. "Then you must find me a chaperone."

He was silent for a full three seconds this time. "A chaperone, my lady?"

"Dem it, Gregors, I could have sworn there was no echo in this house last we spoke. I do not approve of the way so many demireps go about unescorted these days, and I'll not be one of them."

"Commendable, I'm sure," he said. "But be that as

it may, I fear I have no access to someone suitable for such an—"

"I will have a chaperone, Gregors," she vowed. "Or you will be carrying the cabriolet to Darlington on your back. Do you understand me?"

Apparently he did because not two hours later a chaperone arrived. She was approximately three hundred years old. As far as Savaana could tell, the lady was totally bald, though most of her pate was covered by a powdered wig the size of a bushel basket. Beribboned and plumed, it sat askance on her oversized head.

Gregors introduced them himself. "Lady Tilmont, may I present Mrs. Edwards."

Savaana inclined her head and wondered vaguely if the poor old fossil was about to fall dead at her feet, but Gregors seemed oblivious to the possibility of death and soldiered on.

"Mrs. Edwards was the lady in waiting for—"

"My lady!" The old woman's voice boomed through the house like an errant cannon blast. "I am Mrs. Edwards."

Savaana opened her mouth to speak, but the other shrieked on.

"I was a lady of the bedchamber for Queen Caroline."

"Caroline of Brunswick, the Regent's queen?"

"Not Prinny's tramp, of course," Edwards yelled. "George the Second's lady wife."

Savaana quickly tried to figure out the implications of

that fact but was boggled by the possibilities. Caroline of Brunswick had died more than seventy years earlier. "Well . . ." She gave the old woman her most refined smile. "Let us be about our business, then."

Darlington was little more than a bevy of hovels stuck together with wattle and pig manure. But it had a decent dry goods store, which seemed to sell a bit of everything. They stopped there first.

Gallagher had changed from his rough leather breeches into Knollcrest's gray and black livery. She was quite sure he should look servile in the uniform, but somehow it managed the opposite, making him seem like nobility playing in peasant's clothing. He handed her down, grinning roguishly. Their fingers met for a moment, but she refused to acknowledge the spark of something that zapped between them. For God's sake, she hadn't tumbled out of the turnip cart yesterday, she reminded herself, and tugged her hand impatiently from his grip.

Her grocery purchase took all of fifteen minutes, because, truth to tell, she couldn't care less if Knollcrest's larders held nothing more than crickets and dust. But she wouldn't think of her true reasons for being there. Not yet. For now she would remain firmly in character. She glanced about. A blue bonnet was displayed at a cocky angle on the newel post of a railing near the front of the store. She ran her fingers over its brim.

"'Tis a comely piece," Gallagher said from behind her.

She gave him a glance over her shoulder. Didn't drivers usually stay with the damned wagon? she wondered, but had found no reason to insist that he remain there. Even Mrs. Edward had hobbled in and sat nodding away in a corner of the store near the window. Maybe he had merely come in to assist the elderly woman. Then again, for all she knew he might have a penchant for women's garments. For a moment she imagined him in naught but her cotton drawers.

He raised one brow as if he could read her thoughts, but Lady Tilmont was not the blushing sort. Savaana was certain of it.

"'Twould bring out the color of your eyes," he said, and she forced herself to meet his gaze.

"As it happens, Smallwick, I rather like the color where it is," she said, and he laughed.

"'Twould be my pleasure to purchase it for you."

Savaana glanced toward the shop's proprietress. She was a middle-aged woman with a no-nonsense look about her. Luckily, she was too busy hanging dried herbs to notice their conversation.

"Need I remind you, yet again, that I am a married woman?" Savaana asked, returning her hard gaze to the Irishman's.

He shook his head, never breaking eye contact. "I believe that is what the lass in yon corner is for."

She scowled.

"Wee Mrs. Edwards," he said, though it was entirely possible her chaperone weighed more than the two of them together. "Did ye not bring her along to keep yourself from the likes of me?"

"Are you implying that I find you irresistible?"

"Aye," he said, and smiled . . . irresistibly.

"Well, I do not."

"Then why bring the enchanting Mrs.—"

"I hired Mrs. Edwards to keep things proper."

"Did you now?" he asked, and took a step toward her, crowding a little, though in truth there was a full two feet of space between them.

"Yes, I did."

"You know what I find improper, lass?"

"No," she said, "and neither do I care."

"Improper and improbable and unimaginable?"

She wrinkled her nose as though offended by his scent, but in truth he smelled of leather and sunlight. "Bathing on a weekly basis?" she guessed.

His full lips quirked up again. "The fact that your husband could leave a fair beauty like you alone after so little time in your bed." Reaching out, he took her hand in his and skimmed his thumb slowly across her knuckles.

Feelings sparked through her like naughty fireflies, but she refrained from yanking away as if burned. She also refrained from dragging him to the ground like a wolf on a hare. Instead, she lifted her gaze slowly to the busy proprietress, then shifted it regally back to his.

"Unhand me, sir," she said, though in truth, she could not quite find the motivation to pull from his velvet clasp. "Or I shall be forced to take appropriate measures."

His dimples flicked into place, and though he moved no closer, she felt as if they shared the very air they breathed. "Such as taking me to your bed?"

The suggestion made a thousand rampant thoughts thunder through her head, but she banished each one. Angry at her own wayward imaginings, she said, "Such as kneeing you in the crotch."

For a moment he was speechless, and then he laughed. The sound was low and beautiful, rumbling erotically through her soul. The proprietress glanced toward them. Savaana cleared her throat and tugged her fingers from his, though, in truth, their hands were well hidden behind a display of men's hats.

Still, she glanced nervously toward Mrs. Edwards, who had awaken with a start and a snort. There seemed to be something about the Irishman's chuckle that brought every woman alive to her senses.

As for Gallagher himself, he was watching her, eyes laughing, making no attempt to move closer, no pretense of moving farther away. "You are not what I expected. That I admit," he said.

"Oh?" She raised a brow and watched the proprietress

distractedly hang a bouquet of borage beside a cluster of dried rosemary. "And what did you expect, Mr. Wickerheimer? Some besotted chit so brainless she would drop into your bed like a wilted daisy petal?"

His lips cranked up another notch. "'Tis not too late," he said.

"Believe me, it will take more than a few sultry glances to get me to your bed."

"Would kisses help?" he asked. "For I'm willing to part with a few."

"Try it and you'll—" she began, but just then the proprietress wended her way between a burlap bag of fine ground flour and a wooden stand bearing a burnished sidesaddle.

"Is there something that has caught your interest, my lady?" she asked, and Gallagher raised his brows, as if mimicking her question with a glance.

Savaana raised her chin. "This bonnet," she said. "Would you mind if I tried it on for a moment?"

"Not a'tall, my lady," the woman said, and taking it from the newel post where it rested, handed it over.

Savaana perched it immediately atop her head. The shopkeeper nodded soberly.

"Very flattering," she said. "It brings out the color of your eyes."

Shifting her gaze to the Irishman's, Savaana refrained from saying where she'd like to keep her color.

"I shall purchase it, then," she said.

"Very good, my lady. Is there anything else I can do for you while you are in our fair village?"

She glanced about, remembering her persona. "What with the incessant rain of late, I have been rather bored. What have you to alleviate that?"

"Well . . . we are not London."

Savaana didn't bother to comment. Instead, she raised an understated brow.

"But we do have our share of attractions."

She raised her other brow.

"A troupe of entertainers just arrived in town."

"Entertainers?" Savaana felt her heart rate pick up.

"Gypsies, I believe. But I hear they're quite good," said the proprietress. "One of them is nobility, I believe."

Savaana kept her expression placid, her tone skeptical. "Nobility in a traveling troupe?"

"Well, you know how Gypsies are. They all believe themselves to be descended from kings. But one of them is said to be a duke."

"Oh?"

"Yes, the Duke of Natsia or some such."

# Chapter 7

It was nearing dusk when Gallagher eased the quiet chestnut to a halt in a little glen at the north edge of Darlington. A crowd had gathered on a grassy hillock. In the softly muted background, maple trees marched along the curving course of the river. Gold and scarlet leaves fluttered gently against the darkening sky, sweeping in an undulating arc around the north side of the hill, almost reaching the growing cluster of onlookers.

Mrs. Edwards, seated snuggly between Savaana and the Irishman, straightened her ancient back, peering out over the sea of heads. "It appears to be a carnival of sorts," she said.

"Yes." Savaana tried to hold onto Lady Tilmont's haughty demeanor, but it was slipping away, being swallowed by the Gypsy girl that ran wild in her mind.

It was all she could do to retain the carefully cultured voice, to keep from leaping from the vehicle in search of her grandfather. For during the previous night, alone in the dark of her bedchamber, she had come to the only logical solution: Tamas had been her attacker. There was no other explanation. She had thought for a time that perhaps the villain had been someone from Lady Tilmont's past, but after reviewing the conversation a hundred times in her buzzing head, she was certain Tamas had come to retrieve her.

Savaana had no idea how he had found her. She had informed no one but her grandfather of her plans, and though he had been reluctant to let her go, he understood her need. Indeed, he had supplied her with a small pistol to keep her safe.

As for the remainder of the troupe, she had simply told them she would be gone for a fortnight. She had long known, however, that Tamas foolishly thought of her as his own, his mistress saved for a later date. She had not, however, thought he would threaten her grandfather to get her back. Then again, maybe his words hadn't been a threat at all. Maybe they were a warning. Perhaps Grandfather's health was deteriorating and Tamas had but come to inform her. She had to find out. But she was not willing to quit the charade, not until it was absolutely unavoidable. There was too much at stake.

But Grandfather was nowhere to be seen. That much was apparent at a glance. Only the caravan was visible. It stood off to their right, nestled in a copse of rowan. Swirls of rich burgundy and muted greens embellished its lavish design. Narrow steps led up to the small, arched door, but the shafts stood empty. El Rey was nowhere in sight. Without her act, he would not be needed, but she longed to see him, to leap aboard his back, to breathe in his homey scent, the very essence of her people.

"I say, there must be a carnival in town," Mrs. Edwards repeated loudly.

"Yes." Savaana could feel Gallagher staring at her. Grappling wildly with her image, she got a stranglehold on Lady Tilmont's snooty nature just as Tamas strode onto the hillock. He carried a trio of knives in one hand, a torch in another, and in that instant he tilted his head back and belched forth a flaming inferno into the darkening sky.

There were gasps of alarm and amazement as he straightened, chuckles as he grinned and greeted the hushing audience.

Savaana's shudder was not entirely fake. "A shabby Gypsy troupe, by the look of things," she said.

Mrs. Edwards glared out over the crowd, antiquated hoop lopsided beneath her heavy gown, not hearing a word. "Perhaps 'tis a Gypsy troupe."

"Perhaps," Savaana said, and allowed herself to search the grounds, but she recognized no one else. Might Grandfather truly be failing?

A thrush warbled its evening song. The torches had already been lit and placed on wooden poles above the ground. A few entrepreneurial townspeople had set up booths. One sold mincemeat pies. Another hawked baked apples.

"What did they call themselves?" Gallagher asked. He was still eyeing her, but she refused to squirm.

"Duke something. Though I hardly think him noble," Savaana drawled, looking at Tamas. "I but thought Mrs. Edwards could use a respite from the jostling of this lumber wagon before returning to Knollcrest."

"Dook?" Gallagher said, scowling a little. Tamas had thrown the torch aside and begun to juggle wooden handled knives that flashed in the torchlight. "Doesn't that mean magical in the Rom tongue?"

Savaana stared at him, surprised, but she calmed her heart and raised a quizzical brow. "Tell me, Mr. Wickingshire, are you, by chance, one of their lost brethren?"

He smiled at her snide tone. "Doubtful," he said. "But I do know the odd word. I think this troupe is called the Magic Gypsies." He was watching her a little too closely. "Might you be familiar with them?"

She gave a ladylike snort. "Do I look the kind to consort with—"

"Perhaps this is the troupe called Dook Natsia," shouted Mrs. Edwards. "I've heard they're quite good."

Gallagher turned from Savaana with a grin, but there was something in his eyes. Something bright and curious. "You've a sharp memory, Mrs. Edwards. Have you an unobstructed view from your seat there?"

The elder lady patted his arm affectionately. "I had a dog once, too, lad. Licked himself incessantly."

He smiled as if the world made perfect sense and lifted his gaze to Savaana's. "And what of you, my lady? Are you comfortable?"

Tamas had pulled a sword from the scabbard at his hip and was adding it to the twirling cutlery, and though her every nerve was jumping with impatience, Savaana remembered just in time to say something rude. "As comfortable as can be, I suppose, in these rustic circumstances."

"I could obtain seats for you nearer the front of the throng if you like."

"At the front?" Where Tamas could see her? Where even his children might recognize her? No. She hoped to make certain all was well with Grandfather while maintaining her adopted persona. Perhaps, if she were truly lucky, her performance at Knollcrest had convinced Tamas that she was, in fact, nothing more than what she appeared to be . . . a proud baroness caught in lowly circumstances. "And leave me exposed to this rabble?" she asked.

"I would stay close if that would calm your nerves," he said, but the look in his admiring eyes did no such thing.

"Just see to the horse," she said. "I've no wish for her to die of thirst before our return to Knollcrest."

"Certainly, my lady," he said, but his answer was barely heard above the crowd's applause. Tamas was taking his first bow. "I'll fetch water immediately." The carriage rocked as he dismounted.

She gave a brief nod, though she knew for a fact that the wooden pail usually secured beneath the footman's seat was gone.

He turned toward the rear, then returned in a moment. "The bucket seems to have gone missing."

"Missing!" She sharpened her scowl as a thousand worries gnawed at her. "That cannot be."

"I would have thought not, my lady. And yet, it is."

"You must have forgotten to bring it along."

He looked at her strangely for several seconds, but finally bowed gallantly. "I'm certain you're right," he said. Behind him Hanzi and Luca were hastily stringing up their father's high wire. "My apologies. I shall ask about to see if there might be another vessel I might use."

"You'll do no such thing," she said. "I'll have no servant of mine begging about like an abandoned cur. Take the mare to the river off to the left there. It will be good to get our weight off her back."

"What's that?" he asked.

"Unhook her. The pad is galling her withers," she said, and dammit, he was looking at her strangely again. She refrained from clearing her throat. "Not that I care," she assured him, "but I've no wish to be stranded at Knoll-crest without a carriage horse."

"As you wish, my lady."

It seemed to take him forever to unhook the traces, longer still to release the shafts, but finally he was leading the chestnut away. Savaana waited, breath held. Beside her, Mrs. Edwards was nodding off toward sleep again.

The world seemed to be moving in slow motion, but finally their chaperone was snoring and Gallagher was out of sight, hidden by the towering maples.

Savaana delayed only an instant longer. Then, lifting her skirts in one gloved hand, she stepped from the carriage and glided regally toward the river.

"Will you have an ice, my lady?"

She remembered to look down her nose at the vendor, but her haughty persona was all but shattered and she could not trust her voice. Thus, she merely shook her head and moved on.

In a minute she was in the cover of the trees. Once there, she spared a single glance behind her before grabbing up her skirts and racing through the underbrush. Dodging rocks and roots, she sprinted a circuitous course through the woods until she stood hidden in the foliage directly behind the brightly colored van. Pausing, she listened. It was dim there and quiet. Mira was setting up camp. The little girls were gathering firewood. Off to her left, Uncle Shandor was hobbling El Rey in a patch of wild clover. The big piebald lifted his head and whickered at her, but none of her kin took note.

Grandfather was nowhere to be seen. Where was he? Could Tamas have been telling the truth? Was his health failing? Savaana clenched her fists and glanced toward the silent van.

Not a sound issued from that vehicle. Perhaps she should simply ask Mira about Grandfather's well-being, but Mira would surely report Savaana's odd appearance to her husband, proving his suspicions and subsequently ruining her fragile plans. Thus she waited, crouched behind a tree.

The children wandered farther into the woods, chattering as they went. Mira followed them. In a minute the trio was out of sight. Savaana then dashed toward the van. Flattening her back against the brightly painted side, she waited, breathing hard, but no one had seen her. Thus she finally eased out of hiding and quietly opened the back door.

"Grandfather?" she whispered, but no one whispered back. "Hello?"

Her eyes adjusted slowly to the dimness. The bed was empty. She glanced toward the hook that usually held his mandolin. It was bare. He rarely played for the crowds these days, but he liked to sit by the river and harmonize with the rush of the waters.

Either he had taken it or—

But she heard Tamas laugh as he moved through the woods toward her. Luca and Hanzi must be performing their tumbling act, giving him a few minutes to cause trouble.

One quick glance outside assured her he was yet out of sight. But he would be there in a moment, and if he saw her, he would surely reveal her true identity to the staff at Knollcrest. Standing on the ledge of the van, she weighed her options. She was several paces from the nearest maple.

"So you have never seen a performer's traveling home?" Tamas was saying.

"I have never even seen a performer." The young woman's voice was soft and breathy.

Had Savaana been herself, she would have sent the girl packing. Dook Natsia didn't need trouble with irate husbands and worried fathers. Nor did poor Mira need Tamas to be an ass. But just now she had other worries. In a handful of seconds Tamas would round the corner and find her there.

"Come back and see—" he began, and in that instant, Savaana leapt for the nearest branch. She soared through the air, grabbed the horizontal limb and swung her body into the lush underbrush.

Landing on her feet, she crouched and froze, absolutely silent, listening.

"What was that?" asked the girl, voice wispy.

"What?" Tamas's voice was as smooth as the proverbial paved road to hell.

"I thought I saw something fly into the trees."

"A thrush, most like."

"No. It was . . . it was big."

"Then it must be a *mulani*."

"*Mulani*?"

"A ghost." His tone was eerie. "You'd best stay close to me," he warned, and the girl giggled.

Savaana rolled her eyes and straightened. If Grandfather was well, he would have gone down to the water to harmonize with the bustling waves. But where exactly? She scanned the riverbank. A stag glanced up, water dripping from its muzzle, then turned and dashed into the woods behind it.

So no one had scared the deer before her own approach. Perhaps Grandfather had gone in the other direction then. Or maybe—

She heard a noise and raised her head, listening. Was it Grandfather's ethereal music? Turning to the right, she hurried through the woods, stopping periodically to listen. There it was again. Lifting her skirts high, she ran now, following the wending course of the river. A hill rose up ahead of her. The river dropped away. To her left, the bank became steep and muddy, but she kept to the high ground, only stopping every few yards to listen again.

Then she heard it, the haunting refrain of Bach's Bour-rée singing through the trees. She glanced across the bustling river. And there he was, sitting amidst the singing leaves, eyes closed, lost in the beauty of his music. He was well. He was happy. "Grandfather," she whispered in relief, and stepped forward.

"Hello?"

*Gallagher!* She froze at the sound of his burred voice.

"I didn't mean to frighten you," he called. Bracken rustled at his approach.

Dropping to a crouch, Savaana jerked her attention toward the noise. He came into view, dark tousled hair just visible above a nodding spray of elderberries, and in that second she did the only thing she could think to do. She leapt, diving off the embankment toward the steep slope below.

Perhaps she imagined it, but she thought she heard his intake of breath as she disappeared. There was no time to think of that, however, for she was free-falling, gliding downward until she tucked into a ball. Tumbling onto a bed of autumn leaves, she gained her feet. A hidden branch caught her toe, twisting her ankle. But she ignored the pain. Tucking again, she rolled behind a nearby boulder.

"Sweet suffering saints." She heard his voice from up above and tried to control her breathing. "Is someone down there?"

She didn't move. Didn't answer. A crackle of noise sounded on the far side of the boulder. She jerked, pressing her shoulder against the warm granite and breathing deeply as a gravelly voice echoed up from the water's edge.

"What's that?" Hidden from her view, the old man above her was not more than thirty feet from where she hid.

Gallagher answered back. "Ahh, hello. I thought I saw . . . I thought I heard someone from below. It must have been you."

"Oh, aye, I like to do a bit of fishing here." The old man's voice had a slow, steady rhythm. "While me old team drinks."

Savaana remained as she was, not daring to make a move, though her ankle hurt like the devil. Gritting her teeth against the pain, she remained absolutely silent, waiting.

"'Tis a fine day to spend with the fishes," Gallagher called. "How be the trout hereabouts?"

Holy hell! Trout? Now?

"Truth to tell, they're scarce enough, but there are bream aplenty if Ned here don't scare 'em off." She could hear splashing as one of the horses pawed at the water. "Go on now, you daft bugger, quit stirring up the mud. There's others want to drink."

"Bream you say," Gallagher called. "'Tis good to

know. For now I'd best fetch me own cob before she wanders off, though."

The fisherman didn't answer, and in a minute Savaana heard Gallagher move away. She took a deep breath and closed her eyes, relaxing against the boulder. He had gone for the mare and would have no reason to return to the water's—

But suddenly her eyes snapped open wide.

He was gone. Which meant he could be heading back to Mrs. Edwards at this very minute. Cursing silently, she rose to her feet. Her ankle screamed. She almost did the same, but clamped her teeth on her bottom lip and swallowed the pain.

Dear God, there was no way she was going to be able to beat the Irishman back to the damned carriage. Unless. . .

Peeking past the rough boulder, she glanced in the direction of the fisherman. He had settled his back against a toppled tree that had come loose from the loamy earth at the water's edge. Its roots, broad and spidery, still clung to the upturned soil, while its leaves remained intact. The old man's feet and knees were visible past a leafy bough, but his torso was hidden.

Savaana shifted her gaze from his worn shoes to his horses. They were heavy, honest looking animals, haltered and relaxed. Dragging their leather leads behind them, they foraged amidst the sparse grasses. One was dark but graying with age around his broad muzzle. The closer of the two was a blue roan with flickering ears and a wily expression.

He would be the faster of the two.

The thought shimmied through her head. For a moment she tried to shoo it away, but the animal was wandering closer.

Keeping her gaze on the fisherman's feet, Savaana tore a tuft of soft grass from the boulder's roots and rose to her full height. Stepping from hiding, she reached toward the roan. A well-aged log lay between her and the gelding, but he lifted his head and pricked his ears, gazing placidly over the moldering bark. Shifting her gaze toward the fisherman again, she noticed no movement there and kept advancing. But at that moment the older gelding plopped into the sand to roll. Grunting with happiness, he kicked his heels against the sand. It sprayed out, splattering the downed tree.

"Hey now, leave off," yelled the fisherman. His feet shifted. As the roan turned toward the sound of his master's voice, Savaana sprang toward the log that stood between herself and the nearest animal. Using it as a springboard, she landed on her hands, launched into the air, then twisted onto the animal's serviceable back. Shocked from his investigation, the roan sprang up the escarpment like a hunted hare, leather lead flying behind him.

Savaana snatched it up.

"What the bloody hell!" yelled the old man, but she had gained control and was already hustling the horse over the lip of the slope and into the woods beyond. For a moment she was certain she heard her grandfather's laughter float behind her on the breeze. And after that it was a wild ride through the trees, branches slapping at her face as she reined the gelding in an arc toward the Gypsy camp. In less than a minute she was directly beside Knollcrest's horseless vehicle.

With a breathy thank-you and a pat to the animal's solid neck, she launched herself from his heaving back before he leapt from the cover of the trees. Vendors gasped and scattered as he careened riderless onto the grassy knoll.

Savaana winced as she caught her weight on her good foot and straightened.

Startled from her nap, Mrs. Edwards came to with a jerk and a snort just as Savaana snatched an ice from the abandoned booth and sauntered, teeth gritted, toward her chaperone.

"Here now. What's the fuss?" The old woman blinked as she caught sight of the roan, calming now as he dropped to a trot and shook his massive head. "Why is that horse loose?"

"I'm not entirely certain," Savaana said, and rose painfully to her seat beside the widow. "But not to worry. It looks as if the townspeople have the situation well under control. Here then," she said, and handed over the newly stolen treat. "I thought you might like something to cool your throat."

"Oh . . . well . . ." Mrs. Edwards harrumphed a little as she accepted the offering. "That's quite thoughtful of you, my dear. I don't know why people say you're such a—"

Savaana smoothed her skirt and raised a regal brow.

The old woman cleared her throat and took a bite of ice just as Gallagher led the chestnut into the clearing. His gaze shot immediately to Savaana. An unusual frown marred his brow as he shifted his gaze to the roan. The gelding had already dropped his head to graze.

"What's afoot?" he asked, approaching their vehicle.

"We are," Savaana said, and raised her chin a notch. "Until you get that screw harnessed. So let's not dawdle."

He watched her. "You've no wish to watch the performance, then?"

"In this backwater circus? I think not."

"But I thought—"

"And I wouldn't advise you to waste time doing so again anytime soon," she said, and glanced toward the trio of men who carefully approached the stray roan. "Now, let us be off before we are trampled by an entire herd of loosed animals."

He was still watching her. "Certainly, my lady," he said. "But would you care to have help freshening up a bit first?"

She pursed her lips, perusing him. "What's that?"

"I know how you like to care for your clothing."

She managed to refrain from glancing down at her perfect ensemble. Indeed, she stared with single-minded concentration at him, though she felt her persona slip just a notch, like a cog in a machine that's too tightly wound. "Are you a lady's maid now, Wicker?"

He grinned, eyes sparking. "If my lady wishes."

His dimples pulled her in. They were enchanting, all but mesmerizing. But she fought off the effects. She'd seen charming before. "She doesn't," she said, and disdainfully removed an imaginary fleck from her skirt. "You're barely fit as a driver."

He watched her for an instant, then laughed. "'Tis God's own truth," he said, and sobered just a tad. "I but thought you might wish to be rid of the mud that sullies your slippers."

# Chapter 8

**S**avaana held her image with an iron grip. Two days had passed since their trip to Darlington. Two days since Gallagher had looked at her so strangely and inquired about her slippers. What kind of man would concern himself with a little mud on one's footwear when in her company? She was a comely woman. A rare beauty, in fact. A hundred men had told her as much. But what did she expect from a rough-cut Irishman?

She sighed. Beneath her, Daisy plodded serenely along. Savaana refrained from glancing wistfully at the dark gelding beside her, for she would not make the mistake of riding him again. The Irishman must do something to earn his keep, after all.

"Is something amiss, my lady?" he asked, turning to gaze at her.

She didn't glance to her right. She knew how he would look. Devilishly handsome and ridiculously jovial, with that quirky smile playing around his evergreen eyes and satyr's lips. Earlier in the ride he had rolled back his voluminous sleeves. Muscles would be dancing along his forearms as he kept the restive gelding at bay. She didn't need to see that.

"Yes," she said, and shifted her ankle a bit. It was still a little sore. "Something is most certainly amiss."

"Can I do aught to set it to rights?" he asked.

There was concern in his tone. She wondered if it was real or fabricated. More than a few had faked concern in an effort to win her favor.

"Absolutely," she said, and finally turned toward him. And dammit, his idiotic muscles *were* dancing. "You can cease with the seduction."

His brows rose. "What?"

"The seduction," she said. "It won't work."

His eyes lit up like mischievous fireflies and his lips quirked at the corners just as she'd suspected they would. "You think I'm trying to seduce you, do you?"

She raised a single brow. "Yes."

"And what makes you think as much?"

He was dimpling. She didn't tell him what that did to her equilibrium. That when he smiled like that it made her chest feel too small to accommodate her lungs, made her toes curl in her carefully cleaned riding boots. "I have not just arrived off the boat," she said. "Perhaps your pedestrian charms will work on some apple-cheeked country bumpkin, but not for me. In fact, why not dimple up to Emily?"

She stared straight ahead. The sun was shining on the countryside as if it were the first day of creation. And despite the fact that she had worn a riding habit too warm for the weather, the heat felt good against her face. She had removed her gloves some time ago and wished she could do the same with the jacket. But she wouldn't bare any more skin than absolutely necessary. Still, even overdressed and undermounted, it was heavenly to be out of doors, away from walls and the accoutrements of a civilization she had eschewed for as long as she could remember. The rain had cleaned the air. A crested lark sang from atop a stone wall as sheep grazed around them or scampered away at their approach.

Gallagher laughed, drawing her attention from the perfection of the day. " 'Dimple up'?" he said.

"Yes." She didn't turn toward him. Didn't smile, though the sound of his laughter made it difficult to resist.

"Dare I hope you enjoy my dimples, lass?" he asked.

"No, you may not," she said. "But perhaps Emily is the sort to go dreamy-eyed when you turn up your charm."

"But not you."

Although she didn't look at him, she could tell he was smiling. Dear God in heaven, he was always smiling. Except when he was looking at her as if he could see straight through her undergarments.

"Certainly not me," she said.

"And what makes the likes of you so hard?" he asked.

She did turn now. Turned and raised a carefully plucked brow. "Perhaps you have mistaken hardness for discipline."

"Is that what you call it, then?"

She looked at the unfolding country around them again. "Need I remind you that I am not the type of woman who would be attracted to an Irishman with too little funds and too much . . ." She waved a hand at him. " . . . good cheer?"

He laughed again. "Constantly," he said. "In fact, it seems, at times, as if you are two different women entirely."

She felt herself blanch but kept her back perfectly straight, her expression unchanged. "Tell me, Wickerbell, have you been getting into Lord Tilmont's port?"

"In Darlington, for instance," he continued as if she remained mute, " 'twas you who wished to see the entertainment at the start. But 'twas also you who decided to leave shortly after the beginning of the performance."

She shrugged. "Perhaps you have not heard that it is a woman's prerogative to change her mind."

He was watching her again. She didn't like that. It made her skin hot.

"I am told that their acrobat is rather handsome," he said.

What was he getting at? she wondered, but kept her voice steady. " 'Their' being . . . ?"

"The Gypsies," he said.

"Ahh." She nodded. "I should have known a man such as yourself would be interested in the wild Rom."

He was silent for a second, maybe considering the fact that, once again, it had been her idea to see Dook Natsia at the outset.

"So you are not?" he asked finally.

She raised a haughty brow at him. At least she hoped it looked haughty. Maybe it only made her appear peevish. "Interested in the Rom?"

"Aye."

She laughed. Holy hell, the effort all but made her face bleed. 'Twas not easy being a harridan every minute of the day. "Is he titled?" she asked.

"The acrobat?"

"I believe that is who we were discussing."

He shrugged. "I asked around a bit. I am told Tamas is, in fact, descended from kings."

"Well, he lies," she snapped, and felt the silence thrum around them like a heavy drumbeat.

She could feel his confusion, though she dared not turn toward him.

"You know this Tamas?"

She felt her heart twang in her chest. How could she be so foolish? she wondered frantically, but kept her expression stoic, her eyes straight ahead. "Ahh, so you have found me out. Well, I might as well confess all, then. As it turns out, I am having quite a lurid affair with him. Just as I am with the tanner and the shoemaker and the hermit who lives under the bridge by the river."

He was examining her, his gaze as steady and warm as the sunlight. God help her, he had eyes like a song. "My apologies," he said. "'Tis just that there seemed something familiar about him."

"Well, perhaps he is your long-lost brother after all."

"I have only one brother."

She raised a shoulder. "A by-blow by your father, perhaps, then. Not someone your sire admits to. It happens, I'm told, that babies are left with Gypsies on a fairly regular—"

"I'll not have you defaming my family, lass."

She turned toward him. All traces of humor had disappeared from his face. And in the sinking light of the sun, he almost looked sinister. Almost dangerous.

"My father had his faults, 'tis true, but he cherished my mum with every fiber of his being. Cherished her until the day he died." There was something about the way he said it. Something about his fierce defense of the woman who had birthed him that brought tears instantly to her eyes.

"I'm sorry." The words were out before she could stop them. "I wasn't . . ." She drew a deep breath and reminded herself who she was, but it made little difference. She couldn't stop the apology. Loving mothers were a rare and precious thing. None knew that better than she. "I'm sorry," she said again.

Though she dared not look his way lest he see the tears in her eyes, she felt him soften. "She was . . ." He paused, and now she couldn't help but glance at him. He was gazing into the distance as if lost in some earlier time. In some kindly memory. "She was sunlight," he murmured.

His voice was soft and reverent, his eyes dreamy. Savaana found herself lost in his misty emotions. But she found her sharp-edged demeanor with an effort. "Not literally, I assume," she said, and he smiled crookedly. A dark shock of hair bent upward gently before falling forward with cocky happiness onto his forehead.

But who would not be happy if she could touch him with such easy regularity? Surely Lady Tilmont herself would have been unable to withstand his come hither charm.

"All but," he said. "Da was sure the day did not truly begin until she had smiled on the horizon."

Something tugged at her heart. She tugged back. She was not one to be sappy, and Lady Tilmont even less so, but her throat still felt a little tight, and her eyes stung. Best to make small talk.

"She is . . . gone, then?" She stole a glance at him. He was studying the distant woods. And with his profile toward her, it was all but impossible to look without reaching out to touch.

"She was taken two years past."

"I'm sorry," she said, but certainly not even the most heartless could blame her for *that* apology. You'd have to be a rock not to say it. Surely Lady Tilmont wasn't a *rock*, she thought, then caught herself. She *was* Lady Tilmont, but her facade was cracking badly.

"And your da?" Damn it. She should never use such a quaint colloquialism, but she had a tendency to pick up accents without meaning to. He didn't seem to notice her slip, however, for he was lost in his own thoughts, almost scowling as he studied the verdant hills that rolled away from them like swelling waves.

"It was hard for him. First Mum, then—" He stopped abruptly and faced her.

"Then what?"

He shook his head and found his infamous smile. "I didn't mean to sour the mood."

Did he jest? Surely he realized Lady Tilmont's mood had been soured for life. "What happened?" she asked, but he only shrugged.

"'Tis naught but a bit of trouble with me brother. You know how these family matters can be."

"No," she said. "I fear I do not."

He watched her, expression soft in the evening light. "You have no kin?"

Dammit! She had learned little to nothing about Lady Tilmont's lineage, despite her best efforts. All the lady had said was that she would not be bothered by either relatives or friends during her sojourn at Knollcrest. "None in this country." 'Twas a wild assumption, but she had to say something. "Thus you can understand why my marriage is so very important to me." Best to remind herself of the lie.

"You're eager to have wee ones of your own, are you?" His tone was somber now. She matched it with her own.

"Certainly."

"And might you be needing some assist with that?"

She jerked toward him and he laughed.

"Me apologies," he said. "I but think it shameful that your husband is not here to keep you safe."

"Safe?" she asked, and hoped to God he couldn't tell that she was flushed. "Safe from what?"

He shrugged. "While returning from the river in Darlington, I glanced through the trees and thought for a moment that you were gone from the carriage. You can't imagine how I worried."

"I *was* gone," she said, keeping her tone steady. "I went to fetch an ice for poor Mrs. Edwards."

"And that's how your slippers became soiled?"

For a moment she was sorely tempted to concoct some intricate excuse, but she stopped herself. "Tell me, Wickney, are you always so concerned about ladies' footwear?"

"Only when the lady in question is as bonny as you."

She resisted rolling her eyes back in her head. "Do you never give up?"

"Not when the lady in question is as—" he began.

She snorted and he laughed. "I but jest," he said. "In truth, I find it quite admirable that you are so devoted to your spouse."

"So devoted that I can even resist *you*?"

His grin quirked up. "You could *pretend* it's difficult."

"Maybe if you had a title and a decent—" She stopped as she noticed a ewe lying flat out, unmoving on the ground before her. Its abdomen was distended, its neck outstretched. Facing them at an angle, it was sure to be aware of their approach. Nevertheless, it failed to move even as they rode closer.

Savaana halted her mount. "Is it dead?" she asked.

Gallagher was frowning. "Dead, no, I think not, but—" he began, and in that moment the ewe emitted a low, agonized bleat. Her huge belly spasmed and her legs, straight and stiff, jerked spasmodically. "I believe she's in labor."

Savaana nodded. She realized now that she could just make out two tiny hooves protruding from beneath the animal's tail.

They sat their horses in silence. The ewe lay still, panting, pink tongue extended below toothless upper gums.

Savaana glanced behind them. Perhaps she was hoping to see someone riding to their rescue, but there was no one. "What shall we do?"

Gallagher scowled. "These things usually work themselves out, don't they?"

"These things being lambs?"

He was frowning. "And other young."

The ewe bleated again and strained. The tiny hooves moved a half an inch, then settled back where they were near the head of the mother's tail.

"It doesn't seem to be working."

"No. It doesn't." It was Gallagher's turn to glance toward Knollcrest, as if he were no more comfortable than she with the animal's distress. "Perhaps the babe is coming wrong."

"Well . . ." She felt agitated and tense. "Fix it." The words could not have sounded more demanding if they had been spoken by Lady Tilmont herself.

"Fix it?" he said.

"Yes. You're Irish."

He leaned away from her as if struck. "What the devil does that have to do with birthing lambs?"

"Irish." She waved her hand, unnerved by the animal's pain. "Sheep. They're a match."

"I'm a match for sheep?"

"Surely you know what to do."

"Surely I don't. Our laborers—" he began, then stopped abruptly.

She scowled at him. "You had laborers?"

"I mean to say, the neighboring farmers, they cared for the sheep."

Savaana's mind spun. Who was this man? "And what did you do?"

He opened his mouth but the ewe bleated at that moment, stopping his thought. "I hardly think that's the point just now," he said.

She tightened her hands on the reins, jarred from her suspicions by the animal's agony. "We could ride back to Knollcrest for help."

"By the time James returned here, it will be well dark."

True enough. "Then you'll have to do something yourself."

He winced. "I don't . . ." he began, and paused.

"What?"

"The truth is, I don't much care for blood, lass."

"Are you serious?"

He scowled at her, looking honestly peeved. "Perhaps you drink it for breakfast?"

She stared at him for several seconds, brows raised, then dismounted. Dropping the mare's reins, she approached the distressed animal slowly. Too absorbed in her own troubles, the ewe remained as she was, eyes staring, mouth open and panting.

"There now," Savaana crooned. She had lost Lady Tilmont's supercilious accent, but she hardly cared, for she had just noticed one obvious truth: while there were, in fact, two visible hooves, as seemed appropriate, one was pointing up while the other pointed down. "All will be well," she said, though she was far from certain that was true.

"My apologies," Gallagher said and touched her arm.

She turned to find him behind her, and he drew her gently back.

"I shall do what I can."

"What about your squeamishness?" she asked.

"Suffering saints, I suspect you'll never let me forget that."

"Doubtful."

He shook his head. "Perhaps you could hold the horses."

She nodded, walked away, and retrieved the animals' reins as he eased toward the ewe. The animal lifted her head for a moment, then lay back down, defeated. Reaching under her tail, Gallagher touched one little hoof, then, grimacing, slid his fingers along the slippery leg, but in a moment he glanced back toward Savaana.

"I think there may be two little blighters trying to come out all at once."

Savaana worried her lip. "Can you press one back, perhaps?"

He tried, then shook his head. "My hand's too big. There's no room."

She cursed quietly.

"What say you?"

Savaana glared at him, dropped the horses' reins and began unbuttoning her jacket. "Back away."

"What?"

"I said, back away," she ordered, and tossing the garment to the grass, rolled up the starched lace of her sleeves.

"And what might you be doing, lass?"

"What you cannot."

He was grinning as he rose to his feet. "You'll soil your clothing."

She glanced down. It did seem a shame. On the open market she could sell the ensemble for a good bit. Why, the frilly blouse alone would buy six months of Grand-father's medicine. "Give me your shirt," she said.

He turned his head slightly, slanting his ear toward her as if he couldn't have possibly heard her correctly. "I beg your pardon?"

"Your shirt," she insisted. "If I ruin it, I shall purchase you a new one."

His lips twitched up a notch. "Might this be naught but a ploy to see me in me glorious altogether?" he asked, but the ewe moaned again.

Savaana grimaced. "This is an opportunity for you to quit being an ass," she said, and he laughed as he opened his buttons.

# Chapter 9

Gallagher watched the lady's expression of distaste as she squatted behind the ewe. But in a moment she settled down to business. Her mouth set in a resolute line and her brow furrowed in rapt concentration. For several long moments she remained squatting behind the animal as she tried to release the unborn, but finally, perturbed but determined, she stretched out flat on her stomach.

Sean said nothing. He merely watched in fascination. Who was this earthy wench who had stolen the body of the stiff-backed Lady Tilmont? Alastar had said she was unpredictable. Indeed, he had lauded her as unique and kindly and beautiful, with the face of an angel and the soul of a saint, but until this moment, he'd doubted most of those descriptions. Now, however, he wondered if Alastar hadn't been right all along. Only a saint or a shepherd would—

"Damn, bloody, son of a whore," she snarled.

Sean grinned. Very well, then. A saint she was not.

"They're just so demmed . . ." She paused, breathing hard. "There *are* two of them. I'm sure of that," she rasped, and screwing up her face, she pressed farther into the ewe. One tiny hoof disappeared. Deep in concentration, the lady poked her tongue from the corner of her mouth and eased an additional hoof into the open air. Both pointed downward, but the ewe lay perfectly still, too exhausted to move. Scooting onto her knees, Clarette scowled at her handiwork. Nothing changed. The ewe remained unmoving, the lambs unborn. Reaching out reluctantly, she tugged gently at the lamb's knobby fetlocks with both hands. They slipped out a scant half an inch, and now, feeling the unhindered movement, the ewe's belly contracted. The little cloven hooves eased out. They were followed by a pair of bony knees. A tiny head was squished between the forelegs, and a second later the wee animal sloshed to the earth like a loosed trout.

It lay there inert, absolutely unmoving.

Clarette glared at it for all of two seconds, then shook her head. "Oh no. Oh no, you don't!" she rasped, and retrieving the lamb by the hind legs, gave it a firm shake. It wobbled in her hands, then hung limp, smeared with all kinds of unspeakable fluids and as flaccid as a woolen rag. "Listen, you daft little bugger, you're going to live!" she ordered, and drawing back her right hand, smacked it on its ribs.

There was a moment of frozen silence. Then the little

creature snorted, lifted its ridiculously pointy head on its ridiculously scrawny neck and bleated from its upside-down position.

The ewe, exhausted but revived, blinked and rolled onto her chest. After that it was all magic. Another lamb slipped effortlessly into life, wriggling immediately. As for the lady, she carried the firstborn to the mother's head and flopped him onto the ground. In a moment the ewe staggered to her feet. Deep-throated, maternal noises rumbled from her chest as she cleaned her babies with quick strokes of her agile tongue. And they, in turn, responded by doing the seemingly impossible—rising on their gangly legs in a matter of minutes.

During all this, the lady remained absolutely silent. Her expression was one Gallagher couldn't quite place, but her eyes were wide and seemed unusually bright above the smudged beauty of her face.

"Now where did you learn how to do that, lass?" he asked finally.

She all but jumped at the sound of his voice. As if she had completely forgotten his presence. But in a moment she found herself, lifting her chin and clearing her throat.

"Well . . ." Glancing about, she spotted the wending creek not far away and turned abruptly toward it. "It's not very complicated, is it?"

He watched the little family. One tiny twin had

already found its mother's udder and was gleefully wiggling its curly tail as it nursed. "I would have thought so, aye," he said, and seeing she had already left, strode off behind her.

"Well . . ." She raised her nose and descended the escarpment down to the water. "You would have been wrong again, then, wouldn't you, Wickerhauser?"

Squatting beside the stream, she dipped her hands into the water and scrubbed vigorously. He did the same. In a minute or two she rose, shaking the wetness from her fingers before unbuttoning his shirt. Removing it, she handed it over with just a momentary glance at his bare chest.

"Shall we go?"

"Shall we . . ." He lifted a hand toward the sheep, then shifted it toward her. "Who the devil are you?" He tried to keep the frustration from his voice but there wasn't much hope.

She raised a regal brow at him. "Have you suffered some memory loss, Wickster?"

He ignored her wit or lack thereof and waved rather erratically toward the sheep. "One minute you're all starched and pointy, and the next you're . . . you're giving birth."

"Let us not be overly dramatic, Wickerhound," she said, and turned away. "It was not I, after all, who—"

But he stopped her with a hand on her arm. "Who the fook are you?" he asked. There was more passion in his tone than he had ever planned to allow. Tension strummed between them, but in a second she pulled her arm from his grasp.

"I'm a married woman," she said, smoothing the sleeve he had recently crushed. "And married women care for their husbands' property, do they not?"

"Well, aye, I suppose . . ." he began, but she was already striding past him.

In a matter of moments she had buttoned on her jacket and mounted the mare. As for Sean, he was still wrestling with this new turn of events. Alastar had said nothing of her being skilled with livestock. Indeed, he said she was polished and elite and sophisticated. Which made him think perhaps she was not the woman he had been searching for at all. Perhaps. . .

"I assure you I can control myself," she said.

He shook the thoughts from his head and glanced toward her. "Your pardon?"

She motioned dismissively toward his naked chest. "There's little point in you standing about half dressed. I'll not be bedding you."

"Oh, aye," he said, and distractedly pulled on his shirt. "So . . ." He was nodding foolishly as he fastened the wooden buttons. "Born to humble crofters who kept their sheep like children, were you?"

She stared down at him. "Tell me, Wickerly, might you have been dropped on your head as a youngster?"

He scowled at her for a second, noticing that despite the proceeding ordeal, not a single strand of her hair had dared stray out of place. Her bonnet was perfectly placed atop it, her frilly cuffs still crisp and white. And though it seemed entirely unlikely, her fingernails appeared to be absolutely spotless.

"All right. Very well." He tucked his shirt rapidly into his trousers, caught his gelding's reins, and ventured a wild guess. "You have an inexplicable connection with sheep and—"

"Sheep stink," she said, and didn't deign to glance at the wee lambkins she had just delivered.

"Well, aye, they do that." He scowled. "So perhaps you were a midwife before your marriage and—"

"Please!" She was scoffing.

"Your first husband was extremely involved in animal husbandry."

"This *is* my first marriage."

"You were once a poor milk maid."

"I've never been a poor anything."

He felt frustration build in him like a burbling fountain. "You're a doctor. A farmer. A wolf in lamb's clothing."

She frowned down at him. "What's wrong with you?" she asked.

He stared up at her. She couldn't be the woman who had scorned Alastar. She couldn't. Yet, a good deal of evidence suggested the opposite. "I'm not entirely sure," he said.

"Well, mount up," she suggested. "Perhaps you shall figure it out on the way home."

He nodded and did as suggested, but for just a moment she sat in silence, watching the lambs' tails quiver with excitement as they nursed. Her chin was raised, her mouth slightly pursed, but in her eyes there was something that looked remarkably like unfettered joy. Like hope and pride, with just the tiniest hint of longing. Until she realized he was watching her, then she turned without a word, tapped her quirt against the chestnut's right haunch, and cantered toward Knollcrest.

There was little he could do but follow.

"Gallagher." The sun was just setting over the lacy leaves of the western woods when she finally spoke. Sean turned toward her, mind spinning. "Perhaps it would be best if we did not speak of this business of the sheep to the staff," she said.

Who the bloody hell was she? he wondered, but carefully kept the fascination out of his tone. "And why is that, me lady? I think you were quite heroic."

She breathed her disdain. "I helped birth a pair of lambs. Nothing more."

She'd birthed lambs! He couldn't even place that fact with the remainder of what he knew of her. "Then why not speak of it?"

"It's my place to direct the servants. If they think me no different than they . . ." She lifted an elegant hand. "They will not respect me. Surely you see that."

"No, lass, I don't."

Her scowl was firmly back in place when she turned toward him.

He smiled. "Indeed," he added. "I believe they would think the more of you for your efforts."

She raised both brows in unison. "And you believe I care what they think of me?"

He studied her in silence for a moment. It was no difficult task. "Aye, I do at that."

For a moment he almost thought her expression softened, but then she pursed her lips and scowled. "If that's the case you are even more ignorant than I believed!" she snapped. "Nevertheless, you will keep this news to yourself." They were just entering the farmyard. "Do you understand?"

Somehow it was almost as much fun seeing her angry as it was seeing her enthralled. He shook his head as if bemused. "I cannot say that I do, me lady," he said.

"Well, it would be in your best interest if you did," she said, and pulling the mare to a halt, dismounted unaided. "Or you will find yourself on the road without a farthing to your name." Leaving the reins dangling, she lifted her skirts in one hand and pivoted sharply toward the house.

Sean watched her go.

"And what was all that about?"

He turned quickly, only to find Emily just stepping out from behind a stack of loose fodder. He examined her. She was bonny and harmless, and he could think of no reason to keep the truth from her . . . except that Clarette had asked him to. Which was a damn good reason to do the opposite. After all, wasn't that why he was here? To ruin her life just as she had ruined his brother's? But perhaps the timing wasn't right.

"What are you doing out and about?" he asked, and made sure he said the words sound like *oot* and *aboot*. Catching up the chestnut's reins, he led the horses toward the stable.

"Me?" The comely maid gave him a sidelong glance as she fell in beside him. "Ain't that a question better put to your own self?"

"I was riding horse with the lady," he said. "As you very well know."

"You sure that's all you were a'ridin'?" she asked, and grinned lasciviously.

He turned to watch her. "Whatever do you mean by that?"

She snorted a laugh. "A bloke like you don't know?" she asked, and something inside him balked.

"I fear I don't."

She scowled, looking surprised and a little miffed. "You come back with your shirt soiled and Lady High and Mighty looking like she got her tail caught in a wine press. Don't think I don't know what's happened."

"Nothing happened," he said.

"Very well," she agreed, trailing one finger along the top of the nearest stall. "And you ain't hopin' to change that?"

He considered lying again, but it seemed like a stretch. "Even if I were, Miss Emily, the lady is married, and not the sort to break those holy vows."

She stopped abruptly, staring at him. Anger and disappointment were stamped on her pretty face. "And here I thought you wasn't the sort to be made a fool by a trim figure and an uppity title," she said, and turning abruptly away, stomped off toward the house.

Sean stared after her, stunned. Truth was, he had rather thought the same thing.

What the devil was happening to him? Tugging the mare into her stall, he removed her bridle before doing the same with the gelding. Could it be that the lady was actually getting under his skin? Could she be duping him just as she had his brother?

To hell with that. He had loved and lost prettier women than . . . Well, maybe not prettier, he thought, remembering the light in her heaven-blue eyes as she'd watched the lambkins rise on shaky legs, her smile as she'd gazed after the fleeing gelding. And certainly no woman had been more intriguing. But he'd slept with ladies with fancier titles. That was for damn sure. And he'd bloody well sleep with her.

# Chapter 10

It was as dark as sin beneath the towering walnut trees. No moon yet brightened the blue velvet sky, but Sean remained staring at Clarette's window nevertheless. He planned to breach her chambers. But not in the hopes of finding her there. In fact, it was quite the opposite, for he'd had some time to consider the situation, to calm down after speaking with Emily.

Indeed, he'd found himself sleepless and restive, with too little to do and too much time to dwell on his peculiar circumstances. Just past full dark he had fired up the old forge that stood in a three-sided shed just east of the byre. Midnight found him pouring the boiling liquid into a cast he'd carved out on another restless night. 'Twas what he had long done when sleep eluded him. But that hallowed time did little to clear his thoughts, for the situation was too muddled. Too uncertain.

On the one hand, the lady in yonder, thatched manse looked all but identical to the portrait of one Milicent Hennessey, the woman who had broken his brother's heart, broken her word, broken their father's will to live. Likewise, all evidence he'd garnered from the man sent to investigate the woman suggested that she and Clarette were one and the same.

When Sean had met Lord Tilmont some weeks earlier, all the pieces of the devious puzzle seemed to have fallen neatly into place. Careful inquiry had led him to one of London's infamous gambling hells. He'd intentionally taken a seat next to the table where Tilmont was playing a hand of piquet. After buying the baron a drink, he'd taken his departed opponent's seat and proceeded to lose money with conscientious regularity. By the time the second bottle of gin had arrived, the baron had divulged a dozen little details that matched the description of Alastar's supposed wife-to-be.

But on the other hand . . .

Memories of his time with Clarette crept in on Sean with quiet feet, softening his thoughts, hardening his body. It wasn't her beauty that called to him. Well, perhaps that had a wee bit to do with the situation. But there was more. Her wit. Her boldness. Her softness. Her. . .

He drew a slow breath. In truth, he was no longer certain she was the woman for whom he searched, for whom he planned revenge. But there was one way to be sure. Alastar had given Milicent their mother's ruby, the ring their grandfather crafted in his ancient forge near a hundred years before. Even without the sentimental value, it was a precious jewel and not something a woman with Milicent's grasping ways would easily be rid of.

No, if Clarette and Milicent were one and the same, the ring would be in her bedchamber even now.

But he could hardly search her rooms with her watching from the settee. Could not rifle through her jewelry case while she lounged on her divan. He had come here every night since his arrival to watch her window and debate the best time to ransack her property. To attempt to—

His roiling thoughts stopped abruptly. What was that? He leaned forward, peering into the darkness. Had something moved on the tree outside her balcony? He stood, keeping to the shadows of the ancient walnut. Was someone trying to reach her chambers? he wondered. Perhaps she had a lover. The thought pierced him like an arrow to the heart, but then he caught himself. What would it matter to him? It would only confirm what he had come here to prove: that she was poison.

Nevertheless, his fists clenched at the images that raged through his mind.

If she wished for a lover, why not him? He had employed all his best banter, his most winsome smiles, his most charming—

But his thoughts stopped again, for suddenly he realized that the shadow was not ascending the tree. It was *descending*. Whoever was there was already *leaving* the house.

Merciful saints, it was barely past midnight. Whoever was there couldn't have spent much time. If it were himself—

But now he stopped the thought intentionally. What the devil was he thinking? This was his chance to prove what a conniving vixen she was. All he had to do was inform Gregors about her philandering and he could leave this place.

He was moving in a moment, edging through the deepest shadows, hurrying toward the house. But by the time he reached the horse chestnuts that skirted the yard, the dark figure was already gone. He remained as he was, frozen, thinking. Had he imagined it? Or—

But no. There! A movement on the ground. He peered into the blackness, watched the figure rise to his full height. Bloody hell! The bastard wasn't even tall. At least she could have chosen a manly lover. Someone with dark Celtic looks and— He gritted his teeth, driving the idiotic thoughts from his head as he stepped forward, but in that second the other disappeared. Like a wraith, like a dream. He was there, and then he was gone.

Sean hurried across the yard as silently as he could, searching the shadows that surrounded the house but finding nothing out of the ordinary. Thus he backtracked and tried another direction. But there was no one.

He stood in the exact spot where her lover had, trying to divine how he had disappeared. Then a new thought struck him. Maybe the silent wraith wasn't a lover at all. Maybe he was a miscreant of some sort. If Lord Tilmont was coldhearted enough to hire someone to *seduce* her, what was to say he wouldn't hire someone else to do her harm? Perhaps he hoped to be rid of her by even more nefarious means in case the seduction plan failed.

Sean was already heading toward the tree that towered over the balcony. He had no great affinity for heights and was no master at climbing, but he could hardly go through the front door to inquire about her health at this hour of the night. All kinds of ridiculous questions were apt to follow.

Thus he pried off his boots, set his bare feet against the rough bark, and ascended with painful slowness. By the time he reached the bough that grew parallel to the balcony, his arms ached and his lungs felt scoured. Glancing down, the earth seemed a lifetime below. Strengthening his flagging resolve, he inched onto the branch. No noise came from the darkened bedchamber before him, but he would have answers.

It was a leap of six feet to the balcony. He made it without an inch to spare, clung to the stone railing like a discombobulated spider monkey, and finally wrestled himself over.

By the time he reached her door, he was certain he must have awakened the dead. But not a sound was heard from inside the manse. That realization brought relief and trepidation all in one hard rush. What if she *was* inside? What if she was injured . . . or worse?

Able to wait no longer, he opened the door as quietly as humanly possible.

"My lady," he whispered. No one answered. He stepped forward, impressed by his own silence. "Clarette, are you well?"

There was a lump under the covers but it remained absolutely still.

"Clarette!" Panic was rising. He reached out, touching the coverlet, and in that movement realized, even in the darkness, that there was no head on the pillow. He scowled and tugged the blankets aside. The bed was empty.

What the hell was going on? Straightening, he glanced toward the door as a dozen unlikely thoughts screamed through his buzzing brain. She'd been abducted. She was hiding in her wardrobe. She—

Bloody hell! The truth came suddenly: it had been Clarette herself whom he'd seen climbing down. It must have been.

But that was ridiculous. It had taken all his skill and strength to breach her chambers. Surely she could never have managed such a feat. But then, where was she? Certainly not in this room. He glanced about again, as if she might magically appear in a puff of smoke. But she was gone. Absolutely absent. If she was wandering through the house, she would have had no reason to close her door. And she would have taken a light. There had been no light in any of the windows. The entire house was as black as pitch.

What did it all mean?

The truth dawned on him with harsh certainty: Her lover hadn't come to her. She had gone to meet him!

Anger squeezed through him, followed by frustration and foolish righteousness and a few other emotions he refused to admit, but he pushed them all aside, for obviously he had been afforded a great opportunity. Her rooms were empty. No one knew he was there. 'Twas the perfect time to search for his mother's ring. To prove for once and for all that she was the woman who had ruined his brother's life.

Feeling his way silently along a wall, he found a lamp on the bedstead and carried it to the window. Once there, he pulled the heavy drapes across the thick panes. It was darker still now, but in a moment he had a tiny flame burning beneath the curved globe. And by that flame he saw the jewelry box atop her bedstead.

In a moment he was skimming the contents. Pearl ear bobs, a pair of hat pins, and a half dozen rough stones strung on a leather thong. For a woman of Lady Tilmont's wealth it seemed a paltry collection. He glanced around the chamber again. Surely she had more. Perhaps she kept his mother's ruby hidden from her husband, not wanting to explain it. Or maybe she was even more heartless than he believed and had pawned it off as if it was of no more consequence than a bauble won at the fair.

The thought tore his heart, but suddenly the door to the hall shifted. He jerked toward it.

Clarette stood in the opening. Her gaze leapt to his. Her lips parted. Water sloshed from the glass she held in her hand.

"I can explain," he said. "Don't scream."

For a moment he thought she would, but finally she pursed her lips, stepped inside and closed the door behind her. They stared at each other. No more than four feet separating them.

"Very well. You may begin," she said, but for the life of him he could think of nothing to say. It wasn't as if he had never been found in a woman's bedchamber before. It was simply that the lady in question was generally well aware of his presence at the outset. Seconds ticked away. "Wickerdoodle?" She raised her left brow the slightest degree. "Are you going to explain or shall I have you removed from this property?"

"Ahh, yes, explanations." He cleared his throat and wondered how exactly she would have him removed. Piece by piece or all in one dead lump? "I thought I saw someone climb up to your . . ." He tilted his head toward the balcony. " . . . to your room."

The second brow joined the first near her hairline. "Was it you?"

He managed a low laugh. "No, Lady Tilmont." It seemed a good time to use her title. Familiarity was likely to encourage that piece by piece removal he had contemplated earlier. "No. I was watching your—" He stopped, saw the trap, and tried to back away. "I was outside, enjoying the night air, when I saw someone in the chestnut beside your window. I attempted to ascertain—"

"What were you doing watching my window?"

"I wasn't 'watching' your window, my lady. I simply—"

"It just happened to be in your line of vision?"

A hundred ridiculous explanations zipped through his brain, but he squelched them all, trying to catch his balance. "Have you a wish to hear this or not?"

Taking a careful breath, she set the water on her bedstead and seated herself on the mattress. "I've always enjoyed a good yarn."

He scowled at her. "How did you get so jaded?"

She tilted her head a little, as if asking if he really intended to try that tact, and he lifted a hand in concession.

"Very well, then. I admit this looks . . . Well . . . one might think . . ." He cleared his throat. "This isn't what it seems."

"And how does it seem, Lowwick?"

Suffering saints. "Well, one might believe . . ." He shrugged, not quite able to control his grin. " . . . that I hoped to seduce you."

She delayed several heartbeats before she spoke. "And you don't."

He opened his mouth to assure her that he did not. But he was trying to convince her of his innocence, not his stupidity. "Well . . ." He chuckled a little. " . . . any man with a pair of . . ." Wrong strategy. He smiled. Her eyes were very steady, as if she had not a fear in the world. Should she not be afraid to find a man in her private chambers? At least a little? "I don't deny that I am drawn to you."

The slightest hint of a smile tilted her summer raspberry lips. As if she had no desire to be flattered but could not quite help herself.

He took a careful breath. "You are not exactly beastly to look upon, after all."

"Go on."

He found his stride carefully. "I am certain you're aware of your comely countenance, my lady."

She shrugged one shoulder and suddenly seemed like nothing more than a timid girl softly blossoming to womanhood. Lovely, kind, innocent. "If I am such a rare beauty, why does everyone leave me?" There was sadness in her tone now, uncertainty in her eyes.

"Everyone?"

There was a beat of silence, then, "My husband for one."

"He must be mad," Sean said, and found that he almost believed it to be true.

She smiled forlornly. "He is not mad."

"Foolish he is, then," he said. "For you are beauty itself."

She glanced away. "I'm passing fair, I suppose. But . . . well . . ." She paused. "Perhaps you have noticed that I can be a bit . . . a bit *sharp* at times."

The understatement somehow tickled him. He chuckled quietly. "The sharpness only makes the softness more appealing."

She flickered her eyes to his. They were as big as the walnuts that grew near the byre. Soft and lovely and deep with hope. "Do you mean that?"

"Certainly I do. Look at you. You have . . ." He paused, finding he had somehow lost his breath as his gaze settled on her lush mouth. "You've the most kissable lips I've yet to see."

"I do?"

"Aye," he said, and taking the few steps between them, slipped a hand behind her supple back. "Your lips beckon—" he began, but in that moment she lifted a dagger from some unknown location and poked his belly with the tip.

"What the devil are you doing in my room, Wickson?" she asked.

# Chapter 11

**S**ense came slowly back to Sean's feverish brain. He closed his eyes and gritted his teeth. How the fook had he possibly forgotten who he was dealing with? She was the woman who had stolen his brother's dreams, who had promised his family a future, only to abscond with their past.

"Ahh, well," he said, glancing carefully at the dagger she held in one competent hand. "As I've said, a body should never be—"

"Without a *foine* blade." She mimicked his brogue with disturbing accuracy. "But that's not what I asked, is it, lad?" she said, and pressed the tip of the dagger a little harder into his shirt. He stifled a grimace.

"There was someone in the tree outside your window," he said, easing back a half an inch.

"So I'm told."

"I feared for your life."

She shifted the blade the slightest degree and almost smiled. "Did you?"

"Yes."

"And where do you suppose we might find the miscreant now?"

Here's where it got tricky. "I don't know."

"Perhaps you should have followed him instead of coming here."

"I feared he might have done you harm."

She arched a dubious brow at him. "And it never occurred to you to come through the front door to check?"

She held the dagger like one who knew how to use it. He, too, was fairly well schooled in the use of blades, but where the bloody hell had she been keeping this one? "I had no wish to frighten anyone."

Her lips twitched a little. "So you slithered through my window."

"Irishman rarely slither," he said. "Sometimes we slink. Occasionally we—"

She pressured him further with the dagger tip. "Why are you here?"

"As I've told you, lass—"

"I'd like the truth."

Her eyes were as steady as the steel. Indeed, she rather looked as if she might actually pierce him. "As I said . . ." he began, but then something clicked in his head. He scowled. "Tell me, my lady, have you an aversion to cotton?"

"What are you talking about?"

"This . . ." He raised a hand, indicating her ensemble. It was entirely black. Except for her feet. They were bare. And, oh . . . she had rather enchanting toes. He brought his mind back to the moment at hand. "Not that I would have any way of knowing, being a confirmed bachelor as I am, but aren't most nightgowns made of cotton? *White* cotton? And isn't the belt a bit uncomfortable while you're abed?"

For a moment something flashed in her eyes. It might have been fear, but it was more likely irritation. The knife disappeared with the slightest flick of her wrist. How the bloody hell did she manage that?

"I have no wish to cause problems," she said.

He watched her, waiting for more.

But she only sniffed as if he were entirely daft. Which might or might not have been true. "You said yourself that I am irresistible."

"Comely," he corrected. "I said you were comely."

"You said I was beauty . . ." She paused, all but rolling her eyes with impatience. "I don't want to tempt the servants beyond their endurance."

He stared at her, finally raised his brows and hoped to hell she would go on. She didn't. "And?"

"And so I dare not wander out unless I am fully clothed. Even to fetch a glass of water."

He waited, fascinated, for her to continue, but she

refrained. "So you're a'feared of arousing Gregors's baser nature should he see you in less than your full regalia."

She paused a moment, as if trying to think of others whose base natures might be aroused. "Yes."

He managed to keep a straight face. "What of your feet?"

She scowled.

"Your feet," he said. "They're naked."

"I think he can probably—"

"And quite adorable," he added.

Curling her toes, she made them disappear beneath her dark hem. Sean could no longer resist a grin as he lifted his gaze to hers.

"He's a hundred years old, you ken."

"Who's—"

"Gregors. He's a hundred if he's a day."

She pursed her lips. "I doubt he's far past eighty. Besides, I've little reason to believe men become more disciplined with age."

"What of rustier?"

She raised a brow.

"Perhaps he'd like to . . ." He waved a hand at her darkly attired form, including her tiny toes. "I simply don't believe he could," he said, and damned if it didn't almost seem as if she blushed.

"Who are you?" he asked, and watched irritation flash again in her eyes. It wasn't until that instant that he realized she'd *never* looked frightened. Not even when she first opened the door. She'd managed surprised, perhaps, but not fear. "You knew I was here," he breathed.

"What are you talking about?"

"When you came in . . ." He motioned toward the door. "You were expecting me."

She laughed softly, as if he were predictably foolish. "Perhaps I am as irresistible as you—"

" 'Comely,' " he corrected.

She gave him a curved smile. "Perhaps I am as irresistible as you think, but that doesn't mean I often find strange men in my boudoir."

"But it does happen." His tone sounded strange. Jealous almost.

"What?"

"*Sometimes* you find strange men in your . . ." he began, but when her eyes flickered with amusement, he managed to return to the matter at hand. "Why the devil are you fully dressed?"

She was all but laughing out loud now. "Hoping to find me otherwise, Wickerhammer?"

"No. I—"

"No?"

"I . . . Fook it!" he said, and pushed splayed fingers through his hair. "Aye, I was."

She was staring at him.

He laughed at her expression. "Suffering saints,

woman, you've the tongue of an adder, but the body of a goddess."

She blinked, actually blinked, perhaps taken aback for the first time since he'd met her.

"So . . ." He shrugged expansively, taking advantage of her silence. "Do you wish to lie with me or nay?"

Her mouth formed a perfect O. Her eyes were just as round. "Are you . . . Is that really why you came here?"

He'd considered a couple other reasons. They had sounded ridiculously unbelievable. Even if they were true. "Why else?"

"I . . ." She shrugged. "I don't know. To rob me, perhaps?"

He drew a deep breath. "I'm not much of . . ." He shook his head, thinking. "Thievery . . . me da would be sore disappointed."

She plopped down on her bed. "But he wouldn't mind if he knew you were trying to seduce a married woman?"

"I wasn't jesting when I said you were irresistible."

She looked at him askance. "I thought you'd only said I was comely."

He grinned. "You must drive your husband mad."

She scowled a little. "Do you think that's why he left?"

Her voice was soft again, but there was no way of telling if she was sincere or conniving. He was going to have to assume conniving. "'Tis as good a guess as any," he said.

She shifted her gaze slowly to the jewelry box. "She *is* rather abrasive isn't—" she began, then snapped her gaze back to his.

He stared at her in bewilderment. "'She'?"

"I meant— Oooh!" she sobbed, and pulling her feet onto the bed, dropped her head into her palms. "You're right. Absolutely right. Sometimes it seems as if I *am* two different people."

All right then, this was rather surreal. "How so, lass?"

"I have to be . . ." She pulled her head out of her hands. There were tears in her eyes. He reminded himself that she was the devil, but holy saints, there were *tears*! "I have to be so strong." The words were whispered.

He stepped a little closer to hear her.

"Strong?"

She waved to her surroundings. "You think I want to live like this? Alone? Surrounded by servants who hate me? Who know—" She stopped, swallowed, lowered her voice. "Who know my husband wants nothing to do with me."

"I'm sure that's not true," he said, though in fact her husband had said just that. Nevertheless, he sat on the edge of the mattress and reached for her hand.

"He wasn't here a full day before he fled."

"Well . . ." Her skin was marvelously soft beneath his thumb. "He was called away on business, most like."

She blinked up at him. Her lashes were wet. "He doesn't love me."

No. He didn't. And suddenly that truth seemed oddly sad. "Maybe he just hasn't had time to come to know you," he said.

She shook her head, cleared her throat. "His father had to pay him to marry me."

That, he hadn't heard. "Come again," he said.

"The old duke." She managed a smile. It was weak at best. "He wants an heir. Apparently he thought I'd make good breeding stock."

"I'm certain you're wrong."

She blinked, lashes heavy with silver droplets. "You're certain he doesn't think I'll be good breeding stock or—"

"I'm certain your husband finds you as enchanting as I do."

"The duke said that if my lord could produce a child in a year's time, he wouldn't disown him. But even with that, Richard wants nothing to do—" She cleared her throat and shrugged.

He canted a brow.

"Well . . ." She used her free hand to sweep the far side of the mattress. It was notably empty. "He's not here, is he?"

"But surely he . . ." He paused, trying to think how to say it. "The two of you have—"

She blushed brighter. The autumn apples of her cheeks bloomed with color. If she wasn't honestly embarrassed, she was a damned fine actress. "Yes, of course." She wouldn't look at him. "And I had hoped . . ." She paused, then shook her head. "But I'm not with child."

She looked so sad, so beautiful and fragile and brave, it all but broke his heart. He squeezed her hand.

"Might you want help with that?"

Her gaze smacked into his.

"Me apologies. I don't—" he began, but in that instant she leaned closer to him. He felt his desire tighten painfully as she gazed up through dewy lashes.

"You, ummm . . . you *don't* want help with that, do you, lass?"

For one wild moment he almost thought she would answer in the affirmative, but finally she glanced down and pulled her hand from his. "I was a courtesan, Mr. Gallagher. Did you know that?"

"A—" He'd run out of words. Alastar hadn't mentioned that fact, and it seemed fairly significant. "A . . ." He shook his head.

She drew a deep breath. "You can't even say the word."

"You were a courtesan?"

"It sounds so much better than whore, doesn't it?"

"And your husband, lass, does he know?"

She nodded. "As does his father. Perhaps that was why he thought I could be so easily bought."

He could think of nothing to say. So she was a prostitute. And yet, looking at her now, he couldn't blame his brother for being besotted. She was enchanting, mesmerizing.

"In actuality, I'm the daughter of Count von Racowitza and a peasant woman named Luiza."

"A count and a peasant."

She smiled disarmingly. "I am told Luiza was quite beautiful."

"So you've noble blood." His tone was dubious.

"'Tis not a story easily believed, I know."

"If you're aware of your heritage, why not petition your father for funds instead of becoming . . ." He shook his head again.

"A prostitute?" She shrugged. "The countess has been known to hold a grudge." The corners of her mouth lifted a little. "And a gun."

He drew a deep breath and scowled.

She chuckled at his obvious doubts. "'Tis just as well you don't believe me." She wiped her nose with the back of her hand. "If you were to repeat it, I would deny everything."

"Why?"

"We've done what we could to become lost in this

country. Taken various names, kept moving." She scowled, immersed in thought, drowning in years far past. "But they might yet find us."

"I suppose . . ." he began, then, " . . . 'us'?"

It took her a moment to find his gaze again, but when she did, her eyes were as steady as steel. "I don't actually know if my sister yet lives."

"You had a sister?"

She pursed her lips, watching him but seeing something else. "Yes."

"Did she look like you?"

"She was but a child when last I saw her."

"'Tis safe to guess that she lacked your enchanting curves, then," he said.

She came back to the present, and he smiled, lost in her eyes. But he couldn't afford to be such a fool.

"I have no idea if you're telling the truth," he admitted.

Her lips twisted the slightest degree. They were very close to his. "I know."

"And you don't care?"

"In truth, I quite prefer it that way."

"You're a complicated woman," he said, and couldn't help but lean toward her.

"Yes."

He felt his body tighten. "A complicated woman who needs to produce a child."

"Not *your* child." He could feel her breath against his lips. It felt hopelessly erotic.

"Maybe we could simply practice then, lass."

Her lips twitched again, as though an actual smile might break the careful facade she had built around her. "You forget my former occupation."

Prostitution. Ah yes. But was it all a lie? he wondered, and found, oddly, that he could not quite care. "One can never get too much practice," he said, and kissed her.

# Chapter 12

His lips felt like lightning against hers, burning on contact, muddling her senses. Perhaps she had immersed herself too deeply in her role, for it was no longer clear who she was. Sinner? Saint? Courtesan? Gypsy?

Hot kisses slipped to her throat, unraveling a skein of tangled desires, and suddenly it didn't matter *who* she was. The confusing identities blurred to nothingness. All she knew was that they were alone, and that he was temptation itself.

Reaching for his shirt, she yanked it out of his trousers. He didn't stall her, didn't detain her. Indeed, he drew back, allowing her full access to him, to his clothing. She pulled the shirt up over his head, easily baring smooth dark skin over layers of taut muscle. Beneath his steel buttons his erection pressed eagerly against his leather breeches, but his chest distracted her.

"Holy hell," she said, and rising to her knees, pushed

him onto the mattress. He went without complaint. She kissed his chest, his nipples, the hard hillocks of his belly, and moaned as she worked her way lower.

"Fook!" She heard his groan like a swell of agony, and suddenly his hands were on her arms, pushing her up. "Merciful saints, woman, slow down or—"

She kissed his mouth. He had the sexiest mouth in all of Christendom. He kissed her back, but in a second he was pushing her away.

"Just . . . just give me a moment to . . ."

"To what?" He was holding her hands in a tight grip. How had he gotten her hands? She needed them to touch him, to stroke him, to . . . Hell, if she knew what she had planned, but it was going to feel good. She skimmed his chest and licked her lips.

"For the love of God . . ." He shuddered. "Don't do that."

"Do what?" she asked, and dropped her gaze to the swell in his pants.

He swore quietly, reverently. "Slow down," he warned, "or I'll be no good to you whatsoever."

She had no idea what that meant. "Remove your breeches." Her voice sounded odd. Low. Husky.

His was similar. "Is that an order, lass?"

"Yes." Too strong, probably. Too bossy. But if so, why did the bulge beneath the leather swell even larger?

"Very well, then." A dark shock of hair had fallen

across his brow. His eyes were half closed and his jaw clenched, as if he kept himself in careful check. "But you'll be keeping your hands to yourself for a wee bit."

She felt her lips twitch up. He swallowed. A muscle ticked in his jaw, and the chiseled strength of his biceps flexed.

"I mean it, lass. Do I have your word?"

She managed a nod, even leaned back against her heels on the mattress, maybe to help him feel secure, maybe to give herself a better look.

He stepped from the bed. His fingers looked long and brown and powerful as they undid the steel dome buttons. She waited, breath held, and then he was pushing the garment downward. His hips were as lean and firm as a thoroughbred's. And when his cock sprang from confinement, she actually gasped. Her lips opened of their own accord, and when she spoke, her voice sounded raspy. Purred low and possessive.

"Come here." Bossy again. But he came, stepping out of his clothing to move toward her.

She curled her hand around him and squeezed gently. A droplet oozed from the swollen tip.

He groaned something inarticulate. She glanced up to watch him tilt his head back, and when she gripped his balls with her other hand, he sucked air through his teeth and tightened every fascinating muscle. He was a god. A revered statue made of flesh and bone.

Still watching him, she bent to lick off that one solitary

drop. His thighs bunched with power, his hips arched forward, inviting her, begging her. Leaning in, she took him into her mouth. He cupped the back of her head in one hand and pulled her nearer, moaning as he did so. But no one had ever accused her of being the selfless sort. She was certain of that, and eased away from him. His fingers loosened, skimming through her hair as she watched him through lowered lashes.

He stepped back a pace, chest rising and falling with each hard breath, muscles clenched tight and lovely.

"Well?" Her voice was little more than a growl now. "Do you plan to take me or not?"

"Since the day I found you," he said, and dipping his head, came to her.

She could feel the motion in the pit of her stomach, in the arch of her feet, and scooted back onto the bed, so ready, so willing, so—

The lantern shattered, bursting onto the hardwood. Savaana jerked wildly in that direction. A tabby cat was just skittering to a halt on the walnut secretary. But oil had already spattered onto the carpet. Flames licked at it. She gasped. Gallagher cursed.

And then they were both scrambling toward the fire, he naked, she breathless as they beat at the flames with various articles of clothing.

The fire sputtered out, but not before they heard footsteps on the stairs.

They froze in tandem horror.

"Get dressed!" she hissed, but he was already ripping his shirt over his head, already struggling with the charred breeches she'd tossed at him. He'd nearly managed to pull them over his hard-packed hips when someone rapped on the door.

"Madam!"

"Gregors!"

They mouthed the name in unison, eyes wide with terror.

"My lady! Is something amiss?"

"No," she said, but then a little tongue of flame sparked near her foot. She loosed a small shriek and jerked sideways.

Gallagher stomped it out.

"I'm coming in," Gregors announced.

She spun toward the doorway as the old man lurched inside, lantern held high.

"This isn't what it seems!" she rasped, but the butler only stared, brows high and expression haughty as he took in the scene before him.

"So the cat did not cause the lantern to fall?" he asked.

"Yes, but . . ." she began, and glanced to the left. Gallagher was gone. Completely absent. Vanished. It took all her willpower to resist peering under the bed. "Yes." She drew in a tight breath and pressed her fingertips together in front of her body. "Yes, it did."

He was watching her with a strange expression. "You should not leave your window open at night, my lady. Who knows what might come through?"

She managed a nod, but nothing more.

"I shall send Emily to clear away the mess posthaste," he said, and turned toward the door.

She nodded again, then froze, sense scrambling for a foothold in her discombobulated brain. Had she just been squeezing the Irishman's . . . Holy hell! She wasn't *really* the jaded baroness. Didn't *really* seduce laborers in her bedchamber while her husband was absent. But she'd been intent on rushing back to Darlington to ascertain her grandfather's well being when she saw Gallagher ascend the chestnut tree. Thus, she'd hurried through the house, back to her rooms, while gathering her borrowed persona around her like a too-quickly spun web. By the time she stepped through her door, her mind was torn between what she was and what she might be. The Irishman's hot presence had only confused her more. Like too much warm brandy on a chilly night, he had fired up her body and—

"No!" she gasped, coming fully to her senses with a jolt. "Don't bother her!"

Gregors pivoted stiffly back. "I beg your pardon?"

"I've no wish to wake . . ." she began, and remembering herself, pursed her snooty lips. "I've no wish to be bothered by her bumbling efforts this time of night. I need my sleep."

Gregors narrowed suspicious eyes. "Certainly, my lady, but there are other beds where you might reside for a short while."

And leave Gallagher hiding under the . . . wherever the hell he was hiding under? "I don't want another bed," she said. Her voice was appropriately haughty, but her hands were unsteady. She clasped them together. "I want my own."

For a moment she thought the old man would argue, but finally he nodded stiffly. "As you wish," he said, and placed his own lantern on the desk where the other had stood only minutes before. "Until morning, then," he added, and turned away.

She snapped her gaze rabidly to the left, searching wildly for the Irishman, but Gregors was already turning to close the door behind him, his expression as solemn as death.

She schooled her face and nodded. "Until morning."

He was gone in a moment. The flame flickered slightly in the whispering breeze.

Savaana turned like one in a dream, searching, then saw the Irishman squeeze out of her wardrobe and rise to his full height. His pants were firmly in place, but his shirt was open, exposing most of his well-muscled chest and belly, like a banquet after a long fast.

She closed her eyes and wondered what the hell was wrong with her. "Get out," she said softly.

But he shook his head and stepped toward her.

Gregors's footsteps were already inaudible.

"What if he watches the balcony?" Gallagher whispered.

"What?" The word was nearly soundless.

He pressed a finger to her lips. "Your balcony's visible from the window in the library."

"How do you know that?"

"Shhh," he hissed, but continued quietly. "I can't leave yet. He might see me."

Panic soared through her at the memory of what she'd been like just minutes before. What she'd been about to do. And do happily. "You don't expect to stay here."

His brows rose in conjunction with his lips. "I thought you wanted to—"

"That was before." She hissed the words, cutting him off abruptly.

"Before what?"

"Before—" she rasped, then glancing at the bed, snatched a blanket from it and shoved it up against the bottom of the door, even though it would be all but impossible for anyone to hear from the hallway. Knollcrest's walls were a solid foot thick, its doors made of hardy walnut. "Before I came to my senses."

He scowled. "I think I liked you better nonsensical."

She gave him a look. He grinned and took a hopeful step forward, but she placed a hand firmly to his chest. It stopped him in his tracks, but did nothing to calm the raging sensations that skittered up her arm to every tittering nerve-ending. Still, she managed to give him a stern scowl, even though his skin felt like sun-warmed marble beneath her fingers. His nostrils flared a little. She shook her head and pointed to the opposite side of the room.

He raised his brows. "What are you thinking? That I'll stand there like a good little soldier until you decide it's time for me to take my leave?"

"Exactly."

He grinned a little at her tone, and though her boggled mind had no idea why, it almost seemed that he enjoyed her brassy nature. Then again, it wasn't really *her* nature. Was it? Holy hell, she needed time alone, to think, to figure things out without him there to confuse . . . everything.

He leaned into her palm, increasing the heat that steamed between them. "But that might be hours," he said, and smiled when she swallowed weakly.

"What kind of soldier are you?" she asked. Her voice sounded pale.

He grinned a little. "A randy one?"

She tightened her lips as if she were doing the same with her self-control. "Against the wall."

"I can't remain standing all night," he said. "I'll need to rest. The climb is difficult."

She snorted softly. "Don't be ridiculous. I just—" she began, but stopped herself abruptly, horrified that she nearly admitted she'd tried the climb herself only a short time before. He watched her, but she only shrugged and frowned. "Standing is too taxing?"

"I fear so."

"Yet you didn't think . . ." She paused, trying to come up with a word that wouldn't make her want to throw him on the floor and rip off his clothes with her teeth. There was no such word. "You didn't think *copulating* would be overly arduous?"

He thought about that for a second, then shrugged simply. "I was willing to make the effort." He reached up, touching her cheek. "For you."

For a moment she almost melted, but she caught herself. "Oh for God's sake. Fine! You take the bed. But only until the moon goes under," she said, and turned toward the chair.

He caught her arm before she'd swung completely away. "Not without you."

She swiveled back, breath held, scowling a question, and he stared at her, looking ridiculously sincere.

"I'll not get a bit of rest knowing you're uncomfortable, lass."

"Are you serious?"

Something sparked in his devilish eyes. "Me da raised me better."

She stared at him. He grinned. His expression looked foolishly boyish juxtaposed against his granite-hard body. But she resisted . . . everything.

"Very well," she snapped. "But you'll remain on your side of the bed."

"Of course," he agreed, and almost controlled his grin.

# Chapter 13

**S**ean stared up at the ceiling, fingers linked behind his head, shirt open down the front. And why not? He seemed to be perfectly safe from her lusty nature now. Indeed, she had not so much as glanced his way since they'd reclined on the bed. And why was that? He rolled toward her, but she was lying on her side, facing away, fully clothed but for those tiny, titillating toes.

"Where'd she go?" he whispered. His lips were inches from her ear, and despite everything he knew of her, he found that he wanted quite desperately to kiss her, to bring her alive once again.

She rolled to her back, looking peeved, even in the darkness. "What are you talking about?"

"The umm . . . enthusiastic lass what wrestled me out of me clothes," he said. "I but wondered what might have happened to her."

"She came to her senses."

He almost laughed, but even with the servants stowed

some distance belowstairs, he dared not chance the noise. "'Tis a pity."

She stared at him, all somberness, then cleared her throat, pursed her lips and lowered her eyes. "Perhaps I owe you an apology."

Nothing could have surprised him more. Actually, he'd been considering thanking her. Turned out, there wasn't much that was more flattering than seeing a strong woman weaken just because of a few discarded articles of clothing. Well, actually, it had been *all* his clothing, he thought, and almost grinned at the memory. "An apology, lass?"

"I wasn't myself."

"Truly?"

She flickered her gaze to his, anger already snapping in her ice blue eyes. "Yes."

"Then might I meet that other woman again?" he asked, and touched her face. Her skin was as smooth as fresh cream.

"I can't . . ." She paused as if desperately searching for the right word. "I can't lie with you." They were whispering, though her tone was harsh with angst.

"You seemed quite capable just a few minutes back, lass," he murmured.

"I said I was sorry."

She didn't sound sorry. Indeed, she sounded peeved and impatient, and that truth amused him. But in a moment a new thought accosted him; he sobered abruptly.

"Who is he?" His own voice was soft, but imbued with more feeling than he had intended.

She scowled at him. "What are you talking about?"

"The man you are willing to give up others for? Who might he be?"

She leaned away a little to study him. "Do you forget that I'm married?"

He almost wished he could. Almost wished he could disremember everything he knew of her and start afresh. But she was what she was. And yet he wanted her. Or at least parts of him did. Damn those opinionated parts. "Someone came through your window, lass. It was not your husband."

She raised one brow at him. "Are all Irishmen so delusional?"

"I saw him leave with me own eyes." He kept his tone as neutral as possible, but felt dark emotion stir like a sleeping serpent within him. It almost seemed akin to jealousy. Which was ridiculous, of course. For he had not come to win her heart. Hardly that.

"Believe this," she said, "none came through yonder window while I inhabited this room."

She was either sincere or an excellent liar. Possibly both. "You think someone ventured here after you left your chambers?" he asked.

"No," she said. "I do not."

"Then—"

"I believe you created an intruder in your mind so that you might have an excuse to come here yourself."

"You think me that devious?" he asked, though it was, in fact, something he might do.

"Yes," she said, and he chuckled softly as he stroked his thumb across her perfect chin.

"How is it that someone as lovely as you has become so jaded?"

"By knowing men as conniving as you."

He kissed the corner of her mouth. Not because he planned to. Not because he hoped to seduce her. But because he couldn't stop himself. There was something about her looking so peeved and so lovely at the same time that made her strangely irresistible. He wanted to touch every feather soft inch of her, wanted to kiss every lovely hollow and swell. But she was still fully dressed.

And why was that again? He'd never obtained an acceptable answer to that query.

"So, the gown . . ." he said, skimming his hand down her sleeve. "Tell me again why you wear it?"

She raised her chin the slightest degree. "And all the while I thought clothing was a fairly standard practice these days," she said. "Even in the more backward regions. Such as the Isle."

Good saints, she was mean, he thought, and managed to stifle a grin. "Some have taken to the idea, I'm told, but I, meself, have never been in favor of it," he said, and skimmed his fingers along her arm.

"Shall I assume you don't sunburn easily, then?"

He did grin now. Why fight it? "Some consequences are well worth the cost, lass."

For a moment he almost thought her smile would win the day, but she managed to stave it off like one might the black death.

He raised his brows, watching her from inches away. "Quite certain, I was, that you believed the same a few minutes ago."

She cleared her throat as he skimmed his fingertips across her knuckles. "I am fairly sure I already apologized for what happened a few minutes ago."

"Ahh yes. I believe you did."

"Then as a gentleman you are required to accept my contrition and not mention it again."

"But I am not a gentleman," he said, and kissed her.

And glory be, she kissed him back, her lips warm and needy and as soft as a dream against his.

The moment stood still, bathed in moonlight, washed with desire until she pulled gently away.

"What are you, then?" she whispered.

Her eyes were wide now, and though he knew himself a fool, he couldn't help but think she looked as innocent as the tiny lambs she'd drawn into the world.

"I thought we had discussed meself already," he said,

and slipped his hand down her neck to her shoulder. It was a beautiful shoulder, as smooth as satin, as warm as mulled wine.

"You are not a simple blacksmith," she said.

Leaning forward, he kissed her just where her bodice crossed her clavicle. Good saints, she smelled like magic. "I don't believe I ever said I was simple, lass."

"Who are you?" She breathed the question, and he drank the words in.

"I might ask the same of you," he said. "One minute you are tearing the clothes from my wee shivering body and . . ." He meant to make light of it, but found that despite it all, he couldn't quite breathe for the feelings the sharp memories elicited. Pausing for a moment, he scrambled for his equilibrium. And what the devil was that about? He was no stammering farm boy, after all. No bumbling lad out for his first tumble. "Well . . ." He found his stride after a moment. "Suffice it to say you were doing some rather fascinating things."

Her gaze flickered nervously away, and try as he might he couldn't decide which side of her he preferred, the bold baroness or the mild maid. He stroked the tender length of her elegant throat.

"Where, may I ask, did you learn such things, lass?"

She cleared that elegant throat and forced herself to look at him. "Might you think there's a school for such things?"

He chuckled low and quiet. True, she was as change-able as a Highland wind, but none would call her boring. "If there is, I think you could apply as tutor," he said.

"I don't believe my husband would approve."

From another woman perhaps the statement would have been amusing. But he was not amused. Indeed, the thought of her wed made his heart squeeze tight in his chest.

"Tell me true, lass, why do you resist?"

She fiddled with a fold in his sleeve, then slipped her fingertips onto his bare chest, slowly, as though she couldn't quite help herself. But all the while she refused to meet his eyes. "Resist what?" she asked.

"Taking me inside yourself," he rasped.

The blatant question seemed to shock her. Her eyes grew wide and she ceased to breathe, but in a moment she steadied herself.

"I don't deny that I've been a bit . . . unorthodox in the past. But now I am wed," she said, and slipped her pinky over his left nipple. He let his eyes fall closed but managed not to whimper like a hopeful hound. "And I have every intention of making this marriage last."

Steeling himself, he considered her answer for a moment but found it impossible to believe a word of it. Perhaps it was because she was caressing him with mind-bending tenderness as she spoke. But maybe it had some-thing to do with what he knew of her past. "Is it because I am not a great lord?" he asked.

"I don't know what you are." She pressed his shirt aside ever so slightly, granting her greater access and smoothing her palm across his pectoral. "You refuse to tell me the truth," she said, and flickered her gaze to his.

Their eyes met with a clash of sharp feeling.

"I'm beginning to fear I could refuse you nothing," he said, and felt suddenly that it was not just a foolish line, but a painful truth.

"Then tell me who you are." She skimmed her fingers feather-light down a groove between his ridged muscles, but he managed to find some lucidness.

"I'm a worker of metal, a trainer of horses, a lover of women."

"You're a liar."

He grinned. "If I were not, would you make love to me?"

"No."

"Then I have little reason to change. Give me some hope," he pleaded. "I am only a rough-cut stone now. But if I were polished, might you love me?"

"What you are is a—" she began, and stopped abruptly, immobilized. "What did you say?" Her voice was breathy.

"I believe I was begging for your—"

"Before that?"

"I asked for hope."

"After that."

He scowled. "I was talking about . . . me stones?"

"Stones," she hissed, and suddenly she was upright, standing beside the bed like a general about to direct his subordinates. "Holy hell. The stones!"

He stared at her, wondering if she was, perhaps, completely out of her mind. Wondering, too, if that would make her any less desirable. "In truth," he said, "not every woman becomes so excited about me stones. But I'm pleased to see—"

"Get out!"

"I beg—"

"Now."

"I didn't mean to offend—" he began, but she was literally dragging him from the bed, and damned if she wasn't the strongest little baroness who had ever tried to drag him anywhere.

"The moon is gone now."

"But it might—"

"Hurry!" she said, and shoving him out the door, locked it firmly behind him.

# Chapter 14

"**W**hy London?" Sean asked, but kept his gaze steady on the winding road ahead. Daisy was a fine steed, but had a tendency to hit every possible pothole if left unattended, and he had no desire to see his passengers dumped into the ditch. Even though Clarette Tilmont was obviously as mad as a spring hare.

She had insisted that Mrs. Edwards accompany them yet again. Thus the three of them were squashed onto a seat built for two. Their chaperone, bulky and lax, should have been an effective buffer between them, especially considering the baroness's obvious derangement. Yet he could feel her effects on him as clearly as if he was touching her skin, kissing her lips. And how bloody stupid was that? He was *not* attracted to this woman. Well, not beyond the mere physicality of it, at any rate. Oh yes, he still intended to seduce her, but not because he wanted to. Well, he *wanted* to, but . . . fook it, he was as daft as *she* was. And why the devil were they going to London?

Was she meeting a lover there? And if so, why the hell wasn't *he* that lover?

"My lady?" Giving their snoozing chaperone a nudge to keep her upright, Sean kept his tone even, though God knew he wanted to shake the haughty baroness until her teeth rattled. Especially when she turned toward him as if he were of no more significance than a bothersome gnat.

"What is it, Lowlywick?"

He gave her a smile. He knew it might have been a little tight. Perhaps he'd been a bit frustrated since . . . meeting her. "I asked why we are traveling to London."

She raised her brows slightly. "Might that be your concern in some unimaginable way?"

Damn right it was. She was driving him mad. He smiled again. "I but hope you are not in some sort of trouble."

As if shocked by his words, she leaned away a little. Any farther and she might well tumble over the low side. He was ashamed to find the thought entertaining. Maybe.

"Whyever would a lady such as myself be in trouble?" she asked, and steadied their chaperone with one gloved hand.

Why? Because she *was* trouble. Damn her, he couldn't even think when she was near. And when she *wasn't* near . . . Why the devil had she chased him so abruptly from her chambers the previous night? She had wanted him as much as he'd wanted her. Hadn't she? Or was it all an act? A devious ploy to drive him from his—

He stopped himself, calmed his thoughts. "So all is well?" he asked.

"Of course."

They rattled along for a few more seconds. He willed himself to be silent. After all, he was the driver, and little more. But the words came out unbidden.

"Is it a man?"

She turned back toward him with a snap and jerked her gaze to the widow, but the old woman was as limp as a cabbage leaf, her head bouncing loosely with every beat of the chestnut's staccato trot.

"Must I remind you, yet again, that I'm a married woman?" Clarette's voice was hushed but audible.

"Perhaps you should remind yourself," Sean said. He felt petty and itchy.

"I've done nothing to break my husband's trust," she hissed.

He raised his brows.

She rushed her gaze back to Mrs. Edwards, but that one's mouth had fallen open. Clarette pursed hers. The sight of those succulent lips did something ridiculous to his . . . everything. He pushed his gaze back to her eyes with an effort, but couldn't forget how her mouth had felt as it enclosed him. His body tightened traitorously at the memory.

"You've a curious definition of nothing, lass," he said, and though he tried, he couldn't seem to keep his attention from the fullness of her lips.

"Quit that!" she ordered.

"What?"

"Looking at me like that." She snapped her gaze back to the old woman who now snored between them. "She may be deaf, but she's not blind."

"Tell me why we go to London."

For a moment he thought she'd refuse to answer, but finally she spoke. "I have a bit of business there," she said, and reaching out, returned Mrs. Edwards's flopping right hand onto her plump lap.

"Business?"

"Yes."

"What kind of business?"

"Am I mistaken, or are you yet in my employ?"

"I can assure you I'm doing me best to service you." He hadn't exactly meant to make that sound suggestive, but damn it, it was impossible to think in any other terms where she was concerned. Now, however, she merely stared at him, scowling a bit, as if she didn't understand the reference. Which was damned strange for a courtesan. "But you ejected me from your room."

"Will you hush your mouth." Her words were barely audible, but it hardly mattered. He could have guessed her sentiment just by seeing the outrage on her face, and for some reason that brightened his mood.

"I will if you tell me the reason for this journey."

She glared at him for several seconds, lowered her attention to the old woman again, then sighed. "Very well, but you must swear secrecy."

He refrained from holding his breath, but his attention was so intense on her that for a moment he forgot entirely about the mare. The tilbury bumped unceremoniously through a pothole.

Awakening suddenly, Mrs. Edwards squawked in terror. As for Clarette, she grabbed the mounting handle and braced her hip against the old woman to keep them both upright.

"Watch what you're about, lad!" their chaperone scolded.

"Me apologies," he said, and in a matter of moments Mrs. Edwards was snoring again.

"I believe you were about to divulge your reasons for this journey," Sean said, and kept his attention on the road disappearing between the mare's chestnut ears.

"And you swear not to tell another?"

"You've me word as a . . . blacksmith," he said, and gave her his best smile. There was no reason to allow her to know that she was driving him out of his mind.

"Very well, then," she said. "I plan to buy my husband a gift."

He wasn't sure what he had expected, but this wasn't it. "A gift."

"Yes."

"And why is that?"

"Because he is my husband."

"Then perhaps he should not have left you alone at—" he began, but she held up her hand. It was gloved, but he couldn't forget how her velvety fingers had felt against his chest, his belly, his. . .

She cleared her throat, doing the same with his lurid thoughts, then scowled at Mrs. Edwards, whose head was lolling around like a walnut on a thread of yarn. "Sometimes I can be a bit . . . impatient."

He stared at her. "What?"

She glanced away as if peeved. "Perhaps you have not noticed, you being a . . ." she waved a hand at him dismissively and shook her head once. "Whatever the hell you are. But at times I can be rather . . ."

"Mad?" he guessed.

"No."

"Shrewish, annoying, petty?"

"Superior," she said, face deadpan.

"Are you saying you *are* superior or that you *act* superior?"

For one wild moment he almost thought she would laugh,

for her eyes lit like magic and her mouth quirked, but finally her impassive expression was firmly back in place.

"Both," she said.

"So you're apologizing for acting superior even though you *are* superior."

"Some believe the nobility are supposed to be . . ." She sighed, looking put upon. " . . . accommodating to the little people."

"Little people. Such as gnomes?"

"Such as blacksmiths."

He wouldn't kill her. That would be wrong. But he had no compunctions about embarrassing her. "A woman of your experience must know better than to think me little, lass," he said.

She raised a brow at him.

"After last night," he explained.

"Good God, have you no shame?" she hissed, and though her expression became increasingly haughty, her cheeks reddened in concert.

He couldn't quite stop his chuckle, for her outrage made him near ecstatic. "Not about that, surely."

"How is it that you've not been flayed within an inch of your life by some lady's irate husband?"

"Generally the ladies in question have sense enough not to announce our affair," he said, and failed to miss a bump in the road. Mrs. Edwards's eyes flickered open.

"Truffles!" She all but shouted the word.

Clarette jumped, Daisy jerked in her traces, and Sean lowered his attention to the old woman's eyes.

"What say you, Mrs. Edwards?"

"Chocolate éclairs," she muttered, and nodded back into oblivion.

"We're not having an 'affair,'" hissed the baroness, and nudged the big woman's bulk toward Sean.

"What's that?" he asked, though he had heard her perfectly well.

"We are *not* having an affair."

"What would you call it then, lass?"

"A mistake!"

He narrowed his eyes at her and kept the lines steady. "Is that what you always call it when you put your mouth around a man's—"

"Shut up!" she hissed, and he laughed.

"Where are we going?"

"What?" she looked as flustered as a scolded child. Her expression made him want to kiss her . . . or shake her. Maybe both.

"To get this gift for your lauded husband. What is our destination?"

"*We* are not going anywhere. You'll wait outside."

"Very well," he said, "unless it's a bordello. You're not buying him a prostitute, are you?"

"Of course not. What is wrong with you?" she gasped, and he laughed.

"For a courtesan, you seem strangely prudish." He reconsidered that for an instant. "Sometimes," he added, and she blushed again.

He watched the color dawn on her cheeks, then continued. "If not a prostitute, what?"

She looked annoyed. "He's quite fond of cuff links."

"So you're going to a jeweler?" Hope surged in his chest. He knew a little shop that would be perfect for the occasion.

"If that's acceptable to you."

He smiled. "Far be it from me to overstep my boundaries and give an opinion regarding my lady's plans. Which shop do you intend to visit?"

She paused for a moment. "You're a metalsmith. Which do you recommend?"

"Please, me lady . . ." he said, exaggerating his brogue. "I am naught but a humble blacksmith."

She scowled at him. "I doubt you're a humble anything. Have you a shop to recommend?"

He pricked his ears at her tone. It almost seemed edged with uncertainty. "But surely there is a store you favor."

She shrugged and glanced at the country that rolled past them like a verdant panorama. "Naturally, but I can hardly visit one my husband frequents. It might well ruin the surprise," she said.

He longed to question her further, for she still seemed

tense, but he dare not lose this opportunity. "There's a shop on Oxford Street that some find pleasing."

"Some who?"

He stared at her.

Her scowl darkened. "Some women?"

It actually took a moment for him to recognize the jealousy in her voice, but when he did, he smiled. "Dare I hope that you would care?"

"No, you may not," she snapped, and he laughed.

"I assume there have been one or two of the fair sex who must have approved of Smith's Ornaments," he said. "But just now I cannot think of a single name."

She caught his steady stare for a second, then turned away, almost flustered. "Take me to this shop, Wicken-minor."

"As you wish," he said, smiling at her pique. "If you'll tell me who you truly are."

"Whatever are you talking about?" Something flashed in her eyes. If he hadn't known better, he would have almost thought it was fear, but he had seen her moments after tumbling from the high-strung gelding's back. Fear wasn't something this woman would comprehend.

"Are you the woman who lies on her belly in the mud of the wild fields to deliver lambkins or are you the one who refers to the laboring class with ringing disdain?"

"Both," she said. "If the lambs are my own and the laborers in question are . . ." She shrugged. " . . . disdainful."

Anger coursed through him. It wasn't an emotion he was oft familiar with. Not unless it concerned his family, at any rate. But then, she *did* concern his family, didn't she? "Well, it's good to know you found nothing disdainful about me last night."

She glanced at her chaperone again, but when she raised her eyes, they were level and, yes, disdainful. "If that were true, do you think I would have tossed you from my chambers?"

"Give me another chance," he said, "and you'll beg me to stay."

"Right now I'm begging you to keep your mouth shut."

He lowered his gaze to her mouth. "I'd never do the same to you," he said, and watched those gorgeous lips part, watched her expressive eyes dilate.

"Do you never give up?" Her words were no more than a whisper.

"Not until I hear you sing for joy," he said.

"I believe I told you earlier that I am not the singing sort."

"Then you've been with the wrong men. And that I'm willing to prove."

"If you'll but shut up, I'll recite the Hallelujah Chorus."

"Next time we're alone I'll be as quiet as an Irish rose," he said.

"There won't be a next time."

"Your husband had best return home soon, then, lass, for a woman like you can't wait too long," he said, and turned his attention from her steaming eyes to her puckered lips. But just then they struck a bump and Mrs. Edwards slumped to the floor of the tilbury like an overstuffed pillow.

# Chapter 15

**W**as she insane? Gallagher probably thought so. And maybe he was right, Savaana thought as she glided toward the jeweler's shop.

She'd received a missive from her grandfather just that morning. It had been short and suitably guarded in case others intercepted it, but she was now sure beyond a shadow of a doubt that he was safe and well. Thus she had been allowed to consider other things. To travel to London, in fact. But that hardly meant she had the right to act like an impetuous strumpet. Which she had. Or rather *Lady Tilmont* had.

Blushing at her potent memories, Savaana wondered dismally if perhaps she had allowed her part as the baroness to go too far. Or maybe . . . maybe she had simply wanted to touch the Irishman and used her current identity as an excuse to do so. After all, despite his host of irritating qualities, his sexual appeal was undeniable. Kissing him had been intoxicating. Touching his chest had been exciting. Stroking his— But no, she wouldn't think of that.

Indeed, she would think of nothing but the task at hand.

The stones in her beaded reticule seemed inordinately heavy. She glanced behind her as she strode purposefully down the foot pavement. Smith's Ornaments was just around the corner, or so Gallagher had said. But Daisy had picked up a stone in her forefoot just short of there, and the Irishman insisted that they stop a block or so from their destination, which suited her fine. She was more than happy to have him occupied so she could see to her business alone.

Before rounding the corner to Oxford Street, however, she chanced upon another shop. Gallagher's gaze met hers as she glanced back, sparking a thousand lurid memories, but the squeak of the jeweler's door put a merciful end to her roiling thoughts.

A scrawny man stood behind the counter helping a young buck in a dark tailcoat examine cuff links. The spectacles perched on the proprietor's hooked nose made him look narrow-eyed and peevish, regardless of his stylish jacket and starched cravat.

Savaana waited, perusing hat pins and feigning patience as they discussed the merits of the various pieces. Her heart pounded in anticipation against her overtight ribs. But finally the customer left. The tall jeweler stashed the links away and turned toward her with elegant lethargy. "Can I help you, madam?" His accent was French. Maybe. What the hell did she know of French accents? For all she knew it may have been Mesopotamian. After all, it wasn't as if she had studied in Paris. Or anywhere.

"I do hope so," she said, and permeated her tone with an accent of her own. It, too, might have been French. "I have a . . . a bauble I would very much like you to examine."

He nodded, saying nothing.

Faking a bored mien of her own, Savaana drew the necklace out of her reticule and set it carefully on the glass. It lay between them, half a dozen thumb-sized stones pierced by a simple leather thong.

He stared at them a moment, but didn't touch, as though he had no wish to soil his hands. "And what is this, madam?"

"It's . . ." She felt foolish suddenly, like the Rom she was, trespassing where her betters trod. But Gallagher's words about polished stones had awakened a suspicion in her mind; she had set off at the first possible moment to investigate. "Just a little something I received from an admirer," she said. "I thought perhaps you could advise me as to its value."

Lifting the necklace finally, he fingered the stones. "Well, madam, I fear the only advice I can give is to find yourself a better grade of admirer."

Her stomach dropped. She'd been so sure that she had underestimated them, just as Lady Tilmont had. "So they're—"

"Nothing but pebbles, madam."

"Oh." She swallowed her disappointment, straightened her shoulders. "Well, thank you," she said, and grasping the necklace, prepared to leave, but he touched her arm.

"Still, they are . . ." He sighed as if loath to waste his time on such paltry rocks. "They are interesting stones. If you'd like, I could take them off your hands."

Her breath froze in her throat. She canted her head a little, as casual as he, though her veins thrummed with hope. Since her earliest memory she'd performed in carnivals and markets and festivals. And from those experiences a litany of the same sort of words sang through her mind. *You're stealing me blind, luv, but . . . I shouldn't do this, but for a 'andsome bloke like you . . . Me 'usband'll kill me dead if'n 'e finds out I done this, but. . .*

Savaana drew a careful breath and reminded herself to exhale. "How very kind of you," she said, and felt herself tremble just a little. "What could you give for them?"

He shrugged. The movement was outwardly relaxed, but there was something in his eyes, a shining avarice she'd seen more times than she could count. Shame on her for forgetting her upbringing.

"I saw you admiring the hat pins near the door," he

said. "Perhaps you'd like to trade this little trifle for one of them."

She glanced toward the pins as if debating, but her mind was spinning with questions, with ideas. "They *were* quite lovely."

"Indeed, and well crafted," he said, and now his voice almost warbled. It was like the howl of a wolf about to pounce.

She scowled and caught her lower lip between her teeth with girlish dismay. "But come to that, my admirer is rather special. Perhaps I'll keep the necklace after all," she said, and plucked at the piece.

The proprietor's bony fingers tightened on the stones. "Two then," he said. There was a desperate note to his voice now, and his face looked pinched above his snowy cravat. She could have named a dozen country fishwives who would have played this game better.

"I beg your pardon?" she said.

"Perhaps I could part with *two* hat pins. Though you're robbing me blind."

"No," she said firmly, and pulled the necklace from his hands. "But I appreciate your time more than I can say." That much was the absolute truth.

He watched her go. She could feel his attention on her back as she stepped from the store. Her breath was coming hard, as if she'd just completed the performance of her lifetime. And maybe she had. She glanced toward the carriage in a haze and saw that Gallagher was busy adjusting the mare's overcheck. She looked to the right, longing for another opinion. Perhaps Smith's would be just the place.

The Irishman was positioned on the far side of the animal and wouldn't see her if she slipped down the paved walkway to the next store. The less he knew of her affairs, the better, she thought, and making a speedy decision, hurried around the corner and down the street to Smith's.

A little bell tingled merrily as she stepped through the door. A middle-aged woman wearing a starched apron over a powder blue gown greeted her. She was dusting a display of snuff cans and silver cups that graced an elegant, ivory tabletop. Introducing herself as Mrs. Fellowhurst, she proclaimed that their store offered unique ornaments of all sorts: jewelry, tableware, even locks and etched door handles.

"Indeed? How interesting," Savaana said, though it was all but impossible to keep her tone casual. "And what type of gemstones do your craftsmen work with for their creations?"

"All sorts. Rubies, brilliants, sapphires. Whatever you wish."

"So you're familiar with most of them."

"Certainly."

"Perhaps you can tell me something of these, then," she said, and pulled the necklace into view.

They looked dismal and dull against the ivory table-top. But the woman behind it drew in a sharp breath.

"Put them away!" she ordered.

Savaana raised her brows, but Mrs. Fellowhurst was pushing them toward her. "Away," she repeated.

Glancing nervously toward the door, Savaana dropped the stones back into her reticule. "What is it?" she asked. "What's wrong?"

The woman pulled in a heavy breath, clasped her hands in front of her apron and looked toward the street as if expecting to be mobbed at any given moment. "An interesting piece," she said finally, relaxing a little. "Might I inquire where you obtained it?"

"They were given to me," Savaana said, mind roiling. "Why? What do you know of them? Have you seen them before?"

"No," the woman said, and shifted her gaze to the reticule where they rested. "Nor have I seen their like, I think."

"What can you tell me of them?"

"Maybe I'm wrong." She shook her head as if she were dreaming. "'Tis impossible to say for sure without a closer look. Perhaps . . ." She glanced up, her eyes shining with a bit of the same light that had glimmered in the old man's just moments before. "Perhaps you'd like to leave them with me for a time so I can examine them more closer."

Savaana stared at her, point-blank. "I think not," she said, and the other grinned sheepishly.

"You cannot blame me for trying."

"I would have done the same myself," Savaana said. Perhaps she was admitting more than she should, but haggling brought out the earthy Gypsy in her soul. "What are they?"

Again the proprietress glanced toward the street. Then she motioned toward the back and turned away. Savaana followed. Once out of sight from the window, Mrs. Fellowhurst pulled out a glass and examined the stones. An imaginary clock ticked inside Savaana's head, but finally the other woman looked up. Her face was pale.

"Tell me," Savaana ordered.

"I believe they're . . ." She cleared her throat. "It's impossible to say for certain without further examination."

"But—"

"I believe they may be paragons."

Savaana shook her head.

"Brilliants. Diamonds." Her voice had dropped even further. "Of exceptional quality."

"All of them?"

"That's my guess from a cursory inspection."

For a moment Savaana was tempted to inquire about their value, but it hardly mattered. By the paleness of Mrs. Fellowhurst's face, she could deduce that they were indeed rare. By the same token, she could guess that Clarette had no idea of their value, for she had left them behind. But of course that meant little. Certainly it was no sure indication that the baroness had obtained them from her mother. No reason to assume she hadn't gotten them from an admirer, just as she herself had claimed when speaking to the old man. But what kind of gentleman would give such a gift and not indicate its true worth?

"How likely is it that someone will recognize them for what they are?" Savaana asked.

"Unless the person in question is trained . . . quite unlikely."

"So they could have been worn openly without risk."

"Yes."

Savaana nodded. Lifting the stones, she opened her reticule.

"Don't keep them there." The woman's voice was hushed and gruff, her gaze caught on the dangling rocks.

Savaana glanced up. "Am I at risk because of them?"

"I'd rob you myself if there were no repercussions," she said, and finally found an uncertain smile.

Savaana nodded. "My thanks," she said. "You've been more than helpful."

"Don't be too grateful," said the other. "I may yet decide to take the risk."

Savaana almost smiled, then with a quickness her

sedentary life had not yet robbed from her, she slipped the necklace into her bodice and turned. Stepping outside, she pulled the drawstring reticule closed as she did so.

But she had not taken a dozen strides before she was approached.

"My lady," said a voice from behind.

Anticipation trembled through her, but surely she was only being paranoid. Raising her chin, she clutched her reticule close to her abdomen and turned.

The man behind her was short, neatly dressed, and smiling. His mustache was trimmed close, his top hat just so upon his graying head, which he bobbed in a quick bow. "I was wondering if I might have a word with you, madam."

"A word?" She raised one brow and gave him a regal stare, though her heart was beating overtime. "Regarding what exactly?"

"Just a . . ." He shrugged, looking benign. "A business matter."

Something deep inside her made her long to clutch her necklace to her chest, but she remained exactly as she was. "What sort of business do you have in mind, sir?" she asked.

"One of some import," he said, and suddenly she realized they were alone on the street. Gallagher was well out of sight around the corner, and she was carrying the most valuable item she had ever imagined.

"I'm certain your offer is quite generous, but I'm a bit rushed at this time," she said, and turned away.

A giant of a man loomed behind her. The sight of his scarred face spurred a dozen ragged memories through her agitated system, and it was in the fraction of a moment before she passed out that she realized it might not have been a bad idea to let the Irishman accompany her.

# Chapter 16

"Hello," Sean said, and stepped fully into the jeweler's shop. Dammit, he hadn't intended for her to come *here*. Indeed, he had been entirely uninformed about this store's presence.

Glancing about, he couldn't immediately see Clarette, and for reasons completely unknown to him, that made his heart race rather oddly in his too constricted chest. "I'm looking for a woman."

The man behind the counter was as lean as a hickory stick and only half as charming. "You and most of the pinks in Londonderry," he said, and barely sparing a glance from his narrow spectacles, went back to polishing a ring he'd lifted from beneath the counter.

"This is a particular woman," Sean said, and kept his tone light with some difficulty. "She entered just a bit ago looking for a gift for her husband."

"So you're looking for another man's wife, are you?" asked the other, but Sean's nerves were surprisingly frayed and he found he had no wish to trade either barbs or witticisms.

"Where is she?" he asked simply, but the other shrugged his sharp-boned shoulders.

"No generous wife has been here this afternoon," he said, and stepped out from behind the counter.

Sean scowled. What went on here? He had watched Clarette enter this very shop. "She's a handsome woman," he said, sure that if he explained, things would be set right, "with—"

"I didn't think you'd be searching for a homely woman." The jeweler glanced down his nose. "Your type seldom is. Now if you'll excuse me . . ." he said, and turned away, but Sean caught his arm and turned him back around.

"Her hair is dark and her gown lavender."

The proprietor pursed his lips. "What are *you,* then?" he asked, eyeing Sean's humble attire with distaste. "A seducer or a thief? For you're surely not the one who gave her those stones?"

Sean's breath caught tight in his throat. Something was happening here, and he didn't like the feel of it. Did Clarette have his mother's ring after all, or were they talking about something else entirely? "What stones?"

The proprietor gazed owlishly down at him. "Unless you were ignorant of their value."

"What stones?" Sean asked again.

The jeweler laughed, but the tone was tinny and peeved. "The ones she'll receive a fortune for from someone else."

"When did she leave?" His mind was spinning, and though he knew he should be concerning himself with his mother's property, he couldn't bear the thought of Clarette in danger. This was no place for a lady to be walking unescorted. He should have known better than to allow her to go alone. But he'd had no desire to be recognized by those on Oxford Street. Dammit! How had he missed her exodus? "Where'd she go from here?"

"I can't imagine. I'm the only jeweler in the entirety of this city," said the other, and turned again, but this time Sean caught him by his starchy cravat.

"Tell me which way she went," he gritted, and tightened his grip, constricting the other's scrawny throat.

"Very well. Ease up," the man croaked. "She turned right, then took a right at the corner."

"My thanks," Sean rasped, and turning rapidly, sprinted toward Smith's Ornaments.

A little bell tinkled. Mrs. Fellowhurst glanced up.

"Where is Lady Tilmont?" His voice sounded odd, harsh and strained.

"Mister—" she began, but he stopped her.

"A beautiful woman," he said. "Lavender gown, dark hair."

"Is she in trouble?"

"She hasn't returned to the carriage."

She didn't ask more. Instead, she nodded quickly. "That way," she said, pointing to the left. "Some minutes ago. Are you quite—"

He was out the door in an instant. The light was fading. Reaching the cross streets, he slowed to glance right. An old man was sweeping the cobblestones. To the left a gray-haired gentleman in a tidy top hat glanced his way. Their eyes met for just a moment and then he stepped into a nearby alley.

Sean was running before he thought, sprinting down the walkway toward the alley. "You! You there!" he called, but the man didn't step back into view. Tearing down the uneven path, Sean careened to the left, and there, not forty strides away, two men were bending over a prostrate form. He slowed, breathing hard, lungs tight in his chest, heart hammering a threatening beat.

"If you've hurt her, I'll kill you." His words sounded even and matter-of-fact in the still alleyway.

The smaller of the two men straightened and raised his hands. "Not to worry, friend," he said. "She seems to have fainted. We mean no harm."

But Sean saw the other man was crouching over her, touching her shoulder as if he meant to turn her onto her back, and in his other oversized hand he held a knife. Something contracted in Sean's gut, but he kept walking.

"Leave now," he ordered, "And you may have a chance to see the dawn."

"We've no wish for trouble," said the fellow with the hat. The other man straightened to his full height. He filled the alley like a tidal wave, seeming to rise forever.

Sean swore in silence and glanced about for a weapon, but in that second all hell broke loose. One moment their victim was flat on her back, head lolling to the side, and the next she was hurtling through the air like a loosed wagon wheel. Her heels struck the giant in the jaw. He staggered back, arms flung to the side. But she was already on her feet. Somehow, her assailant's knife had miraculously disappeared.

The two miscreants stared at her for several seconds, and then they turned, fleeing down the alley like scurrying rats.

For a moment Clarette remained just as she was, slightly bent, but finally she hugged herself as if chilled. Then she straightened with an audible sigh and turned.

She stopped abruptly when she saw him. "What are you doing here?"

He blinked and glanced behind him. Was this a dream? A nightmare? A ridiculous play of some sort? "I was . . . I was looking for you." Indeed, he had come to defend her, he thought, and found his manly behavior of moments before rather silly suddenly.

"How long have you been there?" she asked.

It felt as though he had stepped onto the stage of a nonsensical drama. "Not long." He made a face, gave a shrug. Why not play along? he thought. The world had obviously gone mad. "Just long enough to see you attack the two thugs who accosted you."

For a moment it almost seemed as if she swore, but she was already striding toward him with purpose and composure. "Whatever are you talking about?"

"Well . . ." He glanced about, vaguely wondering if someone was enjoying this odd performance. "I believe I was talking about the thugs who attacked you. The ones who—"

"Someone attacked me?" she rasped, and stopping even with him, raised her left hand to her throat. It almost seemed to be shaking.

He stared at her point-blank. "What's happening here, Clarette?"

"I don't . . ." She glanced behind, her voice suddenly bewildered, her expression the same. "I was walking along." Keeping her left hand by her throat, she lifted the right wistfully. "I had just left the jeweler, I believe. And suddenly . . ." She gasped, brought her outreached hand to her bosom. "Everything must have gone black because I don't seem to remember anything after that. I . . ." She lifted a fragile hand toward her brow. "Oh. You don't suppose it was—" she began, and fainted.

Sean watched her tumble gracefully to the ground, watched her lie there. For a moment he remained exactly as he was, brows raised. Perhaps he was waiting for the second act. He wasn't certain, but when she didn't rise, he bent over her.

"Clarette?"

She didn't answer.

"Lady Tilmont?" He lifted her hand to feel for a pulse. But gloves covered her from elbow to fingertip. He began to peel off the right one. She moaned then, tugged her hand from his grip and blinked open her eyes.

He settled back on his heels, not sure if he should applaud or escape while he still had a modicum of wits about him.

"Where am I?" Her voice was little-girl soft.

"England."

She scowled a little, already looking peeved.

"London. An alley," he corrected, because who could tell? Maybe she really *had* fainted.

Her eyes narrowed slightly. "Why?"

He shook his head. There was no possible way he could be more confused, but he was certain of one thing: "Not to buy your husband a gift."

"What?" she asked, and pressed her fingertips to her skull.

He considered questioning her, but this didn't seem the proper place. And there was probably no point. "Can you rise?"

"I don't know. I—" She paused and closed her eyes for an instant. "What happened?"

"I'm hoping you'll tell me," he said, and scooping her into his arms, rose to his feet.

"What are you doing?"

"Carrying you," he said, and strode toward the carriage.

"You can't carry me, I'm—"

"Heavy?" He was beginning to pant a little. She wasn't a big girl, but she was no wilting flower either.

"No!"

"Strange?"

"Put me down!"

Frozen images of the past few harrowing minutes were flying through his mind like frightened crows. "A hell of an actress?"

"I don't know what you're talking about. I was attacked." Her head wobbled a little. "Wasn't I?"

"I have no bloody idea," he said, and, finally reaching the carriage, shifted her onto the seat.

Mrs. Edwards awoke with a start. "Oh, there you are, my dear. Is it time for dinner yet?"

"I'm afraid we must return to Knoll—"

"Not tonight," Sean interrupted.

"What are you talking about?" Clarette asked, but he was already striding around to the far side of the carriage.

"We'll get a meal and a place to stay for the night near here." The tilbury tilted as he settled on the far side of their chaperone.

"Are you daft? I am—"

"Very probably," he said, and set the mare into motion.

Clarette gripped the seat abruptly and stifled a wince. Sean gritted his teeth and swore in silence. Whatever had happened, she truly was hurt. And it was his fault.

That thought gnawed at his guts, tightening his hands on the reins and searing his mind until he finally tugged Daisy to a halt in front of an inn. It was a humble establishment made of stucco and brick, but the exterior looked solid and the walkway was free of debris. Stepping from the carriage, he strode inside. A scrawny girl of twelve or so was cleaning a table.

"Have you a room to let for the night?" he asked.

She stared at him a second, eyes wide. "Yes sir. We do, sir."

"And what of a meal? Can we get that, too?"

"Certainly," she said. "If I have to fix it meself, sir."

"Very good. Thank you," he said, and hurried outside. Clarette, or whoever the hell she was, was scowling at him. "We'll be staying here for the night," he told her.

Her scowl turned to a glare. "Did something happen to Prinny?"

He stared at her, a thousand worries scurrying through

his mind at her nonsensical words. "Did you hit your head?"

"I was simply wondering if the Prince Regent may have died and put you in charge."

He almost laughed. In fact, he would have if she wasn't so damned heavy, because he was already lifting her out of the carriage.

"Holy hell," she hissed. "Not again."

"Yes again," he said, and marched her through the doors. The girl was still there, staring with wide eyes. "The lady needs a room," he said. "She's been injured."

"I'm fine," she argued.

"You're not," he said.

"I've . . . I've got a room at the top of the stairs," stuttered the girl.

Top of the stairs. Of course. He glanced up. The steps seemed to go on forever. "Lead on," he said, and rose laboriously to the aviary.

By the time Clarette and Mrs. Edwards were settled, Sean felt somewhat relieved. For a moment he had considered housing them in the same room, but Clarette's head seemed to hurt when she was jostled, and a woman of Mrs. Edwards's size could do a lot of jostling. Thus, he ordered meals for all three of them and insisted that the baroness's be sent to her bedchamber.

"I don't understand," Mrs. Edwards said, pausing

between mouthfuls of pigeon pie as she and Sean ate in the common room. The cream colored satin of her wide tiered skirt had ingested the chair upon which she sat. "What happened?"

"I'm not entirely certain," he said, and pushed his own meal to the center of the inn's scarred table.

"What's that?" she asked, tilting her head toward him.

He scowled, thoughts scampering in a thousand directions. "There may have been foul play," he mused.

"Yes, the fowl is quite good," she said, and scowled, still masticating. "But what of Lady Tilmont?"

He raised his voice. "I believe she may have . . ." He paused; several people had turned toward him. "I think she fainted," he said.

"Sainted? Yes, she is quite nice. Not at all the harridan people think her to—"

*"Fainted!"* Sean corrected, his usual calm shattered.

"Ahh, fainted. Why didn't you say so. Yes, of course. I see. Well . . ." She took a slurp of wine. "She's such a tiny thing. But a good meal will set her right. Unless . . ." She froze, fork halfway to her mouth.

Sean stared at her, stomach twisted with worry. Not much made Mrs. Edwards quit eating. "What?"

"You don't suppose she's . . ." She canted her head in an oddly girlish manner.

Sean scowled.

"You don't suppose she's . . ." Her whisper was as loud as thunder. " . . . in the family way."

"In the—" Fook it all. Pregnant? He hadn't thought of that. Hadn't even *considered* that. But wait a minute. He was beginning to believe his own idiotic stories. She'd been attacked, not overcome by the vapors. Hadn't she? True, the man with the top hat said they wished her no harm, but what was he *apt* to say? *We've clonked her over the head and now intend to rob her blind and perhaps kill her for sport?*

"Oh!" Mrs. Edwards clapped her chubby hands. "Wouldn't Lord Tilmont be pleased?" she crooned, and the day went from bad to miserable.

# Chapter 17

They were running. She was exhausted and hungry and scared. The baby wouldn't quit crying. They should leave her. The evil thought stole like poison through Savaana's mind. They should leave her as they had the others. Though she didn't know where they were going. Didn't know why they ran.

She fell, tripping on a root in the undergrowth. Mother stopped. She was panting. Dogs bayed in the distance. Mother jerked toward the sound, eyes white in the encroaching darkness. A hound howled again.

Savaana snapped her eyes open. A figure stood over her, arm descending. A sword. A giant. Fear! She rolled wildly to the left. The bedding tangled about her legs, trapping her. She shrieked a scream, but it was muffled in the pillow.

"Suffering saints, Clarette, 'tis me."

She scooted to the far side of the mattress and turned back, muscles rigid with terror. "Who?" Her voice was as wispy as a lost child's. A giant grinned in her mind, scarred lips twisted, but was that a memory or a dream? Was he friend or was he enemy?

"Me. Sean Gallagher."

She shook her head, confused.

"Wicklow," he said, and the soft edge of humor in his voice calmed her nerves somehow, brought a semblance of clarity. "I but wished to make certain you were well."

Her senses returned slowly, and with them a modicum of anger, which made her think perhaps she wasn't so very different from Clarette after all. "You scared the stuffing out of me so you could make certain I was well?" she asked.

"Apparently," he said, and smiled a little as he seated himself on her bed. There was a good yard of sagging mattress between them, but still he seemed very close in the moon-kissed darkness. "I'm sorry. 'Twasn't me intent."

Savaana's dark dreams faded slowly, allowing her to catch her breath. She leaned back against the crunched pillow behind her and watched him. "So you're not trying to kill me?"

He studied her in the silent darkness. "I admit I've considered it a time or two."

She flashed her eyes to him and he grinned, his teeth cutting a swath in the night.

"But 'tis obvious, I'm not the first."

Memories of the alley stormed back at her. What the hell was going on? Had one of the jewelers sent someone to steal the necklace? It seemed likely, but ungodly fast. She had barely stepped out the door before the brigands were on her.

"I brought Tuica," he said and raised a small metal cup toward her.

She frowned a little. Sometimes it was damned comfortable living in Clarette's skin. She never had to be nice. It was rather relaxing. "What?"

"Plum brandy," he explained. "'Twas not a simple thing to find." He was watching her closely. "'Tis made elsewhere. Romania mostly. But Delvania also."

Delvania? What did he know of the place? she wondered, but didn't allow her gaze to snap to his. Instead, she studied the mug in her hand. It was crafted of fine hammered steel that shone in the moonlight. The handle was made to look like a rearing horse, mane and tail flying.

"Emily said 'twas your favorite," he said.

"Oh, yes, of course," she said, finally remembering she had tasted it once and found it surprisingly palatable. She and Clarette seemed to have similar tastes. The thought made her feel a little breathless, but she set the thoughts aside. "What an unusual cup," she said, admiring the delicate workmanship. "Where did you get it?"

He said nothing for a moment, then finally spoke. "I tired of shaping nothing but horseshoes."

"You made it?" she asked, and did let her gaze rush to his now.

"Drink your brandy," he ordered.

"Why? Is it poisoned?"

"I would think not," he said. "Take it. It'll steady your nerves."

She scowled, wondering when he had crafted the mug. Wondering where it had been during their trip to London. In the pocket of his breeches? In his shirt against his bare skin? "My nerves are steady," she said. Or they had been until she considered his skin.

"No truer words . . ." he said, and letting the sentiment dangle, drew his feet onto the mattress. Leaning his head against the wall behind him, he watched her in silence before he spoke. "You're a spy," he said finally.

She coughed on her first sip of Tuica and almost spat the contents onto the somewhat frayed counterpane. "What are you talking about?"

He nodded thoughtfully, still watching her. "An agent hired by the prince regent—Prinny, as you call him—to ferret out secrets." He tilted his handsome head. "I've heard of such things."

"How much of this did *you* drink?" she asked.

"You can admit the truth," he urged.

"Very well." She cupped the mug in both hands, liking the smooth feel of the steel against her fingers. "I am *not* a spy. I am Lady Tilmont."

"You can trust me with your secrets," he said.

"How nice." And odd. "What the devil are you doing in my room?"

"You forgot to lock your door."

"No," she said, and took another sip of brandy. "I did not."

"Then the lock must be faulty."

"Hmmm," she said, and raised her head from the cup. "How did you know where to find me?"

"I beg your pardon."

"When I was . . ." The memory made her hands tremble. Perhaps her nerves weren't quite as steady as she would have him believe. "In the alley," she said. "How did you find me?"

"Perhaps I'm a spy, too."

She rolled her eyes. "You really *are* Irish, aren't you?"

He watched her as if searching for logic in her oh-so-obvious statement.

"Prone to bouts of overactive imagination," she said.

"I didn't imagine the giant bending over you," he said, and there was something in his face that gave her pause. An unusual seriousness. A caring.

"You stopped them." Her voice sounded strange, almost broken.

He frowned, as if unsure how to respond, but finally spoke. "What was their intent?"

"I don't know." She took another sip and felt strengthened by it.

"Tell me the truth," he said. His voice was earnest and soft. "This one truth and I shall tell you how I found you."

For a moment she was tempted almost beyond her strength to reveal all, but she had not been raised to be foolish. "Very well," she said. "The truth is, I spoke to two proprietors about a piece of jewelry. When I left the second one, I intended to return around the back street to the carriage. There was very little foot traffic. Very little traffic of any sort." Her throat felt tight. She cleared it and continued. "A man approached me from behind and asked if he could speak to me about a business deal. He seemed—"

"The short man?"

She scowled at him.

"There were two of them," he said. "One was short. The other was huge. Which one spoke to you?"

She tried to recall. Things were fuzzy in her head. "He wasn't tall. He was . . . older . . . with gray hair. He wore a black top hat."

A muscle bunched in his jaw, but he nodded curtly. "Continue."

She shrugged. "There's not much more to tell. I said

I wasn't interested and turned away." She didn't mention the giant or the odd stirrings of uncertain memories that accompanied him. "That's when everything went black."

"That's it?"

He looked as tense as a bowstring. Why? What was it to him? Or—

A new thought struck her suddenly. Perhaps he had somehow been involved in the act? Maybe he had known about the necklace all along. Maybe that's what brought him to Knollcrest. Maybe that's why he was able to find her in the alley. Because he had instigated the crime, hired the miscreants, ordered her disabled. But if that was the case, why would he interrupt the villains before they'd taken their prize? She scowled, thinking hard.

"That's all I remember," she said. "Now it's your turn."

"My turn to what, lass?"

"To tell me how you found me."

"Oh." He looked distracted. "I asked the jeweler."

She waited. He didn't continue.

"That's it?" she asked.

"No. Actually I asked both jewelers. The scrawny cantankerous fellow and the woman at Smith's."

The scrawny fellow *had* been cantankerous, and a woman *had* worked at Smith's. It almost made his story believable. Besides, it seemed too ridiculously simple to be fabricated.

"You're a terrible spy," she said, and drank again.

"I found you, didn't I?"

She rubbed the back of her head. It was a bit sore, but nothing debilitating. If the two in the alley had meant to kill her, they were not very adept. "Perhaps next time you could do so a bit sooner."

"You're planning a next time?"

She gave him an irritated glance.

"I'm sorry," he said, and reaching out, put his hand on her knee. It was pressed tightly to its mate, elevated above her bare feet, and hidden beneath two twisted blankets. Still, his touch felt strangely intimate, and he sounded so honestly apologetic that she immediately felt guilty.

"It's not your fault." She took another sip of brandy and glanced at him askance. "Is it?"

"I should have gone with you."

She grinned a little over the rim of her mug. "I believe I forbade it."

"I believe you did," he said. "And why is that?"

"There are certain things a woman prefers to do alone?"

"Such as getting robbed?"

She took a deep breath and found that her hands were steadier. He'd been right about the brandy. "Not generally," she said. "Usually that's a social event."

He didn't think her particularly amusing. Which was probably best. Clarette didn't seem like the entertaining sort. "Any idea what they wanted?"

She shook her head.

"The big one . . ." He paused as if composing himself. " . . . he had a knife."

She closed her eyes for an instant. That much she recalled. She could see the blade gleaming dully in her shaky memory and wished now that she had not left her grandfather's dagger at Knollcrest.

"When I saw that I . . ." He drew a deep breath. It sounded a bit unsteady. His face was ultra somber, which made her realize how she had come to cherish his smiles, his laughter, even his foolish jests. "He was holding your shoulder as if to turn you over."

She scowled. "What?"

"The giant . . . he was touching you, and I . . ." He cleared his throat, then reached out and squeezed her fingers gently between his.

"You what?" she asked. There had been only a moment's time between her awakening and her attack. She'd been entirely unaware of his presence until after the two had fled.

He watched her in silence for a moment. "I believe I threatened to kill them."

She raised her brows. "You? Every man's friend?"

He shrugged, expression somber. "I may have lost my sense of humor for a moment when I saw them standing over you." He winced. "Are you expecting?"

*"What?"*

He raised his brows a little at the shocked tone of her voice.

"I thought, perhaps, 'twas why you swooned."

She blinked. "I am not . . ." She licked her strawberry lips, embarrassed. He watched the movement, seeming enthralled. "No!"

"You're certain?"

"Yes."

He studied her with something akin to relief in his eyes. "And you're not hurt?" he asked.

"No." How strange—his somberness was almost as appealing as his joviality. Or maybe, at this moment, she simply wanted someone to care. "Well, you know . . ." She glanced at the counterpane, certain he wasn't as attractive as he seemed, somber or jovial. "Not seriously. Just a few scrapes and such."

"Scrapes? Where?" he asked, and lifting her hand, searched it for damage. A tiny laceration had been burned across her knuckles. He kissed it.

Feelings sizzled through her, shocking her with their intensity. "It's . . . it's nothing," she said, and chuckled nervously. "I've had worse on a daily—" She stopped herself just in time. His eyes were as steady as sunlight on her face.

"You've had worse?"

Maybe the brandy hadn't been a great idea. "Hasn't everyone?" she asked, and shrugging her shoulder, tried to tug her hand from his.

"Not everyone who looks like you, lass," he said, and tightened his grip ever so gently on her fingers.

"I hardly think my physical appearance precludes me from—" she began, but he pushed up the sleeve of her borrowed night shift, found a tiny bruise, and kissed her wrist.

"Holy hell," she breathed, and he grinned a little as he raised his gaze to hers.

"Where are the others?" he whispered.

"Other what?" Her voice was no louder.

"Scrapes and such."

She shouldn't tell him. She was sure of that much, but she couldn't remember why. It had been a difficult day, after all, and a little attention would surely not be ill advised. "My elbow," she said.

Slipping up the sleeve of her gown, he lifted her arm slightly and kissed the abraded skin.

"Where else?"

"My . . . my shoulder." She could barely squeeze out the words, which was ridiculous, of course. They were just kisses, but when he slipped her gown from her shoulder, if felt much more significant. His lips were warm against the bruised skin there, his fingers like magic as they smoothed her hair aside to kiss her neck. She turned away a little, offering him greater access. He pressed the garment lower and she lifted one hand, pressing it to her bosom to keep the gown from slipping too low.

"Damn them." He breathed the words against her skin. "Damn them for harming a hair on your head."

She looked past her shoulder at him, really looked, studying him from such close proximity that she could all but feel his emotions. His expression was solemn, his concern earnest. And somehow the idea that he cared touched her a little too deeply, moved her a little too much. For one protracted moment she was caught in his emotion, seized by his fervor. And when he leaned in, she could do nothing but kiss him.

# Chapter 18

**P**assion trembled between them. She was beauty itself. Beauty and softness and quaking desire. He felt it in her kiss, in her touch, in her sigh. He was certain of it, was moved by it. But in a moment she drew back.

"No." The word was barely a whisper. She twisted away. He kissed the corner of her mouth with desperate longing, forgetting himself, forgetting his objectives. She tilted her face toward him, almost returning the kiss, but then shook her head. "No," she said again. "I cannot."

"Why?" Frustration stormed through him. For a moment he had actually forgotten why he was there. But now he remembered all. She wasn't some innocent maid not to be deflowered. She was a fraud, a liar, the woman who had ruined his family. Had given his father hope only to steal it from him.

*"Why?"* She breathed the word with soft exasperation. "Because we're not mar—" she began, and stopped herself abruptly.

"Not what?"

"What?" She turned her eyes toward him, succulent lips parted.

"We're not what?"

*"I'm,"* she corrected, and stopped again.

"You're . . ."

"Married." She breathed the word as if she herself had just now remembered, and perhaps that was the case, for she seemed strangely discombobulated, her pupils swallowing the mesmerizing blue of her irises.

And suddenly he couldn't do it. Couldn't coax her, or defame her, or compromise her.

"Very well . . ." Perhaps his tone sounded childish or churlish or obnoxious. But if so, who could blame him? He had vowed vengeance, only to realize that the woman he had sworn to defile was desire personified. And now, here he was, in bed with desire personified in his arms, only to find he could do nothing about it. "Very well, then," he repeated, and took a fortifying breath. "But might I . . . could I remain here a short while?" Holy saints, he sounded like a fawning child. Like a callow youth besotted by his first love.

She lifted a half clothed shoulder. Her peaked chin brushed her naked skin. "It's not . . . it's not that I don't want you."

Her voice was butterfly soft and utterly honest, stirring something in his soul he thought long dead. Or perhaps had never lived. Some had suggested he had no true emotions where women were concerned. Perhaps they were right. He was a man who had struggled to restore his family's holdings, then labored to hold his family together. Perhaps that was why he had chosen women who would not complicate his life with love or commitment. Women who all but bored him in everything but a physical sense. This woman did *not* bore him. She did, however, drive him mad.

"I do. You are very . . ." She breathed the words and lowered her gaze to his lips. " . . . *extremely* appealing. And I want to . . . I *long* to . . ." She raised her eyes again. They looked bottomless in the moon-shadowed room, bright with desire, deep with yearning. "But I cannot. 'Twould be wrong."

He could press her. Could convince her. He knew that suddenly, as all men do, but now he didn't wish to, for to see her guilt-ridden might well break his heart. He nodded, then slid farther onto the mattress, stretching out on his side against her back.

He kissed her neck, not with any plans to go further, but because he couldn't help himself. She felt so right against him that he could think of nothing else. But he forced himself to do just that. Remembering how she had looked, helpless and broken on the cold ground of the alley.

"Tell me of your training," he said, and with one lucky arm against the sharp curve of her waist, tugged her just a little closer.

She turned her head. Her hair was kitten soft against his cheek. "What?" she asked, and seemed almost disoriented. Was it because of him? Because of his touch? His kisses? The idea was hopelessly flattering.

"In the alley." He remembered the fear he felt finding her there. The anger. The willingness, nay, the *eagerness*, to kill if she were harmed. Surely he would not wish to take advantage of a woman so recently accosted. But certain body parts suggested otherwise. "You fought them like a tiger." He frowned, thinking uncomfortable thoughts. "An acrobatic tiger. I've not seen the like."

He felt her body tighten the slightest degree under his arm. Ahh yes, her skin was as soft as a lover's sigh, but beneath that satiny surface, her muscles were intriguingly sleek and firm. Why was that?

"Don't get me wrong," he said. "It's happy I am that you did. Indeed, if they had harmed you I would have . . ." He drew a steadying breath. "Tell me where you learned those tricks."

"What tricks are those?" she asked, and glanced guilelessly through her lashes at him.

Their gazes met, and though the bodice of her gown had surrendered another half an inch, he kept his attention firmly on her face.

"Lass, you kicked the giant in the jaw."

"I did?" she asked, and blinked, her expression puzzled, her lips parted as if in surprise.

He stared at her in silence, studying every sweet nuance. The blushing cheeks, the wide eyes, the summer berry mouth.

In the end it was the softly parted lips that brought him back to himself. That forced familial obligations to the forefront. That fired up his cynicism. For her act was just a little too perfect, too soft, too helpless. Lady Tilmont, or whoever the hell she was, was about as helpless as a she-wolf.

"Aye, you did, lass," he said, and in light of her stellar performance, found he no longer felt the need to refrain from kissing her shoulder. Then lower. The gown gave way with generous aplomb. Apparently the lace tie at the front had come undone. How fortunate. "You flew at him, end over end, and knocked him back a good three paces. I cannot help but wonder how a lady such as yourself . . ." he began, but suddenly he saw something in the shadowy night. A dark mark against the smooth skin just below her scapula. "What's this, then?" he asked, touching it with a finger. It looked to be in the shape of a crescent moon.

She shrugged, moving her silky skin luxuriously beneath his hand. "As I said, I met the little man in the top hat. Then everything went black. I know nothing more than what I've told you."

He frowned, fingers frozen on the little moon. "Are you speaking of the time in the alley or this mark?"

She turned her head, eyes luminescent in an errant shaft of light. "What mark?"

"This spot on your back."

"Oh. That," she said. Her voice was casual, but there was something a little off, an increased tension in her glorious body. "I've always had it. Was born with it."

"It's rather bonny." He was trying to match her casual tone, but could not quite force out his breath. "Like a tiny star."

She turned again, resting her chin atop her lifted shoulder, eyes wide and gleaming.

"Is it a birthmark?" he asked.

"As I've said . . ." The satiny shoulder shrugged a little. "It has always been with me."

He kissed the edge of it. "It looks almost like a tattoo."

"A—" She stopped herself, then continued smoothly. "Obviously I cannot see it myself."

"You've not seen it in a mirror?"

"Do *you* often gaze at your back?"

He didn't allow himself to be distracted by her chiding tone. "But surely others have mentioned it, lass. Your bridegroom, for instance, what did he think of your little star?" It was foolish, of course, idiotic, but even as he tried to trick her, to goad her into spilling a tiny bit of truth, the thought of her husband made him feel tight inside.

"He said it was not my best feature."

"And the other men in your life?"

She twisted around, facing him, eyes half-mast. "I believe they were not thinking of stars when we were alone together," she said, and smiling with sultry allure, leaned toward him.

Their lips almost met, and then he spoke. "'Tis not a star, lass."

"What?" She breathed the word against his skin.

"'Tis not a star," he said, and drew abruptly away, hurrying to his feet before he became lost in her eyes. "'Tis a moon. As clear as . . ." He pointed angrily out the window. "The *moon*. And you know nothing of it?"

She sat up. The goddamn gown sloughed like a wanton over her breathtaking breasts. "That's not what I said."

"I realize that. But your words claim you were unaware of it until the moment I mentioned it. How can you be totally oblivious to such a mark? How could your husband not have noticed? How could—"

Her sultry expression was gone, overshadowed by looming anger. "Lord Tilmont has other things on his mind."

"Other things than . . ." He motioned erratically toward her. The blue laces that should have bound the gown lay intimately against the thrust of her nipples, stealing the breath from his lungs. "Other than *you*?"

"Yes," she said. "You know 'tis true. We've been wed

only a few months, yet he's gone. He left me, too." Her voice softened and her expression became distant, as if she were seeing things long past. "Why do people leave me?" she asked. Her tone was soft and vague, her expression immeasurably sad. "What's wrong with me?"

"Nothing." The word was drawn from him against his will, for she looked like perfection in the diffused moonlight.

"You lie," she said.

"Well, you're . . ." He grinned a little, remembering a dozen scenes from their recent past. " . . . a bit opinionated at times, I suppose, but 'tis not something one would hold against you. Not when you're—"

"You're right." She looked utterly solemn, sitting perfectly straight in her tangled covers. "I'm selfish. I always have been."

"Not selfish, lass," he said. "You're simply strong willed. Perhaps some men aren't able to accept your—"

"No." She was shaking her head. Her hair, long, dark, and glossy as a wet seal, fell across her shoulders and pristine gown. "I drive others away." Her mouth trembled with sadness. "I drive them all away."

Could this, too, be an act? he wondered. But in that moment a crystalline tear slipped from her eye and rolled with heartrending slowness down her sweetly sloped cheek.

"No, lass," he said. "Don't cry. 'Tis not true."

"Even my mother." Her words were whispered now. "I can barely remember her."

He eased onto the mattress. "I'm sorry."

"Sometimes I try. Sometimes in the small of the night I can almost see her face. Can almost hear her voice. But then I remember . . ." She swallowed.

He reached for her hand. "Remember what?"

"She didn't want me. That's why I make up tales about her. That's why I try to believe I'm something I'm not. That I'm more than I am. Some say I put on airs. But really I just pretend . . . to be loved. To be cherished. To be special. So I don't feel so alone. But I am."

"No." He didn't know what to say, what to do. Broken sadness shone in her glimmering eyes and cracked the rough edges of his heart. "You're not alone, lass."

"She left me." The words were little more than a sigh in the night. "I was not yet five years of age when she abandoned me to strangers." Her slim throat constricted as she swallowed. "I don't know what I did wrong."

"Nothing," he said, and pulled her into his arms. "I'm certain you did nothing wrong. No one could ever wish to leave someone like you."

She stared at him a moment, then winced. "I lied," she said. "I know my error."

He shook his head in bemusement.

"I wanted her to leave the baby."

"Baby?"

"We were running. Hiding. I don't know why." She smiled a little. "I like to believe it was because we were ungodly rich. That we were heiresses and others wanted our wealth, but . . ." She shrugged.

"We?"

"As I've said, I had a sister." Her voice was soft, whispered, entirely at odds with her usual bravado. Indeed, if he did not know better, he would think she was another woman altogether. "I believe she was my sister. But she was loud. Crying. And she slowed us down."

He stroked her hair, feeling her honesty to the core of his soul. "What happened?"

She shook her head. A glistening tear slipped toward her perfect nose. "Mother left me. Took the baby. I never saw them again."

Sadness swamped him. His own family had its share of troubles, but he *had* a family. And they cherished him. "She didn't leave because of your faults, luv. I'm sure of it. She was trying to save you."

She grimaced as if holding back tears. "You don't know that. You don't know *me*."

"But I wish to," he said.

"Do you?" She drew back. Her lashes sparkled with tears. Her full mouth trembled. "Are you certain?"

"More than anything," he said, searching her eyes. They were filled with quaking sadness.

"I'm so lonely," she breathed.

He stroked her cheek, watched her close her eyes, felt her tremble beneath his hand.

"But I . . . I dare not get too close."

"Too close to what, luv?"

"To people." She lifted her gaze to his. "To you."

"That's why you're short with them. That's why you push them away. To save yourself the hurt."

She swallowed and glanced down. The soft curve of her cheek was strangely irresistible. "Everyone leaves."

"I'm here," he said. She raised her gaze slowly to his, then lifted her hand to his face.

"I owe you my life," she whispered. "Yet I've been dishonest and cruel."

"You were frightened."

"Always," she said. "Always frightened."

"Not now. You don't have to be frightened now," he said, and kissed her.

Without thought, he eased her back onto the mattress. She sighed as he swept her hair from her face. Lowered her lashes as he kissed the trembling corner of her mouth.

"You're beauty beyond words, lass," he said. "But I'll not press you if you don't wish me to."

For a moment he held his breath, and then she reached up and undid the top button of his shirt.

"Lass—" he began, but she kissed his mouth, hushing him.

"Give me this moment," she pleaded.

He wanted to. He wanted to give her everything, but he'd been despicably dishonest and she was baring her aching soul. He was sure of it. "There is something you should know."

"Probably several things," she said, and managed a wobbly smile. Her fingers never stilled. Beneath her hand, his flesh tingled with hope.

But he caught her wrist, stopping her. "Lass—" He found her eyes with his.

"What is it?"

He winced. She was magic beneath him. But he'd been wrong to believe he could go through with his scheme. He drew a hard breath. "I've planned this."

"This what?"

"This night. This time together. I've thought of nothing else for a long while."

"Me, too," she said, and slipped the gown from her shoulders. Her breasts gleamed in the moonlight. They *gleamed!* What was he to do?

"Sweet saints," he said, and kissed her.

He was never sure what happened next. One moment he was clothed, and the next he was not. One moment he was telling himself to take things slowly, and the next she was atop him, riding him like a charging stallion.

He growled as the tension built. She shrieked as she arched against him, and then he exploded, drained of every drop of energy. She collapsed against his chest, heart thudding against his, hot and slippery and as sexy as hell against his depleted body.

"Lass . . . I'm sorry."

Savaana remained as she was, knees clasped against his hips, trying to think. What had she done? What had she *said*? "Really?"

"Well . . . that is . . . I didn't mean to go so fast."

"Oh . . . is it . . ." She paused, maybe to breathe. Maybe to *think*. And it was about damn time. Somehow she had begun to confuse herself with Clarette. Had she melded the two because they were much more similar than they seemed. Were they in fact . . . But it didn't matter now. She'd forgotten her mission, and in doing so had admitted too much of her own fragilities, her own weaknesses. But perhaps it wasn't too late to shift back into the baroness's skin, to become the brash noble-woman she was to impersonate. "I didn't know there were rules, Wicklow."

He chuckled a little. She eased onto her side.

"I just meant, you must prefer to go about it more slowly."

"More slowly." She was still breathing hard and refused to look at him as she searched for Clarette's harsh persona. "Yes, well, this was fine, too."

"Fine?"

"Better than fine." She gave him an arch glance over one bare shoulder. "Quite good actually."

"Quite good."

"Ohh." She sighed. "Now I've offended you," she said, and slipped off the bed.

"Is your husband fine, too? Are all men—" he began, rising to his feet, but suddenly his words stopped.

Savaana's heart constricted sharply in her chest. She turned at the abrupt cessation of his words, finding his face in the dimness, just as she tried to find *herself*, to separate the Gypsy from the baroness. But he didn't look at her.

"What's that?" he asked. His voice sounded odd. He shifted his attention to her, eyes accusatory, and suddenly she felt as naked as she was. She reached for her gown.

"Lass." He sounded angry.

She popped her head through the opening of the night rail. "Yes?" she said, but he was staring at the bed.

"It looks like blood."

She yanked her gaze to the stain midway down the mattress and swore in silence. Holy hell! How could that be? She'd ridden astride for as long as she could remember. Had jumped and tumbled and cartwheeled onto every hard surface conceivable. Wasn't that supposed to do something to *something*?

"What the devil's going on?" he asked, and shifted his eyes to hers.

She swallowed, remembered to breathe, shrugged. "I . . . must have cut myself."

"On me . . ." He waved vaguely toward his spectacular nether parts. "On *me*?"

She laughed. The tone sounded a little close to hysteria. "Don't be ridiculous."

"I'll be whatever I damned well wish to be," he said, and stepped from the bed, all naked, masculine beauty. "What the hell happened here?"

"Here?"

"Yes here!" he said, and grabbed her arms. "In that bed. Where the blood . . ." His words staggered to a halt and his face went pale. "You were a virgin."

"What?" she said, and laughed. It sounded like the bray of a wild ass. "You're deluded."

"Am I?"

"I'm a married woman."

"Then where is your husband?"

"He left me. Remember?" She tried to conjure up some tears to distract him again, but really, she felt quite marvelous. Whoever invented sex was a bloody genius. "Everyone leaves—"

"No!" he interrupted, and shook his head. "I'm never believing those soppy tears again."

Dammit. And that was her best act.

"No man could leave you. Not after . . ." He waved wildly at the bed they'd just shared. "Not after . . ." He paced a short two strides and returned. "Who are you?"

For a moment she didn't answer, couldn't, for despite everything, she had no desire to lie. "What?" she asked, and tried to dredge up a modicum of believable anger. "Are you pretending you didn't remember who I was? Didn't know I was married? Is that the lie you're planning to spew should someone learn of this? That you had no way—"

"What is wrong with you?" he asked. His tone suggested he was really quite curious, but she had no answer. She was in over her head and sinking fast.

"If you're . . ." He shook his head, seeming to find thought difficult if not downright painful. "If you were a virgin, you couldn't be the woman who . . ."

She stared at him, breath held. "Who what?"

"What's your wedding date?" he asked, shifting his attention abruptly to her face.

"Are you mad?"

"It looks that way, doesn't it, lass?" he snarled. "Your wedding date, what is it?"

Bloody hell! "That's none of your concern."

"You don't know it."

"Of course I know it."

"Then—"

"August sixth!" she said.

He stared at her, then shook his head slowly. "It's August fourteenth."

Dammit! How could he know that? He . . . Wait a minute, there was no reason to believe he wasn't lying just to draw her out. She forced a laugh. "You're wrong."

"You're a fraud," he breathed, and stepped toward her.

"What are you talking about?"

"You're not Lady Tilmont at all," he said, and grabbed her arms.

"Of course I am."

"Did you kill her?"

"What!" she gasped, and staggered back an honest step.

"The real Lady Tilmont. What did you do to her?"

"I—"

"Come along. We'll see what the constable says about this," he said, but at that moment footsteps pounded up the stairs.

They turned toward the door in breathless tandem.

"Clarette!" someone yelled.

"What—" Savaana breathed, but Gallagher interrupted.

"It's your husband!" he hissed.

"My husband! How would you know—"

"It's your husband," bellowed the man on the far side of the door. "Let me in."

Their eyes met in panic. "Get out!" she hissed.

"Out? How the hell—"

"Clarette! Let me in or I'll be forced to do something rash," said Tilmont, and rattled the doorknob.

"I thought you said the lock didn't work," she hissed.

"I picked it."

"You—"

"I build them. I can pick them."

She shook her head, then pushed him abruptly toward the wall.

"Get beside the door."

"Are you out of your mind? This will never—"

"Beside the door or out the window," she hissed.

He grabbed his clothes, strode to the wall, and pressed his back near the hinges.

# Chapter 19

Savaana's heart was galloping like a runaway in her chest. Dear God, what now? she wondered frantically. But truly, there seemed few enough options. She would play the role given her. 'Twas but another performance.

Gallagher's eyes gleamed with emotion as she whipped the counterpane over the soiled bedsheet, paced to the door, and swung it toward him.

"My lord?" She didn't mean for it to sound like a question. After all, she should be able to recognize her own husband. But she'd been fooled before.

"Clarette." Lifting the lantern held in his right hand, he skimmed her with his eyes—the fragile gown, the disheveled hair. "Are you well? I heard there was a mishap."

"I . . ." she said, and reaching for his empty hand, drew him farther into the room, leaving the door open. "I'm fine."

"Fine!" He followed her with long strides of his

black-booted legs. Fair-haired and lean, his face was flushed with drink. She could see that much as he set the lantern upon the narrow bedstead. "'Tis said you were attacked."

"Well . . ." She didn't glance toward the door, though she was sorely tempted. "I'm not entirely certain what happened. One moment I was leaving the jeweler's, and the next I was quite unconscious. It was . . ." She let her voice shake and lowered her eyes. From beneath her lashes, she saw Gallagher slip from the room and into the hall. "It was rather frightening."

Tilmont was scowling. "Rather frightening! I should think so. But you didn't come here alone. Surely the Ir—" He stopped, changed conversational footing, and continued. "Mr. Underhill accompanied you, did he not?"

What had he been about to say? It almost sounded like 'Irishman.' But that couldn't be. Gallagher had appeared *after* Tilmont's departure.

"I brought Mrs. Edwards, of course, but she was resting in the carriage."

He scowled a little. "Mrs. Edwards?"

"My chaperone."

His brows leapt toward his hairline. "You hired a chaperone?"

"Yes, well . . ." What was going on here? What was he not telling her? "With you gone so long I didn't feel it was proper for me to travel alone."

"You didn't think it proper?"

She lifted her chin, struggling for her shattered persona. "I am, after all, your wife."

He was staring at her as if she had grown a second head, but spoke finally. "What were you doing in London at the outset?"

She cleared her throat and fiddled with a fold in her borrowed gown. "I would rather not say."

"I daresay," he said, and striding forward, bent to look under the bed.

She watched as he straightened, bobbling a little as he did so.

"What are you looking for?" she asked.

He shook his head as if confused, but glanced toward the wardrobe. "I simply mean to make certain you are safe here."

"How thoughtful of you, my lord," she said, and watched as he strode toward the opposite side of the room and threw open the tall dresser doors. It was absolutely empty but for the lavender dress she had hung there only a few hours before.

He made a huffing sound, "I've been thinking," he said then, and turned toward her.

She stepped back. "Have you, my lord?"

"Aye. You're a beautiful woman. Like royalty." He narrowed his eyes at her. "Might you have heard of the Beloreich?"

Her heart thudded, hard and fast, but she kept her face inscrutable. "I believe it's a kind of dessert."

He laughed. "The Beloreich of Delvania are ever haunted by their Ludrick cousins. King Stephan was the last of the Beloreich line. Unless they find the princesses lost long ago."

She felt weak. "Princesses, my lord?"

"Aye," he said, and seemed to lighten his mood a little. "You remind me of that line. Luckily for me, you are my wife and not royalty gone astray." He took a step toward her. She sidled sideways. He drew a deep breath. "I'm considering returning to Knollcrest."

"How wonderful that would be," she said, and gripped the bedstead with white-knuckled fingers.

"Indeed, I was speaking to Rolf regarding just that when someone mentioned the fact that you had been seen at this very establishment." He scowled as if trying to recall a former conversation. "*Why* did you travel to London?"

"If you must know, I wished to purchase a gift, my lord."

"For . . ." He paused as if trying to remember something he shouldn't admit he'd forgotten.

"I know how you enjoy cuff links."

"Oh? *Oh!*" he said.

She clasped her hands and glanced at the floor. "It has occurred to me that I have not been the wife I should."

"Really?" He was staring at her as if she were bi-headed again.

"That is to say . . . a small gift is the least I can do."

He cleared his throat. "'Tis not as if I've been the perfect husband. I've been gone entirely too much. Neglecting you." He reached out and touched her cheek. She had nowhere to go. His smile was eerily tender. "You would be lovely with a babe in your arms."

"A *babe*!" Savaana kept from jumping as she said the words, but only by sheer power of will.

"I thought when I left that perhaps you would turn to . . ." He shook his head. "In fact . . ." Another pause as he glanced toward the wardrobe again. "But I find now that I'm glad you did not."

She didn't attempt to control her scowl. Clarette certainly would not. "That I did not what?"

"Stray," he said, and brushed her hair back from her face.

"Why would you think—" she began, but in that instant Gallagher stepped into the doorway, entirely dressed. Memories of him otherwise swooped in. She groaned inwardly and refused to close her eyes at her own foolishness.

"My lady," said the Irishman soberly.

She nodded and stepped away from Tilmont. He tipped unsteadily toward the door.

"Mr. Gallagher," she said.

"Lord Tilmont, I presume," said the Irishman pointedly, and stared hard at the other man.

"Oh, yes. *Yes*, I'm Lord Tilmont." He grinned a little. "And who might you be, good sir?"

"Sean Gallagher, at your service, my lord," he said, and bowed stiffly. "Gregors hired me to see to Mr. Underhill's duties while he recovers. I've driven your lady wife here to London to see to some shopping."

Tilmont looked momentarily confused. "And what of the task I—"

"Driving your lady has kept me well occupied," Gallagher said, interrupting smoothly. A muscle jumped in his jaw. Savaana jerked her gaze from him to Tilmont and back. What the devil was all this about? Did these two know each other? And if so, how? "I've had time for naught else."

"Ahh."

Gallagher nodded again. "I thought I heard a noise and came to make certain your lady was well." He glanced toward Savaana. She jerked from her thoughts.

"Oh. Yes," she said. "I assure you I am quite well." She cleared her throat. "My husband must have awakened you. My apologies."

"'Tis glad I am to know he's here . . . to keep you safe." His tone was peeved, his body stiff.

Savaana refrained from wringing her hands, from

drilling him with a hundred steaming questions, from throwing a shoe at him. "Thank you, Mister—" she began, but Tilmont interrupted her.

"Yes, well, I don't believe we'll be needing your services any longer, Mr. Gallagher."

"What?"

"*What*?" They said the word in unison.

The baron grinned and raised his brows at the Irishman. "I'm certain Mr. Underhill will be right as rain in no time. What happened to him anyway?"

"I believe he was injured by the gelding," Gallagher added.

"Ah yes, the gelding."

"He's a handsome animal. You'll look quite rakish riding him of a fine morning, my lord."

Tilmont scowled, thinking. "I will rather, won't I?"

Savaana narrowed her eyes. What was the Irishman's game?

"A few more weeks of my time and I'm certain he'll be serviceable for you."

"You think you can have him ready so soon?"

"I am ever hopeful," Gallagher said, and glanced irritably at Savaana.

"Good, good," Tilmont said, and seemed to immediately forget his intentions of sending Gallagher away. "You'd best hasten back to Knollcrest first thing in the morning. Until then I don't believe we have any more need of your services. Do we, my dear."

"No," she said, and wondered if she was going to pass out in earnest this time. "No, but . . . I have had a rather trying day." And needed to have a few moments alone with Gallagher. "Might you be willing to fetch me a bit of brandy to calm my nerves?"

"Brandy. Of course. A bit of the bingo. I should have thought of that myself," Tilmont said, and bowed slightly before turning. "Gallagher, old sport, see to it, will you?"

Savaana gritted her teeth, then smiled wanly when the other swiveled back. "Perhaps you'd like a little something for yourself as well," she suggested to Tilmont.

"I think I will at that. See if you can find me a bottle of ruin."

A muscle jumped in the Irishman's jaw, but he bowed. "Certainly, my lord."

"There's a good fellow," Tilmont said, and turned dismissively back toward his supposed bride. "How very kind of you to think of me. You seem rather . . ." He shook his head, searching for the proper words.

Savaana kept her gaze carefully on Tilmont's face as Gallagher stepped from the room. "Rather what, my lord?"

"Changed," he said.

"Well, we haven't seen each other for quite some time,"

she said, and looking for something with which to busy her hands, retrieved her shoes from the floor near the bed, then hustled toward the wardrobe that stood near the corner.

"Too long," he said, and nodded. "Far too long. But perhaps we could make amends for that so I might get to know who you truly are."

She glanced quickly back at him, wondering what he meant. "I would dearly love to hear of your adventures since last we were together."

"You want to hear about *me*?"

Reaching inside the wardrobe, she set her shoes on the wooden floor. "It has occurred to me that I know entirely too little about you, my lord."

"And I too little of you," he said, watching her, eyes bright. "It seems you're full of surprises."

"Hardly that," she said, and eased out of the corner before he could trap her there. "I'm a simple woman. Boring really."

He stepped quickly to the side. "I rather doubt that," he said, and slipped his arm about her waist.

"My lord!" Gallagher's voice seemed strangely loud in the room. Savaana jumped. Tilmont turned with ragged precision. Gallagher was scowling even as he bowed. "I've brought you the requested libations," he said, and lifted the two bottles he held in his right hand.

"Good God," Tilmont said, and laughed. "However did you return so quickly? And with so much gin?"

"The cellar wasn't locked, my lord."

"Good thinking, Gallagher," he said, and stepped forward to take a bottle from him.

"Thank you, my lord," said the Irishman, and scowled at Savaana. She raised a brow at him.

"But wait," Tilmont said. "I have no glasses."

"Ahh, my mistake," Gallagher said. "Why don't you take a seat, and I shall remedy that situation immediately."

"I was actually thinking of finding my bed," Tilmont said, and slanted a suggestive glance toward the nearby mattress.

Savaana smiled wanly. Gallagher's expression darkened.

"But you've no manservant," said the Irishman. "Have a seat, and I shall assist with your boots."

"Very well," Tilmont said, and turned gracelessly toward the chair, bottle in hand.

Gallagher glared at Savaana. She made a "what?" motion with her hands as Tilmont settled into the narrow wingback with a sigh.

"It does feel good to sit," he said, and let the bottle tumble unharmed to the floor. "When I heard of the attack on my wife, I dashed across town quick as a ferret."

Gallagher had already lowered his gaze to the bottle that remained in his hand and was working at the cork. "If I may ask, sir, how did you hear of her troubles?"

"The usual gossip at Almack's," he said, and Gallagher nodded as he handed over the gin.

"It must have been quite a shock for you."

"I dare say," said the other and took a swig straight from the bottle.

"Well, the gin will calm your nerves. Sit tight," Gallagher said, "while I fetch a glass."

Tilmont nodded and drank again.

Savaana watched, breath held.

"Where are my manners?" Tilmont asked, glancing up. "My father would be sore disappointed. Would you like a drink, my dear?" he asked, and held the bottle toward her.

"No. That's very kind of you, but—"

"Of course, you requested brandy," he said, and already the Irishman had returned, glass in hand as he stepped into the room. If his ploy to see the baron unconscious was any clearer, even Tilmont would realize it.

"It seems you've neglected the lady's drink," said the baron.

"Oh, aye, my apologies," Gallagher said, and retrieving Tilmont's abandoned bottle, uncorked it before pouring enough to drown a camel. Savaana raised her brows as he handed it over. Gallagher gave her an irritated glance, then bowed. "If you'll excuse me again, my lord, I shall fetch your lady's drink."

Savaana all but rolled her eyes as the Irishman stepped from the room.

"You're certain you won't join me, my lady?" Tilmont asked.

"I believe I'll wait for the brandy."

"It seems rude to drink alone."

"Very well, then, I'll have to accompany you," she said, and lifting the bottle from the floor, pressed the green glass to her mouth without taking a drop. "I like to see a man enjoy his drink."

"Truly?"

"Yes," she said, and pretended to drink again.

"I didn't know that about you."

"There is much you don't know," Savaana said, and tasted a droplet of gin.

"But I'm eager to learn."

"Are you?" she asked, and glanced at him through her lashes. "In the past, you've seemed . . . rather uninterested."

"Uninterested? No," he said, then shook his head as if to belay his own words. "Well, I'm . . . To speak the truth, in the past I've thought you . . ." His voice trailed off.

"What?" she asked.

"A bit harsh," he said.

She lowered her eyes. "Sometimes I can seem that way when I'm nervous."

"I make you nervous?"

She shrugged. Best to keep him talking . . . and drinking. "You're a powerful man, my lord. Surely you can see why I might feel the need to put up barriers between us."

"There will be no need for barriers tonight," he said, and prepared to rise, but Gallagher all but leapt into the room.

"My lady's drink," he said, and presented Savaana with a thimbleful of the Tuica he'd found earlier. She refrained from raising her brows at the minuscule amount.

"Now, my lord . . ." Gallagher said, striding to the baron. "Drink up, then I shall remove your boots."

Tilmont laughed as he gazed at the tumbler. It was still half full. "You must think me quite a lush if you believe I can finish this so quickly."

"Not a'tall," Gallagher said.

"Oh no," agreed Savaana. She could feel the Irishman's harsh gaze on her, but she continued, unabashed. "You're simply sophisticated."

"Sophisticated is not quite the term my father uses," Tilmont said, and chuckled. He sounded sleepy. Thank God. And Gallagher, she supposed.

"A sophisticated man is *expected* to drink a good deal," Savaana said. A muscle jumped in Gallagher's jaw. "To maintain his standing in society." Ignoring the brandy, she pretended to take a deep swig from the bottle.

"Yes but . . ." Tilmont began and made to rise.

Gallagher rushed forward, already squatting to pull off his first boot. "There now, my lord, you must be exhausted after your fright."

Tilmont scowled. "I am a bit fatigued. And my shoulders ache something dreadful." They sagged as he leaned back. "The mare father gave me is naught but a screw."

"Yet another reason to train the gelding quickly," Gallagher said, slowly slipping the boot from the baron's foot. "His paces are quite smooth."

"It can't be soon enough, then," Tilmont said, and sighed. "It does little for my reputation when others see me riding such a bone setter."

"Of course not," Gallagher agreed, and moved on to the second foot. If he moved any slower the leather would disintegrate and fall aside on its own, Savaana thought, but finally the boots were placed side by side next to the chair.

"Well, then . . ." Tilmont said, and shifted, but Savaana hurried across the floor.

"Let me attempt to ease your ache, my lord," she said, and stepped behind him to set her hands to his shoulders.

Gallagher rose to his feet, eyes snapping, but she ignored him as she massaged gently.

"Ahhh," Tilmont said, rolling his head to the side. "That does feel quite lovely."

"Try to relax," Savaana said.

"Let me pour you a little more gin," Gallagher insisted.

And finally, after they had schemed and massaged and cajoled, Tilmont fell asleep, his head slumped against his chest like an overused doll of rags.

# Chapter 20

**T**hey stared at each other over the baron's slumped head.

*Let me ease your ache?* Gallagher mouthed the words.

Savaana shrugged, a lifetime of frustration and anger showing in her sharp expression. But he felt the same emotions.

"Just what kind of ache did you have in mind?" he rasped.

"Well, it was successful, wasn't—" she began, then stopped abruptly. "He's my husband," she hissed.

"Is he?" Gallagher began, but then Tilmont rasped a staccato snore, causing them both to start. Grabbing her arm, Sean pulled her toward the door. Opening it a crack, he glanced left and right, then tugged her into the hall. In a moment they were inside his room.

"Who are you?" His voice was raspy.

"Me!" she growled, and twisted from his grip. "How did he know you?"

"What?"

"The baron . . ." She waved wildly toward her own room. "He knew you before you were introduced."

"You're deluded."

"He was about to call you the Irishman."

"I *am* the Irishman."

"He—" she began, then changed tactics abruptly. "How did you know he was my husband?"

"He was pounding on your door, calling your name. I only hope there aren't a host of others who feel they could do the same."

She thought about that for an instant, then shook her head. "You knew before. You knew his voice."

"And you did not," he said. For a moment he thought she blanched. "You are not Clarette Tilmont."

"And you are not sane," she said, leaning toward him for emphasis. "Of course I'm Clarette."

"Then why aren't you with him?"

She hesitated for an eternal breath of time. Her eyes flashed but her face looked pale and earnest. "Perhaps it is because I wish to be with you."

The world stood still, waiting. And damn him, he wanted to believe. "Is that the truth?"

"Yes." Her voice was throaty, her eyes sincere, but he wouldn't be a fool.

"Swear it on your mother's life," he demanded.

"I swear it," she whispered, and suddenly nothing seemed to matter.

He kissed her, her mouth, her neck, her shoulders. She moaned.

"I have to go," she breathed, but he couldn't let her.

"He'll sleep," he vowed, and dropped his forehead against hers, feeling the agony of their impending separation like a hot iron against his soul. "Stay. Just a minute."

"I can't."

"But you want to?"

"More than anything," she said, and they were the sweetest words he had yet heard. So sweet that he couldn't help but kiss her one more time. Slowly now, reverently. And then it seemed like the most natural thing in the world to cup her breasts. He felt her sigh in the very depths of his being and slipped his thumbs over her nipples.

"Wicklow," she gasped, and he smiled as he tugged up her gown.

"Perhaps you could call me by my name just this once," he said, and kissed her nipple through the fabric.

She jerked as if burned. "Holy hell, when you do that I don't even *remember* your name."

"Sean," he said.

"Oh . . ." She exhaled heavily. Her fingers had become tangled in his hair. "That's right."

"What's yours?" he asked, and kissed the underside of her jaw.

"Who cares?" she rasped, and suddenly she was

tearing at his belt. He tried to keep his head, to hold his line of questioning, but there was no hope. In an instant his breeches were open, his erection straining toward her.

She swore like a mule driver when she saw it. He pushed her up against the wall, and though he would never be certain how it happened, she was suddenly wrapped around him, her legs strong and supple, her heels digging into the small of his back. One breast was bare, and his cock was flirting with heaven.

He scrabbled for thought. It was slippery but important. He was sure of it. "Are you who you say you—"

"Shut up!" she hissed, and rounding down to meet his lips, she kissed him.

There was a moment of indecision, a moment of fumbling, and then he was inside.

Heavenly saints, it was utopia. He eased into her heat, trying to savor the moment, but she was already arching against him, sliding around him, squeezing him. He grappled with her weight, holding her up. She ripped his shirt open, balanced on the sinewy strength of her legs alone and sucked his nipple into her mouth.

Fire exploded in his chest and raced toward his cock. He growled, she hissed. He moaned, she swore. They grabbed greedily for satisfaction, then stiffened in unison moments before she dropped her head against his shoulder.

Sean straightened slowly, legs trembling as he carried her to his bed. Setting her carefully on the mattress, he eased down beside her. She scooted over weakly, gown rucked about her thighs, breath coming hard. He followed as best he could, barely able to move, entirely unwilling to think about anything but how she had looked as she found ecstasy. Her head thrown back, her face alight.

"You're beauty beyond words." His voice was raspy, his strength almost too depleted to reach out and touch her cheek.

Her eyes were closed. She turned her face to kiss his fingers. "I have to go."

He pushed the hair behind her neatly scrolled ear. "Tell me your true name."

"Clar—" she began, but he put a finger on her lips.

"I know you lie."

Her sapphire eyes were haunted when she opened them, her mouth tremulous, but she shook her head. "No, you don't."

Perhaps she was right. Perhaps he no longer knew anything but what he wanted to believe. What his body *insisted* he believe.

"I must return to him."

His stomach clenched. "Tell me one thing . . . one truth . . ." They were face-to-face, inches apart, breathing the same air. "One truth and I'll let you leave."

She scowled, no less beautiful for the harsh expression. "If he finds me here—"

"You're not who you say you are."

"I never meant to hurt you. Never wanted to disappoint you."

"You're not married." He felt desperate. Frantic. "You weren't a courtesan."

"I can't change the past. I can't make this right."

"Then what of the blood?" Anger and frustration bubbled inside him like a boiling toxin.

She shrugged. The movement was stiff. "Some women bleed each time."

Was that the truth? He had no way of knowing.

"I'm one of those."

"Then how many men have there been?" He knew he was a fool to ask, to torment himself. Better by far to live with the fantasy he had created, but he couldn't help himself. Apparently he was a selfish man. Maybe even a jealous man.

"Do you really wish to speak of this, Wicklow?" she asked, and turned toward the door.

"Yes, I do." He stood. "I would know something of the woman who has stolen—" He winced at the words he'd almost spoken. At the words he thought he'd never say. "I would know something of you."

She stopped, expression twisted. "We can't—" she began, but he reached her before she could finish the sentence.

"I'm not asking for eternity," he said, and found that it was difficult to push even those paltry words from his mouth. "Just a moment of truth between us. Am I just one of many?"

"No," she said, and reached up to touch his face. Her movements were slow, almost as if she meant to resist. "There's no one like you."

"Even Alastar?" The burning words came unbidden.

She scowled, drawing away. "I know no one—"

"Alastar Buckingham. Surely you remember him if you're who you say you are. You planned to marry him."

"What are you talking about?"

"He was going to be a barrister. Sit in the House of Commons. Until he met you. Until you promised him everything and gave him nothing."

"How would you know that?"

"I know because I sought Tilmont—" He stopped abruptly.

Her face had gone pale. "You *did* meet him before."

He shook his head, though he wasn't sure why.

"You met him on purpose," she said. "To get to Clarette."

"I . . ." A thousand regrets were tumbling in on him, but he reminded himself that she was the one at fault. *She* was the one to blame. "Alastar loved you."

"And so you planned revenge on a woman you had never met."

He winced. It sounded wrong when she said it like that, but he rallied. "He's my only brother. He planned a family with you. A life. 'Twas the first time I heard my father laugh since my mother's—"

"Does Tilmont know?"

"Tilmont!" Rage, rare and bright, seared him. He pulled her close. "You still worry about *him*?"

She jerked away. "Even though it may not be a conventional marriage, it's still a marriage, and . . ." Her voice trailed away. "No." She shook her head, eyes steady on his. "Tell me it's not true."

"Listen, lass—" he said, and reached for her again, but she stepped back a quick pace.

"Tell me he didn't pay you to seduce me."

Sean shook his head, but somehow she had divined the awful, convoluted truth.

"His father promised the baron's inheritance in exchange for faithfulness. In exchange for an heir." Her tone was flat, steady, and sure. "But you knew that already, didn't you?"

"Listen, I'm not the villain here. You—"

"You seduced me for money!" Her voice had risen sharply.

"I never intended to take his money. I planned—" he began, but her eyes had gone incredibly wide in the paleness of her heart-shaped face.

"So it's all true." She turned away in a trance, but

he grabbed her arm, guilt mixing angrily with rage in his gut.

"No!" he said. "It's not all true. Hell . . ." He laughed. The sound echoed maniacally in the room. "You've got me so tied in knots I can't tell truth from lies."

"Well, let me help you out a bit, then, Irishman," she growled, leaning in. "You slept with me for coin."

"And what did you do?" he snarled, self-loathing boiling like tar. "Either you're who you say you are and cuckolded your husband while he sleeps next door. Or you were copping me while lying to me face."

She tried to pull away, but he tightened his grip.

"Let me go."

"Which is it? Adulteress or—" But in that instant, she snapped her knee up. It contacted his groin with the ferocity of a mad bull. He stumbled back, gasping for breath, his face twitching madly. But he managed to glance up.

"At least I wasn't doing it for money," she said, her voice dripping with acid. She turned away, and the funny thing was . . . the really hilarious bit was that he tried to apologize just before he collapsed onto the floor.

# Chapter 21

**S**avaana opened the door to her room as quietly as possible. A slew of inventive lies trembled on her lips. But Tilmont never opened his eyes. He remained slumped in the chair, a handsome man dreaming the saturated dreams of the inebriated.

It took her less than a minute to blow out the lantern, remove the soiled sheet, and shove it under the bed. Only a moment to smooth the blankets over the mattress. Removing the necklace from its hiding place in the sleeve of her gown, she slipped it over her head, letting it fall beneath her night rail.

"Clarette?"

She jumped, heart hammering in her chest. For a moment she almost fled the room. But Clarette's future depended on this moment. And perhaps her own life was intrinsically tied to the baroness's. "Yes?"

"I fear I'm not feeling quite up to snuff."

That was hardly a surprise. He had probably drunk his weight in gin before they plied him with a couple more bottles. Guilt seeped through her. She glanced hopelessly toward the door, but Gallagher had remained where he was, possibly still crumpled on the floor. She stifled a wince. "Perhaps you should lie down, my lord."

"I don't think I can . . . I may be about to bowke, I'm—" he began, and gagged. "Fetch the *po*."

She wasn't familiar with the terminology of the *ton*, but there was a certain urgency to his tone that couldn't be questioned. Skittering across the room, she rounded the bedpost, grabbed the chamber pot, and hurried back to shove the porcelain vessel beneath his face. His stomach rejected its contents in a series of volcanic eruptions. She made a face and backed away until finally he set the pot on the floor and sagged to an upright position.

"My thanks." His voice was weak, as if he might expire at any moment.

"Are you well?" she asked.

"Certainly." He waved a dismissive hand at her. It was blue-veined and frail, reminding her a bit of her grandfather's. "I just . . . My apologies."

"It's quite all right," she said, and easing toward the chamber pot, retrieved it from the floor. "I'll just be rid of this, then."

"You're an angel." His voice was watery.

"Not exactly," she said, and opened the door.

"Clarette?" He glanced up, eyes reddened as she swiveled back toward him.

"Yes?"

"You'll be back, won't you?"

She refrained from glancing down the hall, from closing her eyes, from begging his forgiveness. "Yes," she said. "Of course."

After setting the chamber pot outside the back door of the inn, she ascended the stairs again. Stepping cautiously inside her rented room, she desperately hoped that Tilmont would be sleeping, but he was not. Instead, he was lying on his side, clothes rumpled. He opened his eyes as she moved into the chamber.

"Thank you," he said again.

She nodded, and refrained, just barely, from wringing her hands. "I'll leave you to sleep," she said, but his expression was haggard, his eyes cheerless.

"Where are you going?"

"I don't wish to disturb you," she said, and that might well have been the truest words she'd spoken in weeks. "I'll sleep with Mrs. Edwards."

His mouth quirked up a little. "I didn't mean to chase you from your room."

"It's no trouble," she said, and wondered vaguely what Clarette thought of him. He seemed a decent fellow except for his penchant for alcohol. But who in the lauded *bon ton* was not a sop?

"Would it be troublesome to stay and talk with me for a bit?" he asked.

She kept her hands still, her gaze steady, though she wanted nothing more than to leave. "No. Certainly not," she said, and sat carefully in the chair he'd recently vacated. "Are you feeling much improved?"

He smiled. The expression was weak. "Would you believe me if I said yes?"

"You'd have to put more effort into the lie," she said, and he laughed.

"The blue ruin . . ." He looked philosophical. " 'Tis not a friend of mine."

"At least you realize as much."

"For all the good it does me. Did you know I have a bad heart?"

She shook her head.

"Father doesn't like to have it known. A weakness, you know. One of many."

She wanted to ask what his others were. "I'm sorry."

"The truth is . . ." His face was very somber, earnest and pale in the near darkness as he watched her. "It's unlikely I'll be able to sire children."

"Oh. Oh!" she said, realizing the enormity of that truth. Clarette would be paid only if she had a child, but if she did, Tilmont would suspect it wasn't his.

"I'm sorry."

"Well, it's not . . . not your fault," she said.

He watched her. "I know of the deal you made with Father."

"I don't—" She stopped, sick to death of the lies, but she had made a vow to Clarette, one of the few people to whom she owed true allegiance. Or not. She raised her chin, remembering the other's mannerisms. "I don't know what you're talking about. I've barely met your esteemed sire."

He smiled a little, looking like a lost, disheveled child. "You will gain a fortune if you are faithful and produce an heir."

"I—" She was tired. Too exhausted to parry. "And what of you, my lord? Do you not want a child?"

He smiled again, but in a moment it was lost in sorrow. "I sent the Irishman."

She almost winced. "What?"

"Gallagher. I sent him to seduce you. So that I might keep my fortune to myself."

So she'd been correct, she thought, and wished she could feel good about that, but the truth soured her stomach, and she found she had no idea how a woman should act in such a situation. "How could you?" she asked, and he shrugged.

"I thought you might enjoy him."

She scowled, far out of her depth. "Does holy matrimony mean nothing to you?"

"I owe you an apology."

At the very least. "I should say you do."

"And my thanks, I guess, for being honorable."

She was in hell. "Just because I was a . . . a courtesan 'tis not in my nature to betray a trust."

"That's what *he* said."

"What?"

"Gallagher. 'Tis what he said." Tilmont smiled again, but the expression was wobbly. "Well, not exactly. It was code of sorts. Quite clever if I do say. Perhaps you didn't even notice. The Irishman indicated he had performed no tasks for you other than as a driver."

She opened her eyes wide, as if surprised, and secretly wished she had kicked him harder. "Is that what he meant?"

"Quite so." He looked sick and weary.

She shook her head. "But how did you meet him?"

"Gambling. Rolf introduced us. We were in the same game of piquet. The Irishman is a fair hand at games. I thought he had me, but in the end I beat him out. He owed me a good bit of coin."

"So you traded his debt for my honor."

His face contorted with guilt. "Truth to tell, I didn't know you had any to barter."

"Because I was a courtesan?"

"Because I have so little myself, perhaps, that I didn't expect to find it in you." He winced. The truth looked to be a bitter pill. "Gallagher seemed a decent fellow, and someone interested in you from the outset."

Anger spurred up in her again, but she played the

game. "How do you mean? He knew nothing of me."

"Introductions were made. I told him I was newly married. He said you must be rather hideous if I was willing to leave you alone so early in our union. So I produced the cameo Father commissioned of you. You were quite lovely that day, remember? In your yellow frock?"

He lay perfectly still, but his gaze never left her face. Why?

"Yes, of course," she said.

He smiled a little. "Mr. Gallagher agreed that you were—"

"Was it his idea or yours?"

"What?"

"To seduce me. His or yours?"

"I'm sorry to say it was mine. He merely wished to meet you."

"And you didn't wonder why he would wish to meet another man's wife?" Anger spewed through her again. Apparently there was enough to douse both men. "I doubt you told him how sweet-natured I was."

He actually seemed to blush. "Well, no. But that was before I saw this portion of you. In the past you have seemed rather . . ." He paused, grinned crookedly, as if to say he was none to throw stones. " . . . harsh."

Against her will, Savaana remembered Clarette's sharp tongue. And though she'd been offended by it herself, she found now that she had an inexplicable need to defend the other woman. "I've had a difficult childhood."

"Did you? You never mentioned."

"I don't care to talk about it."

"Perhaps it would be good for you to do so. Cathartic."

She shook her head.

"I'm an excellent listener," he said, and patted the bed beside him.

He must be joking, she thought; she'd heard better lines from the Irishman himself. But Tilmont's face was absolutely solemn.

"Unfortunately, I am not much good for anything else."

"I'm certain that's not—"

"Except for with you that once . . ." He gave her a meaningful glance. Unfortunately, the meaning was lost on her. " . . . I've not lain with a woman for most of two years."

She opened her mouth to speak but had nothing to say. Yesterday she could have sworn she hadn't copulated in all of her twenty odd years. Now all she had was about seventeen minutes.

"Well, I've *lain* with several, but . . ." He sighed. "I lied when I said I didn't find you attractive. There's simply nothing I can do about it. Most times, at least. My apologies."

"Well that's . . . that's all right," she said.

"So there would be no harm in you lying beside me."

She eyed him askance and he laughed.

"I promise to neither vomit nor take advantage."

"I don't—"

"And you'll be afforded more of the bed than you would with Mrs. Edwards. I've seen her on more than one occasion. You might well be crushed."

She glanced toward the door. The truth was, she didn't relish the idea of bumbling about in the dead of night. She couldn't forget the men in the alley. What had happened there? In truth, she had no way of knowing whether the Irishman had been instrumental in the attack. He said he had sought Clarette out of revenge. Perhaps that was true. Who was to say that revenge didn't include theft or worse?

"I but wish to speak to someone while I fall asleep," the baron assured her.

"Very well," she said finally, and eased onto the mattress.

He scooted over a little. She turned on her side to face him.

"You are a rare beauty," he said. "I'll say that much for my father."

Tucking her left hand under her cheek, she watched him in the pale moonlight. "How do you mean?"

"You were his choice, of course. He said that perhaps since you were a . . ." He paused, glancing at her apologetically. " . . . a courtesan . . . you wouldn't mind even sleeping with *me*."

She watched him thoughtfully. "I don't think I care for your father."

He smiled. "That may be the nicest thing any woman has ever said to me. But here now, we're supposed to be speaking of you. What of your family?"

She thought of her grandfather who was not her grandfather. Her sister who might be nothing more than a figment of her desperate imagination.

"What of your mother?" he prompted. "Was she as lovely as you?"

"She had ginger hair." The words came unbidden, blown like an errant breeze into her thoughts.

"Do you, too?" he asked, but his eyes had fallen closed.

"What?"

"Red hair," he murmured. "Shortly after we wed I found the remains of a walnut and indigo pigment in a basin at Father's house."

"Walnut and indigo? How did you identify—"

"Ever since, I have wondered about your true color." He sighed heavily, so near sleep. "It seems a pity. I rather favor chestnut hues. They're quite unusual."

"She dyed her hair?" The words were little more than a thought, not breaking into his consciousness.

He was silent for a moment, lost in sleep, but in a bit

he awoke again. "What of your father? Or siblings?" he asked, voice blurry with gin and sleep. "Do you have other family? A dashing brother, perhaps, or a comely . . ." His words trailed off. His mouth went lax.

"Yes." She whispered the word into the night, certain for the first time. "I have a sister."

# Chapter 22

It was morning. Still, Sean paced his rented room like a rabid hound. He'd been doing so since shortly after he was able to straighten, and he winced now, feeling another twinge in his offended nether parts. If he heard footfalls in the hall, he would step out, casual as a maimed bear, to determine the cause. He had asked the inn's employees, again, as casually as humanly possible, if Lady Tilmont had made an appearance, but they assured him she had not.

Which meant she was in her rented room. With her husband. The thought sent an ache of another kind shivering through his system. If she had gone elsewhere before dawn, he would have known it, for he had prowled the halls most of the night. Now he was frustrated and aching and exhausted.

The sound of a door opening made him spurt for his own. He reached the hall just in time to watch the cause of his impending insanity step out of her room. In an instant he was beside her.

"What the hell were you doing all night?" he gritted.

Never stopping, she raised a haughty brow at him. His balls quivered at her expression, but when she turned away, he grabbed her arm. Bloody hell, he was a brute for punishment.

"I think that is hardly any concern of yours, is it, now?" she said, and lifting her lavender skirt in her right hand, yanked her arm from his grasp and strode for the stairs. He followed like a demented puppy.

"It damned well *is* my concern," he hissed. "I happen to be—" His words failed as she glared at him. Good saints, she could make a boulder quake.

"What?" she asked, voice perfectly even, perfectly modulated. "What are you, Wicklow? A liar and a cheat, surely. But what else?"

"Listen, I didn't know—"

From below, an elderly gentleman glanced up from his task of buttering a muffin.

Sean bobbed in an ingratiating manner and raised his voice a hair. "Shall I bring the carriage round, then, my lady?"

"Yes," she said, gaze never leaving his. "Do that, Weakwick."

He refrained from gritting his teeth. From demanding answers. Or kissing her speechless. "Perhaps my lady would like to stroll down to the mews herself. 'Tis a bonny morning, it is."

She gave him a preening smile. "If I wished to walk to the mews, I wouldn't have a stable boy, now would I, Wickendick?"

Sean flicked his gaze to the patrons below. They all seemed to be engaged in conversation, minding their own business. "Come with me or I'll tell Tilmont the truth here and now," he warned, "Come, or I'll tell *everyone* the truth."

An old woman having a bowl of stewed prunes raised an inquisitive brow at them.

Clarette's nostrils flared, but she acquiesced. "Perhaps a bit of air might be in order after all."

It seemed to take forever to make their way outdoors, longer still to get out of sight, hidden away in an empty stall in the nearby stable. Gallagher trapped her between his arms, hands flat against the rough-hewn planks behind her.

"What the devil happened last night?" He was all but frothing at the mouth. Where the hell had his damned pride gone off to? Or lacking that, a modicum of sanity. He had no right to question another man's wife. But she wasn't a wife. Was she?

"Don't you remember?" she asked. She didn't look trapped. In fact, she looked all but bored. "You took advantage of me."

"Took . . ." The word popped out of his mouth. "Me?" His voice was almost squeaky. "Do you think me mad? Do you think I don't know you distracted me with your . . ." He motioned wildly toward her scrumptious body. " . . . *everything,* so that we wouldn't talk about who you are. About what you've done. About where you've stowed the body of the real Lady Tilmont."

She raised a brow. "Stowed the body?" Her tone was absolutely steady. She gave him a look that made his scrotum quiver. "As a matter of fact, Wickerhound, I think you *quite* mad."

"Am I? Am I!" he rasped.

"Yes," she said, and slipping under his arm, strode away.

"Very well." He nodded, storming after her. "Maybe I am. But if that's the case, then—"

"What?" she snarled, spinning toward him. "What? It's my fault? You blame *me*?" She stepped toward him. Certain body parts strongly suggested that he retreat, but he couldn't quite manage to do so. Something about manhood and masculinity, and what the hell difference did it make if she *did* beat him to a bloody pulp? He no longer doubted that she was capable of it. He just couldn't seem to care. "Did I ask you to prostitute yourself? Did I ask you to come into my life at all?"

He scowled, eyes steady on hers. "Perhaps not, lass. But you *wanted* me to take you. And I agreed, despite your caustic tongue."

The stable went silent. Her face went pale. "If you'll

excuse me," she whispered, eyes downcast, and suddenly he wanted nothing more than her forgiveness. He couldn't help but step forward. Couldn't help but touch her face.

"I'm sorry. Please . . ." He searched for words that weren't there. "Please tell me you didn't lie with Tilmont."

Her gaze met his, blue and tortured.

A dozen hot emotions shot through him. "Tell me you're not his wife." His voice was raspy.

Her face crumbled. "I'm—"

"Clarette?" The baron's voice rang through the stables.

Her eyes darted to the doorway and back, pleading for silence.

Sean gritted his teeth, wanting madly to step forward, to tell the truth, to admit all. But there was anguish in her face, desperation in her eyes. "Go," he said. He expected her to step out of the stall, but instead she glanced up, then jumped. Hooking her hands over the top of the planks, she pulled herself silently over. He was still speechless when he heard her voice from the other side.

"My lord." The stall door beside the one he occupied creaked as she pushed it open. "I didn't wish to disturb you. I thought you'd sleep well into the afternoon."

"After last night I feel . . ." Tilmont paused, sounding euphoric. Sean ground his teeth and tightened his fists. " . . . refreshed."

"How wonderful."

"But what of you?" he asked. "What were you doing out and about so early this fine morn?"

"I just . . ." There was a shrug in her voice. "I but went for a stroll and found myself here."

"In a box stall?"

"The mare inside caught my eye. She's quite beautiful."

"Yes?" The baron's footfalls echoed across the hard-packed floor, never reaching the stall where Sean remained alone. "Ah, I favor a nice gray myself, but I didn't know you entertained an interest in horses."

"There's much you don't know of me." She sounded bright, young, flirty.

Sean closed his eyes against the infusion of pain.

"I've been considering the same thing," Tilmont said. "Indeed, I was thinking I might begin to remedy that this very day."

"So you'll be returning to Knollcrest with me?"

"Knollcrest? I don't see why. So long as we're here, why not enjoy the sights of Londonderry?"

"But I thought you wished for me to care for your estate."

"'Twas my father's wishes," he said, "and I begin to think I've been betwattled by his wishes long enough." There was a pause during which Sean imagined him kissing her hand. His stomach coiled up tight. "Come, let me show you London, and you to London."

"I don't think—"

"Good. We'll not think a'tall. Not for days on end. We'll do naught but dance and eat and drive about the square till everyone from here to Istanbul insists you're the most beautiful woman in all of Londonderry."

"But I'm not—"

"Hush now. I go to fetch the driver."

*"Who? Gallagher?"*

"Who else?"

"I . . ." Words seemed to fail her for a second. Sean was glad to know it could happen. "Do you think that's wise . . . under the circumstances?" Her voice had dropped low. The baron's did the same.

"Under the circumstances that I hired him to seduce you?" he asked.

Sweet saints, the dolt had actually told her that? Had absolutely confirmed her suspicions? Knowing that, he'd been lucky to have survived the morning. Of course, the day was still young.

"I'm terribly sorry for my mistakes, Clarette," said the baron. "But I've turned over a new leaf. You'll see. I've no idea what I was thinking , promising him you, for now I find I'm entirely unwilling to share."

"Then why not just give him a bob and send him packing?" she suggested.

"A bob," he said, and laughed. "No, my love, I'll not treat him so shabbily. The man needs a job. I owe him that much at least. Unless . . . He didn't treat you poorly did he?"

"Poorly?" Her voice was weak.

"I'll not forgive myself if he was too forceful on my account."

"Forceful? No. No, he . . . No."

"So that's a no then?" he asked, and laughed.

"Yes." Her voice sounded weak, but Gallagher very much doubted she had the decency to feel shame, though she'd ridden him like a well-favored jockey. The memory made him feel a little weak.

"And you did not find him attractive?"

"Well, in a brutish sort of way, perhaps."

"Brutish . . ." he said, and laughed. "And here I thought he was a maid's wildest dreams. I'll fetch him. You can stay and converse with the gray if you—"

"No!" She all but yelled the word, then cleared her throat and smoothed her tone. "I believe I'll accompany you back to the inn. It seems I left my reticule there."

"Ahh, very well, then. I just thought you might wish to remain here and admire the mare."

"At second glance I think she may be a bit cat-hammed."

"Cat-hammed you say. Well, then, I'll have to find you another mount. A nice gelding, perhaps. And clothes. We can't have the most beautiful woman in all of England parading about in yesterday's gown, can we? Indeed . . ."

His voice trailed off.

Inside the stall, Sean fisted his hands and dropped his head against the rough planks behind him. Bloody hell, he should never have come here. He should have let his brother handle his own troubles. It wasn't as if Alastar were a child. If he was old enough to get involved with a woman like Clarette Tilmont, he was old enough to work out his problems.

But ever since their mother's death, he had felt responsible for the lad. Had done his best to care for the boy.

But not anymore. He was done. There was no reason for him to return to the inn. No reason to torture himself by driving the Tilmonts around London as if he were their damned lackey.

And yet he knew he would.

He glanced toward the door and gritted his teeth. He would stay, for whether she was baroness or courtesan or raucous street vendor, he was smitten.

# Chapter 23

Savaana felt as if she was in hell. Or perhaps she simply *should* be; not only was she living a lie, she was cheating on her husband who wasn't really her husband, but her sister's husband.

Or was she entirely wrong? Had she conjured this whole debacle in her mind? Was Clarette just what she seemed, a spoiled heiress who had no connection whatsoever to her? Had her own need for family driven her to this?

"That's Mr. Dumfrey," Tilmont said now, leaning in. He had hired a vis-à-vis, saying only an alkithole traveled in a tilbury anymore. Sometimes Savaana didn't understand a word he was saying.

In the driver's seat of their rented vehicle, Gallagher kept the rented hack at a brisk trot.

"No title, but he's dreadful wealthy. 'Tis said he pays his mistress three thousand pounds a year."

"Oh?" She was doing her best to focus on the

conversation, to smile at the right moments, to be gossipy and inquisitive. But her time had run out. She was supposed to meet Clarette near Knollcrest in two days' time. What would happen if she failed to appear? What—

*"Oh?"* Tilmont said, and laughed. "Is that all you have to say?" Smiling, he lifted her hand and kissed her knuckles. "For a courtesan you seem sadly disinterested in money."

"Former courtesan," she reminded him, and he smiled again.

"That's right, you are all mine now, are you not, my love?"

"Yes." She smiled and refrained from glancing toward the Irishman. "We are wed, after all."

"And I never did get you a suitable wedding gift."

Guilt swarmed her anew. "Oh, my lord, you needn't—"

"Richard, please."

"I beg your pardon?"

"My given name, 'tis Richard. 'Twould be a thrill to hear it on your lips."

"Richard." She said the name softly, then jerked as the vehicle struck an unusually deep rut. Struggling to right herself, she managed to refrain from glaring at the driver. "You needn't buy me anything."

But Tilmont only laughed, and the hell continued.

* * *

That afternoon found them at Mrs. Ball's dress shop, where Savaana was measured and prodded and poked.

"Such a lovely bride you have, my lord," Mrs. Ball crooned, speaking from behind the curtain that separated the alterations area from the remainder of the shop.

The woman had coaxed her into a midnight blue gown that boasted lace frilling at the low-cut bodice. Scrolled silver embroidery etched the hem and tight-fitting sleeves. It was ungodly itchy.

"I couldn't agree more," Tilmont said.

"The morning dress you chose will be divine on her certainly, but I'd like you to see her in this as well," Mrs. Ball announced, and swept the curtain aside with dramatic flare.

He smiled when he saw her. "Lovely," he said, but his face looked a bit gray, his eyes bloodshot.

"Is something wrong, my lord?" Savaana asked.

"No. No, not at all. Not when I see you thus."

Mrs. Ball preened. "She is a vision, isn't she? The piece was commissioned for a certain lady who simply *needed* it for a soirée, but she never returned for it." Her nostrils pinched, but she rallied. "'Tis far more fetching on your lady, though. The bold color accents her eyes and will set her apart from those pastel others. Don't you agree?"

"Absolutely."

"Perhaps we could do this later," Savaana said, watching the baron with some misgivings. He'd looked healthier while vomiting into the chamber pot. She wasn't sure of the rules of sisterhood, but she was quite certain it would be in rather bad taste to kill her only sibling's husband while the other was away. "After we've had a bite to eat."

"Luncheon, what an excellent idea," said Mrs. Ball, and clapped her plump hands as if she had just invented food. "We've taken her measurements. It would be easy as falling asleep to pinch this little confection in for her while you eat."

"I really don't need more garments," Savaana said, but Mrs. Ball was not to be countermanded. She had a nobleman in her talons and was not about to let him go until he had coughed up a few pounds at least.

"She could wear it this very night," said the dressmaker, all but ignoring Savaana. "You *will* be going to the ball at Windfell, will you not?"

"I'm not certain," Tilmont said. "I received an invitation, but that was before—"

"But you must go!" Mrs. Ball insisted. "You absolutely must. It will be the perfect place to showcase your lovely bride."

"We really should be returning home," Savaana insisted, but the seamstress flopped a dismissive hand at her.

"Home will still be there tomorrow," she said,

and Tilmont concurred with a laugh, looking a little brighter.

"We'll take it, then," he told the proprietress. "You can have it ready by this evening, you say?"

"I'll have it stitched and pressed by the time you've finished your tea."

After that, Tilmont spent some time paying his bill and extolling Mrs. Ball's expertise, but finally they were exiting the shop.

"I appreciate your generosity, my lord," Savaana said, champing at the proverbial bit as he settled her hand in the crook of his arm. "Truly I do, but I must insist that we return to Knollcrest."

He laughed as they strolled toward the vis-à-vis. "And I insist that you not take your responsibilities so much to heart."

She scowled. "I worry for your health. You don't look well."

"While you look enchanting," he said, and smiled into her eyes.

Gallagher was staring at them from his perch on the rented carriage. She could feel his attention like the glare of the sun and took a half a step away from Tilmont, lest the other launch from his seat like a loosed cannonball.

"I worry for your heart," Savaana said.

"It's not my heart that troubles me," he said, leaning in to smile down at her. "It's the drink."

She scowled.

He smiled wanly. "Or the lack thereof."

"Oh," she said, and realized belatedly that his hands were unsteady as he turned and kissed her knuckles.

"Perhaps it isn't so simple to be off the blue ruin as I had imagined."

"I'm sorry," she said, and found she meant it.

"That I'm a lush?"

"That you're in pain."

"It's not pain . . . exactly," he said, and smiled. "Besides, your beauty makes me long to be better. Now . . ." he rallied, tone brisk, "where would you like to dine?"

"I still think—"

"Chez Henri, it is," he said, and handed her toward the carriage. But he stopped. "Mr. Gallagher, the step please."

Savaana glanced at the Irishman. His eyes bore into hers.

"Mr. Gallagher?" Tilmont said, and Sean turned toward him as if just noticing his existence.

"Yes . . . my lord."

"You cannot expect a woman of our lady's caliber to climb aboard like a sailor on leave. Fetch the step, if you please."

"Of course, my lord," Sean said, and descended the vehicle, but as he set the little stool before Savaana, she dropped her reticule. Their hands inadvertently brushed.

For one endless moment electricity sizzled through her like wayward lightning. She stepped back as if seared, waiting to be burned to ash.

Tilmont watched the exchange but seemed completely oblivious to the emotions that swirled around them like storm clouds. "Thank you, my good man. Now up you go, dearling."

And so the day continued without so much as a moment's reprieve. There was lunch and a walk through Covent Garden, then back to Mrs. Ball's for the gown. Little did Savaana know that the worst was yet to come.

Windfell was the size of a barley field, but lacked the bucolic charm even though it was set far from the city and surrounded by ancient woods. The house itself was graced with every foolish but expensive feature known to mankind, an elegantly etched tear bottle from Cairo, a red Indian's war bonnet from the Americas.

Some hours before, Savaana had found a moment to stitch the rough-cut necklace into the hem of her gown, for her décolletage was far too low to hide it.

She held her head high, her shoulders back, as she entered the ballroom on her faux husband's arm. They were introduced to the gathering by a man with enough starch in his bleached cravat to make a flag stand on end.

The Irishman remained with the vis-à-vis. He'd been practically silent the entire day. But his eyes had spoken volumes. Most of it was profanity. And how could she blame him? She had become the epitome of everything she hated. Sneering at him. Lying to him, then accepting him into her bed. She almost snorted at the idea, for the truth was she'd all but *forced* him into her bed. And had done so moments before welcoming her supposed husband with open arms. Accepting his gifts, sharing a room.

Gallagher must think her the devil incarnate. And maybe he was right.

"He can't take his eyes off you," Tilmont said.

She snapped her gaze to him, breath stopped. "That's not true," she said. "He's simply—" She stopped before flinging herself into the fires of stupidity. "Who might we be talking about?"

He laughed. "The duke, of course. But he's hardly the only one enthralled."

"The . . ." She tried to still the beating of her wild heart. " . . . duke?"

"The Duke of Landsgate. In the corner with the woman who looks like she swallowed a tuna. And there's Lord Balesford. Near the table. The one drooling as he watches you."

She glanced to the left, trying to find her bearings. There actually did seem to be someone drooling. "I think that might be a medical problem," she said, and he laughed.

"I'm going to miss you."

It took a moment for his words to sink in. She turned toward him, meeting his eyes. "What do you mean? Miss me when?"

For a moment he stared at her, and then he grinned lopsidedly. "I suppose I shouldn't be so macabre. This affliction may not kill me. Perhaps I will only *wish* to die."

"Don't talk like that. I've known several people who have lived long and well with heart conditions."

"It's not my heart that worries me," he said, and watched a flute of champagne wander past.

"Oh, I'm sorry." Holy hell, she was a terrible fake wife. Indeed, she had entirely forgotten about his alcoholism. "Listen. We don't have to stay here. We could yet go—"

"Home. I know," he said, and laughed again. "But honestly, the way the Irishman drives I think the trip might kill me well before we reached the edge of town." He raised a brow at her. "You don't suppose he's hitting those holes a'purpose, do you?"

She was going to hell. She was sure of it, but gave Tilmont an innocent if somewhat sickly glance. "I can't imagine why he would."

"To keep us apart, perhaps?" he suggested.

She snapped her gaze to his, heart hurtling along like a frightened bunny's. "Surely not! Why ever would he do such a thing? He wouldn't. That would make no sense." She was babbling and couldn't seem to stop. "That is to say, I barely know the man. I surely have no interest in him." She fluttered a helpless hand. "And he has none in me. Indeed—"

"My love," Tilmont said, voice sounding ever so casual against her frenetic rush, "every man here has an interest in you. Indeed, every man everywhere. Even the ones who can do little about it," he added, and smiling at his own failings, kissed her hand, but when he straightened, he wobbled a little.

"My lord! Are you well? Can I get you anything?"

"Anything?" he asked, and watched the champagne tray pass again. "No, I think not. Far better that I keep my mind occupied elsewhere. Would you care to dance?"

She scowled. The reel had broken up and a waltz began. "I'm not particularly accomplished at the waltz," she said.

"Ahh, but it matters little with a woman as lovely as you on my arm. Come," he said, and led her onto the dance floor.

In truth, she had been dancing for as long as she could recall. Indeed, according to her grandfather, her grace was only surpassed by her sleight of hand. And though that particular talent was used only for magical tricks, she could imagine how this crowd would react if they knew of her inauspicious beginnings.

Still, the dance went well enough, though Tilmont seemed winded and a little shaky by the end of it.

"If you don't mind, I'd like to sit for a bit," she said, though her nerves were jumping like frogs in a frying pan.

"There's no need for you to humor me," he said. "I'm quite capable of humoring myself. Indeed—" he began, but just then they were approached from behind.

"Lord Tilmont."

They turned in unison. Tilmont smiled. "Lord Reardon, you look well."

"And you look as dreadful as always," said the other, "but your bride . . ." He opened his arms as if to encompass her. "This is your bride, isn't it, and not some glamorous figment of my imaginings?"

"Clarette, my love," Tilmont said, bowing a little. "I'd like you to meet Lord Reardon, the most irritating man in all of Christendom."

"My pleasure," Reardon said.

"Always a privilege to meet irritating men," Savaana said, and they laughed on cue. How easy the nobility was to please. Not at all like entertaining a fractious village crowd.

There was a bit more small talk before Reardon asked her for a dance. Tilmont handed her off, looking more than a little relieved to find a seat alone, and she was escorted back onto the marble floor.

"So you've landed the notorious Lord Tilmont," Reardon said as they moved sedately through the crowd.

"Notorious, is he?"

"Yes, quite, but I'll wait for you to figure it out on your own. You seem a bright one."

Savaana mulled that over until the dance came to an end.

"Look after him, won't you?" Reardon said, and bowed as a tall gentleman appeared to her left.

She would have liked to excuse herself, but Tilmont was otherwise occupied, so she turned to the newcomer, who held her a little too tightly as they danced. She was glad when the song came to an end, but already there was another man waiting, standing a little behind.

"Might I cut in?" he asked. His voice evidenced either good breeding or a nasal condition.

"I believe we'll take another spin," said the tall lord, but the other pushed him aside.

"I'm afraid you're mistaken, old chap," he said, and Savaana turned at the niggle of familiarity.

There, front and center, was Sean Gallagher, dressed in frock coat and starched cravat, and looking like nothing so much as a debutante's lusty dreams.

# Chapter 24

Savaana felt her mouth drop open.

"Just dance," he ordered.

"What happened to your brogue? And where—" she began, but he was already leading her into the first steps, his movements fluid and sure. "What's this about?"

He didn't look at her. "I might ask as much of you."

She leaned away from him, watching his face. It looked the same, yet different somehow. His chiseled chin was elevated, his lovely body stiff, his eyes imbued with a confusing mix of anger and boredom. "What are you talking about? Where did you get that jacket?" It fit marvelously across his wide shoulders.

"Why are you here?"

"Why—" She felt well out of her depths and sinking fast. "I'm with my husband, Lord Tilmont. You remember him, don't you?"

"Oh I remember him, but he's not your husband." His posture was perfect as he swept her into a twirl.

"You're deluded." She felt breathless. Maybe it was from the spinning. Maybe not.

"And happily so," he said.

"Do you know what the penalty is for impersonating your betters?"

He glanced down at her, allowing a smidgen of the Irish to shine through. "Are you so sure I'm impersonating, *lass*?" He drawled the last word, employing the damnable brogue.

She tripped. He pulled her tighter to his chest and continued on, forcing her to follow his perfect lead. "Careful there, my lady. We wouldn't want you to ruin your fine new frock."

"What the devil are you talking about?"

"Your frock," he said, eyes blazing as he skimmed her low décolletage. "It's quite nice, by the by. Flattering, if you don't mind showing a bit of your—"

"What do you mean you're not impersonating?" she hissed, and he grinned coldly.

"Ahh that," he said, and returning to his perfect posture, danced her toward the edge of the gargantuan floor. "Well, perhaps you're not the only one pretending to be what she's not," he said.

She shook her head in confusion. "So you're . . ." She managed a shrug. " . . . a woman?"

He grinned a little at her wit, but didn't bother to glance down. Instead, he kept his head turned away, his shoulders drawn back. The muscles of his thighs felt as hard as hewn granite, his hand strong and callused against hers.

"You deserve more," he said.

"I don't know what you're talking about."

"I'd give you more."

"You!" She gasped the word. "You're a liar and a . . . I don't know what you are."

"Maybe I'm the heir to a small fortune."

"You . . . I . . ." She was at a loss for words. "You seduced me for money!" she said, and the song swept to a crescendo. He twirled her away and then into his arms, her back against the hard plane of his chest.

"Not for money."

Her breath was coming hard. "For a bet. You seduced me for a bet!" she hissed, and his patience exploded.

"I seduced you because you're irresistible. Because you're bright and funny and brave and built . . ." He skimmed her bosom again. " . . . like a damned hourglass with legs."

Their gazes caught. Her breath stopped. He was leaning toward her. Their lips almost met, and then, out of the corner of her eye, she saw a brush of movement. A woman turned toward her for an instant. Her dark hair was pulled into a chignon beneath an ivory bonnet. A veil shadowed her features and her gown was high-necked. Pale and lacy, it covered nearly every inch of her. But for an instant, for just a fractured moment in time, she drew the lace back from her face. Their eyes met. It was like looking in a mirror.

"Dear God," Savaana rasped.

"No. Just a good lover," Gallagher said, and leaned down, but she was already struggling out of his grip.

The woman in ivory was gliding toward the door that led to the gardens.

Savaana pivoted in that direction, but the Irishman held her wrist. "I was only joking," he said. "Please—" But she barely heard him and tugged urgently at her arm.

"I have to go."

"Go? Where? Listen, I apologize. We need—"

"Just . . . I need some air. Time alone. Leave me," she said, and pulled out of his grasp. The crowd surged like a wild tide against her, but she pushed through. Outside, the mist had rolled over Lady Reardon's rose garden. But she thought she caught a glimpse of white lace in the darkness. She rushed through the shadows. The outer gate creaked as she hurried toward it.

"Clarette," she whispered. Not a soul answered, just the soft song of pool frogs. "Lady Tilmont," she said, and stepped through the gate. It groaned shut behind her. She glanced toward the house, bright with a thousand candles. Beyond their glittering light the world looked as black as sin. Fear gnawed at her. But a thousand ragged memories pushed her on. She stepped into uncertainty.

Footsteps, light and quick, hurried away, and she followed, down a well laid path of stone that led to the river. The moon shone for a moment on the dropping land below. Freedom called to her. She could leave. Could quit all this. Could return to her caravan, to the people who had accepted her as their own, but blood ties were still strong.

"If you're here—" she began, but suddenly hands grabbed her.

She gasped. Someone was already covering her mouth, pulling her roughly into the black lee of a towering oak. She struggled wildly. The other's grip broke.

"Holy hell!"

Savaana pulled away, ready to run, but at that instant recognized the voice. "Clarette?"

"I think you broke my nose."

"Clarette, is that you?"

"Of course it's me." Her voice was hissed. "Who the devil did you think it was?"

"I don't know. How was I to know you— What are you doing here?"

"What am *I* doing here?" she rasped. "We were supposed to meet. At Knollcrest. Remember Knollcrest, the place where I am paying you to remain?"

"Of course I remember, but you're early and—"

"And what? You decided to enthrall some lusty peer of the realm when you were supposed to make absolutely certain my husband didn't suspect me of having interest in another?"

"He's not a peer."

"What is he, then?"

Hell if she knew. "An Irishman?"

"Well, you weren't supposed to enthrall a lusty Irishman while I was gone either."

"I didn't . . . He's not . . ." Savaana shook her head. "You're the one who left for a tryst."

"And you're the one who was supposed to stay put. What the devil are you doing here in the first place?"

"How did you find me?"

"I saw Mrs. Edwards in *my* tilbury. Naturally I was a bit curious. Why the hell would you hire a chaperone?"

"I . . . It's a long story."

"Well, I've got all night, since *I'm* not flirting with a lusty Irishman."

"Keep your voice down."

"Why? Do you think the Celt will follow you?"

"Him or your husband."

Clarette grabbed Savaana's arm. "Why would my husband follow you?" Her tone was low, threatening.

"I don't know," Savaana snapped, pulling from her grasp. "Maybe he likes me. What's he doing here, anyway? I thought he was supposed to be in Bath."

"He *was* supposed to be in Bath!"

"Well, he's not."

"Why the hell not?"

"I don't know. I haven't had much time to ask him, what with the parties and the clothes and the . . ." Her voice trailed away.

"And the what?" Clarette asked, glaring.

Savaana refrained from stepping back. "Listen, we've got more important things to discuss."

"More important than whether you've been sleeping with my husband?"

For a moment inexplicable guilt flooded Savaana, but she quashed it. "You wanted nothing to do with your husband!" she hissed.

"That hardly means I wanted *you* to do something with him."

"Well, I didn't."

"You didn't sleep with him?"

She tried not to wince, but she had been dealing with sister guilt for as long as she could remember. It was she, after all, who had wanted their mother to abandon the squalling baby. "I . . ."

"What?"

"We slept, that's all."

Clarette hissed air through her teeth. "You're lying."

"I'm not," Savaana countered. "He'd been drinking."

Clarette scowled as if thinking that sounded likely. "Does he know who you are?"

"Of course not."

They stared at each other, then Clarette shook her head and paced away, all nerves and angst and anger. "I should have known better than to trust a Gypsy. They lie. They cheat. It's in their blood like—"

"You're Rom."

Clarette paced back abruptly, then barked a low laugh. "Ah, splendid, and now you're mad as well."

"I'm not mad."

"Well . . ." She snorted a laugh and paced again. "I've been called a lot of things. A whore. A vixen. A liar. A snobbish little marquis once called me an ill-mannered goat. But never a Rom."

Savaana was calm now, as if the entirety of her existence rested on this moment and there was nothing she could do to change the events one way or the other. "Your mother was Rom."

Clarette stopped as if tripped. "You know nothing of my mother."

Savaana took a careful breath. "She had the voice of an angel."

Absolute silence echoed between them for a heartbeat. From somewhere far away laughter twittered through the still night air. It sounded surreal and disembodied on the floating mist.

Clarette shook her head.

"She sang lullabies."

"Every mother—"

"In Delvanian."

"Don't be ridiculous."

Taking a careful breath, Savaana softly sang the words she still remembered, but Clarette stopped her before she'd uttered two lines.

"Who sent you?" Her voice was weak, her face pale.

"She had hair like fresh ginger. The same color as yours."

"My hair is black." The words were whispered.

"Only so you can escape your past."

Clarette opened her mouth to deny the words, then shook her head. "You know nothing of me. Nothing of her. You don't." She repeated the words like a mantra, like one in a trance.

"She gave birth to two daughters," Savaana whispered. "Less than eighteen months apart."

"You're wrong."

"She gifted you with her necklace."

"You don't . . . She . . ." Clarette began, then laughed again. "'Twas the Earl of Ayrshire who put you up to this, wasn't it? He was angry when I left him. That, I knew, but I didn't think he'd stoop to—"

"I found it in your jewelry box."

The air left her lungs like the rasp of a bellows. "You had no right to go through my things."

Savaana almost made excuses, but finally smiled at the ridiculousness of the situation. "But pretending to be you . . . lying to Gallagher, your servants, your *husband* . . . that was perfectly fine?"

Clarette stared at her in silence for a moment. There might have been guilt in her expression. "Who are you, really?"

Silence ticked steadily away.

"I think you know," Savaana said finally.

Clarette shook her head. "This is madness."

"They're not simple rocks."

For a moment Savaana thought she would pretend not to understand, but finally she spoke, her voice low and hushed. "The necklace," Clarette said.

Savaana nodded.

"Mother said they were nothing but river stones Father had collected. She kept them in memory of him."

"I think she lied to keep them safe. To keep *you* safe."

"From what?"

Savaana drew a steadying breath and wondered if she was right or if all her years of searching for the truth were for nothing. Maybe she had fabricated everything to satisfy her own vanity. "The Ludricks."

"I've never even heard of—" Clarette stopped, half turned away, then swiveled back. "You're daft."

"The stones are diamonds. Uncut paragons."

"You're lying."

"I took them to a jeweler. Two, in fact."

"How dare you?" she asked, but her voice was soft.

"I dare because I'm your sister."

Clarette shook her head and backed away. "No. You're making up tales."

"Why would I do that?"

"Because you want the necklace."

"No . . ." Savaana began, then almost laughed at herself. "I *do* rather want the necklace."

"Well, you can't have it!"

"Very well," she said, and remained exactly as she was.

Clarette's brows lowered quizzically. "It wasn't the Earl of Ayrshire who sent you?"

"No."

"Lord Griffin?"

Savaana shook her head.

"Baron Von Brandt?"

"Never heard of him."

"Lord Aramount?"

"Sounds like a biblical mountain."

"Sergeant MacDugal?"

"How many lovers have you had?"

The baroness scowled. "It was Fen, wasn't it?"

Savaana was getting tired. "Fen?"

"He didn't have a title, but he had . . ." She raised her brows suggestively. " . . . something else."

"If we weren't sisters I wouldn't even *speak* to you."

"We're not sisters!" The words came out on a hiss. "I'm Lady Tilmont."

"You're wrong," someone said, and stepped from the shadows.

They jerked toward him in surprise. He was little more than a silhouette in the darkness, but he was there, his black top hat just visible above his gray hair.

"Your mother was Princess Eliane."

"What?" Clarette rasped.

"You're the man from the alley," Savaana said, and stepped sideways, putting herself between him and Clarette.

"My apologies for our unforgivable behavior of yesterday." His voice was very formal, slightly accented.

Savaana's head was spinning. What had she done? After all these years, had she brought trouble to her sister's doorstep? "If it's unforgivable, apologizing seems a waste of time."

The little man smiled. "You've your mother's quick wit, *cea dulce*."

"Who are you?" she asked. Perhaps if she yelled, Gallagher would come running. Funny how minutes ago she had been trying to avoid him.

"My name would mean nothing to you. What is important is that we have found you. But there is little time to talk. We must leave this place," he said, and stepped forward.

Savaana shook her head and inched backward, bumping into Clarette. "Stay away," she warned.

"All will soon be made clear."

"Why not make it clear now?"

"There's no time. It is enough to say that your lives are in danger."

"That I believe."

"But if you cooperate, this will be simpler."

"Your pardon," Savaana said. "But I don't care to make your life simpler."

He chuckled, but something touched her hand. She twisted her wrist, felt the rock in her sister's fingers, and took it surreptitiously in her own.

"Come along now," said Top Hat, and stepped toward them. "I'll not—"

Savaana loosed the stone, but it was darker than sin in the shadows. The missile bounced off his shoulder, but it was enough of an advantage.

"Run!" she rasped, and spinning about, pushed Clarette away from her.

The giant appeared without warning. Big as a mountain, he caught them both by the fronts of their gowns and hoisted them from their feet.

They fought like cornered badgers. Clarette landed a kick to his groin. He grunted, but his grip didn't loosen a whit.

Then a shot exploded from behind. Their captor jerked

and dropped to his knees. The women lurched away, scrambling for footing.

The giant rolled his eyes upward, meeting Savaana's terrified gaze.

*"Iara-ma, cea dulce,"* he said, and toppled face first into the undergrowth.

# Chapter 25

Clarette spun about. Their savior was there, not fifty feet away. His brass buttons gleamed dully in the pale moonlight.

"Thank God you came!" she rasped. But as she stared in his direction, he raised a pistol. Another bullet whistled through the darkness. It grazed her arm and sung into the distance.

She shrieked.

"Go!" Savaana's voice was breathy, barely audible, but Clarette was already running. Skirts gathered in both hands, she sprinted past the giant's fallen form. Two men appeared in the darkness ahead. She careened to a halt. Savaana skidded, almost sliding into her. They changed directions like hunted hare, darting uphill.

"Hurry!" Savaana gasped.

"I am hurrying!" Clarette said, but someone yelled from above.

"There!"

The sisters jerked their attention upward, and then, as

a duo, dashed to the left, cutting downhill, slipping and sliding. But the men were already giving chase.

It was a nightmare of terror. They ran blindly, crashing through the woods. Branches whipped their faces. Another bullet sang past, lodging in a nearby tree.

Clarette jerked, caught her foot on something and tumbled downhill.

Savaana gasped and slid after. She jolted to a halt next to her sister's still form. "Clarette . . ."

"We're on a road." The baroness lifted her head, sounding dazed.

"Holy hell, I thought you were dead."

"A road," she repeated, and jerked to a sitting position. "Someone will find us."

"That's what I fear, too." Savaana grabbed her arm, tugging her to her feet as she glanced frantically down the pale, twisted trail. There was less than ten feet of clearing from one side to the next, but the road shone like a beacon in the darkness.

"I'd say you were needlessly worried, but—" Clarette began. Another bullet shot into the pebbles at their feet.

Without a word they skittered into the woods on the far side of the road.

"Who are they?" Clarette rasped.

"I don't know."

"Well, guess!"

"I—" A snap of noise interrupted her. "They're close.

Hurry!" she ordered, but their pursuers were catching up, bearing down on them like swooping birds of prey. "How can they see—" she began, then caught a glimpse of Clarette's ensemble. Her bonnet was long gone, but her gown gleamed in the darkness. "Go!" she ordered. They ran again, but only a short distance now. Just out of sight of their pursuers, Savaana leapt. She hit Clarette square in the back. Her sister went down with an audible grunt, rolling as she did so. Savaana clasped her hand over the other's mouth.

Clarette thrashed wildly, but Savaana held tight.

"Quiet!" she hissed.

"Let me—"

"They can see your gown!"

The thrashing stopped. Their gazes met.

"Cover up!" Savaana ordered.

It barely took an instant for Clarette to begin burrowing into the rotten leaves.

Allowing herself one quick glance behind, Savaana draped her dark skirt over the two of them.

Footsteps scrambled nearer. Voices scattered around them. Savaana pulled her feet beneath her wide skirt and dropped her head against her sister's face, letting her hair cover everything.

"Where are they?" The man who spoke had a strong, indistinguishable accent. He was nearly upon them.

Savaana felt Clarette jerk, but she held her down, hand tight over her mouth.

"They are close," someone else growled.

"Then kill them," snarled another. *"Acum!"*

Clarette whimpered. Savaana shook.

Heavy footfalls hurried past.

The sisters remained still, barely breathing until the sound of the men's movement was only a whisper of twigs in the distance.

Savaana eased onto her knees.

"Are they gone?" Clarette sat up carefully.

Savaana shook her head, rising shakily to her feet, squatting beside a nearby tree.

"Let's go," Clarette hissed, and eased back the way they had come. Savaana slunk after.

But someone yelled from above.

The women jerked their attention to the left. Three men were sliding toward them.

"Nandy!" someone shouted from behind.

*"Le va esti aici!"* said another, but the women were already racing away, darting through trees, trying to bisect the enemies in a desperate bid to make it back to the road. It was their only hope now. But the trio from above was slicing off their angle of escape.

Pivoting wildly, the girls skittered downward, scrambling, falling, only to rise and rush on, but the slope was becoming steeper, and they could no longer hear their pursuers. Blood pounded in Savaana's ears. Terror tore at her heart. It wasn't fair. She couldn't possibly have found her sister only to lose her now. To lose her because of her own efforts.

"Dammit!" Clarette said, and skidded to a halt, arms windmilling as she tried to keep herself from tumbling downward. Savaana grabbed a sapling to prevent careening into her. And then she realized the truth; it wasn't the sound of her own terror that was pounding in her ears. It was the river. Glancing down, she saw it tumble and roll thirty yards beneath their feet.

"Holy mother!" Clarette's face looked as pale as the moon, a round sickle of fear, eyes wide with terror. She was holding onto a branch with white-knuckled panic.

But Savaana felt hope bloom like a wild blossom in her soul. "This is our chance."

"What? What the hell are you talking about?"

"That tree," Savaana said, motioning toward a fallen trunk before snapping her gaze behind her. No sinister shapes shone in the darkness, but it was only a matter of time. "We'll crawl out on it. Hide. They'll never expect us there."

"You're mad."

"No time to debate that. Go."

"No."

"Clarette." She caught her sister's eyes. "You're the princess of Delvania. Wealthier than you've ever imagined."

There was a moment of absolute silence, then: "I can imagine quite a lot."

"Surely you don't want to give it all up now."

Clarette closed her eyes, swallowed, then dropped to her knees and shimmied onto the log by slow degrees. Savaana slipped out of her shoes, then followed her, crouched in her wake, watching behind, praying in silence. The tree gave a little beneath them, jerking under their weight.

Clarette whimpered, hugging a branch to her chest. Below them the river raced along its wild path to the sea.

From above Savaana heard a murmur of voices.

"Clarette?"

Her sister turned panicked eyes on her.

"You're going to have to jump."

"You said we were hiding here." The words were no more than a hissed accusation.

"We only have a few minutes before they find us. Maybe not that much."

Clarette glanced down. She closed her eyes. "You lied to me."

Savaana glanced behind again. "You and everyone else. Are you ready?" she asked, and skimmed her bare foot forward a few inches.

"What happened to your shoes?"

"Is that really what you want to concentrate on at this precise moment?" Savaana asked, and reaching for her sister's shoes, pulled them off one after the other "Or do you want to think about surviving?"

Clarette's face contorted. "Are they really diamonds?"

"Would I lie to you?" Savaana asked, and grinned.

"If I survive this I'm going to beat the hell out of you," Clarette said, and Savaana almost laughed as she dropped the shoes into the water below. It seemed a lifetime before they splashed.

Clarette tightened her grip on the tree and pressed her face to a branch.

"They're diamonds," Savaana said. "I swear it. More valuable than—"

Voices sounded from the hill above.

"It's time," Savaana said.

Clarette closed her eyes, hugging harder. "I can't do it."

"Then you won't live to see the diamonds cut."

She didn't respond.

"You'll die," Savaana added. "And I'll die with you."

Their gazes met. Then, with painful slowness, Clarette released her right hand and reached for Savaana. "I've never had a sister," she said.

Savaana clasped her hand, steady as a rock. Just another performance. Just another unlikely feat of derring-do. She stretched out her other hand, and Clarette gave it.

"You've always had a sister," she said, and leaping, pulled them both toward the rushing waters below.

# Chapter 26

"**M**r. Gallagher?"

Sean turned toward Lord Tilmont, brow furrowed, mind churning.

"What are you doing here? And . . ." The baron paused in the arched door of Reardon's ostentatious manor. "What the devil are you wearing?" he asked, but Sean didn't acknowledge Tilmont's questions.

"Where is she?" he asked.

"What?"

Worry gnawed him like a starving hound. He should have gone with her. Should have ignored her request for solitude and followed her into the dark garden. "Your wife. Where is she?"

"I don't think that's any of your concern," Tilmont said, but Sean's patience had evaporated.

Taking the one stride that remained between them, he lowered his voice to a growl. "What the hell have you done with her?"

The baron's brows rose in unison with one corner of

his mouth, and suddenly he didn't look so dissipated, so innocuous. "So I was right, then. You're in love with her."

"I'm not . . ." Feelings swirled like fireflies in Gallagher's tortured soul. Terror and hope soaring on the wings of something rather akin to love. "There's no time for that." He scanned the milling crowd. "I can't find her in this damned circus."

Tilmont scowled a little. "Perhaps she returned home."

Gallagher snapped his gaze back to the baron. "To Knollcrest? Why would she leave—"

"That's not her home," Tilmont said. The words *you dolt* seemed to be implied. "Don't you know anything about her, man?"

"What are you talking about?"

"Her *real* home."

Gallagher scowled. "Which is where?"

"How the devil am I supposed to know?" he asked. "I've only just met her."

The world had gone mad. There seemed little reason to be the only sane person there. So Gallagher took a wild stab at the truth. "You know she's not your wife?"

"Good God, man, I'm a lush not an imbecile. My wife's a sharp-tongued shrew."

Gallagher shook his head, trying to rid it of the confusion. But there was little hope of that. "You've known all along she was someone else?"

"Since I stepped into her room at the inn."

"How—" he began, but there was no time. "Where has she gone?"

"My wife or the other . . ." Tilmont paused. "What's her name, by the by?"

Frustration made Sean want to shake the baron till his teeth rattled. "I've no idea."

"Well, what the hell have you been doing with all your bloody time?"

"I've— She—" What indeed? "How was I to know she wasn't who you said her to be?"

"I told you she was a bitch at the outset. You didn't seem to care a whit. You still wished to meet her. Hell, you were frothing to meet her. Why is that, by the by?"

"I thought she was Clarette!"

"Even after you spoke to her? Are you a damned idiot or—" He stopped himself. "My apologies," he said, and held out his right hand. It shook like a tambourine.

Gallagher scowled. "You need a drink."

"More than you know."

"I'll get—" he began, but Tilmont caught his arm.

"Who were the men who accosted her?"

"I have no idea."

"But we can assume her life is in danger."

Sean felt his stomach twist, felt his face go pale.

Tilmont watched, an expression of near pity crossing his face. "You're that far gone, are you, lad?"

"You've met her," Gallagher said, thinking that enough of an explanation as he scanned the crowd again.

Tilmont grinned, expression wry. "Just briefly," he said. "What part did my wife have to play in this, do you think?"

"I've no idea." Frustration bubbled like hot tar in his soul. Half of London must be in that damned ballroom.

"So you don't know her name, where she's from, or why she's here."

Sean suddenly felt like popping the cocky baron in the face, but he gritted his jaw and manfully refrained. "That sums it up."

"Maybe she's avoiding you."

"Why would she—" Gallagher began, then remembered painful pieces of their past.

Tilmont raised his brows.

"I never intended to seduce her." Gallagher's voice sounded sulky to his own ears. "Not once I suspected she wasn't who I thought her to be."

"What *was* your intent exactly?"

Gallagher watched Tilmont for a moment. Impatience gnawed at him, but there were things to be learned. Necessary things. "My brother was to wed. He said she was beauty itself." He clenched his jaw. "Father had been unwell since Mother's death, but the hope of grandchildren rejuvenated him. He smiled for the first time in months when he gave Alastar Mother's ring. 'A symbol of faithfulness and joy,' " he said.

Tilmont's expression was somber.

"She never showed up for the wedding, and the ring hasn't been seen since. I never met this paragon. But Alastar had commissioned a cameo."

"And when I showed you Clarette's portrait you assumed it was she."

"I thought she was one and the same for some days after I reached your estate."

"So the two women must be working together somehow," Tilmont said.

"That's my guess."

"But why?"

"That question has crossed my mind."

"And mine," Tilmont said. "Let us go voice it."

They glanced about, then made a circuit around the ballroom, going in opposite directions before meeting in the middle.

Gallagher's stomach was cranked up tight.

"She seemed unaccountably attached to horses." Tilmont's tone sounded strained, but whether it was nerves or abstinence, 'twas impossible to say.

"I'll check the carriages. You have a look around the garden." Gallagher turned abruptly away. The crowds dissipated in his mind. Worry gnawed at his nerve endings. What had he been thinking? He should have never let her out of his sight. Should have known better than to upset her, then leave her.

The night air felt cool against his face.

Tilmont's rented vis-à-vis stood in a long queue some distance down the yard. Gallagher glanced toward it, but another row of vehicles blocked it from view. Stepping between a shiny phaeton and the cob that carried the brougham behind it, he emerged into the moonlit night. In that moment he realized someone was bending inside their rented vehicle.

"Clarette." Relief sloughed through him, but suddenly the shadowy personage jerked from the carriage. It was a man, garbed in a short jacket with brass buttons. "Who the hell are you?" rasped the Irishman, but the stranger pivoted away.

Gallagher leapt forward, eating up the distance. "Stop!" he ordered, and snagged the man's arm. "What the devil do you think—" he began, but even as the other turned, his dagger gleamed in the moonlight.

Pain stabbed Gallagher, but worry was even sharper. Tightening his grip on the other's jacket, he pulled him closer, gritting his teeth against the agony.

"What have you done with her?" His voice was guttural, his worry all consuming.

The man uttered something foreign and yanked the knife free to thrust again, but this time Gallagher caught his wrist.

The blade shook between them as they struggled.

"Where is she?" Gallagher could barely force out the words. Blackness loomed, but he pushed it back, fighting for lucidness.

"Where none will find her," the man snarled.

"Why?"

"For Delvania," he said, and slammed his free fist into Gallagher's knife wound.

Gallagher staggered backward as the Delvanian turned to flee, but desperation roared inside the Irishman. Gathering all his strength, he leapt. His fingers just brushed the man's coat. But it was enough. He closed his hands and hung on. The villain stumbled to his knees. Grasping his legs, Gallagher clawed his way up the fallen body. The Delvanian kicked. The momentum threw Gallagher aside as the other twisted around, but even as he did so, the Irishman slammed a fist into his face, then climbed atop him. Groping for the hand that now held a gun, he pinned the man's wrist to the ground.

"Where is she?" he rasped.

"Dead! Dead already."

Insanity roared through Gallagher. He struck with all his strength. The man's head snapped to the side, but then he smiled.

"The bitch is dead. The Ludricks will rule again," he said, and squeezed the trigger.

The gun exploded. Gallagher braced for impact, but

the bullet hadn't been meant for him. Instead, the body beneath him jerked and went limp.

Tilmont rushed to a halt beside them, but Gallagher barely noticed. He struggled to his feet. There was something sticky on his hands. Sticky and warm.

"Someone you knew?" Tilmont asked, and bending, calmly took the pistol from the dead man's hand.

Gallagher lurched back a step. The world was beginning to reel around him like a child's whirligig. "I've got to find her." He was never certain if he said the words aloud or just thought them in the depths of his soul. "Got to—" he said, and scrambling for coherence, tumbled into dark oblivion.

# Chapter 27

The water shattered like glass when Savaana struck it. It rushed into her nose, her ears, pushed with painful force into every screaming orifice. It swallowed her up, pulled her under, tumbled her like a leaf in a wind storm. Her head struck something. Darkness blasted inside her cranium, threatening explosion, but the pain in her lungs was all consuming. She contorted, body avulsing, legs spearing downward, and suddenly she torpedoed out of the water.

Air struck her lungs like a lance, but she drew it in, knowing nothing but the sweet agony. Thinking of nothing but staying alive, of breathing.

And then she remembered.

"Clarette!" The name gurgled from her throat. She spun around. Water rushed around her, past her, pushing her downstream, but twenty yards away a dark form floated on the waves. She yelled again and swam toward the shape, but her gown was snagged on a branch. Bracing her feet against a submerged log, she ripped her clothing free, then sliced through the water toward her sister.

Clarette was facedown, arms flung wide. Savaana turned her over, babbling wildly. The face that mirrored her own looked blue.

"No! Dammit, no!" she rasped, and slapped the other's cheek. Her sister remained limp, bobbing on the fleeing waves. "Clarette!" Savaana cried, and slapped her again.

Her eyes opened, angry and squinted. "Slap me once more and you'll wish you were at the bottom of this stinking river!" she warned.

Savaana cupped her sister's face. "I thought you were dead."

"Well, apparently I'm not, so—" she began, then turning her head, spewed the contents of her stomach into the water. Wiping her mouth with a shaky, ice-blue hand, she added, "You'd better get me out of this bloody mess." Her haughty accent had disappeared entirely, seeping into a more earthy dialect.

Savaana laughed, giddy with relief.

Clarette glared. "You haven't gone mad, have you?"

"No. Absolutely not," Savaana said, and grinned. "Take off your clothes."

"Brilliant," Clarette said. Her voice sounded casual, as if they sat together in some toasty parlor sipping lavender tea, instead of floating along toward unknown enemies. "You've got a plan."

"I do. But you have to trust me."

"Trust you. Good idea." Clarette nodded and paddled vaguely, though the current was carrying them at its will. "I don't even know who you are."

"I told you I'm—"

"My long lost sister," Clarette said numbly. "And it must be true, because things have been humming along swimmingly since the moment I met you."

"Swimmingly," Savaana said, and sank beneath the surface for an instant, weakened by fatigue and cold, but she forced herself back up, kicking furiously. "Is that a jest?" Her fingers felt numb and disembodied, but she spun her sister about to claw at the laces that bound her gown at the back.

"You decide if it seems as if I'm in the mood for making jokes." Clarette tipped her head up, trying to keep the water out of her nose. "I'm about to drown . . . if I don't freeze to death first. I've ruined one of my favorite gowns. And my supposed lover, Eduardo Delafonti, is now wed."

"What?" It was damnably difficult to do anything when your fingers felt as thick as pigs' feet.

"Not that that should matter, I suppose. Technically, I'm married, too, but for some unfathomable reason, Eduardo has decided to remain faithful. To his wife. To his *wife*!" She said the words as if they were crazy, then sighed, sank beneath the waves and resurfaced again, breathing hard. "Hence, I'm not bloody pregnant. I just spent a fortnight traipsing around Paris alone, only to return to find you in London. With my husband."

Savaana scowled at the saturated laces, trying to see in the darkness. "I had to learn what I could of the necklace."

"Is that what you were doing?" Clarette's teeth were chattering now and she trembled violently. "Because it looked like you were about to fornicate with the lusty peer right there on Reardon's polished dance floor."

"Well, I wasn't!" Savaana said.

"Already did that, did you?"

"No," Savaana said, and it was technically true.

"Hmmf." Clarette's eyes were closed by the time she was facing her sister again. "Why are you taking my gown?"

"Clarette." Savaana shook her gently.

"Mmm."

"You can't sleep now."

Her head had fallen back in the water. "I could if you'd quit yammering."

"Don't make me hit you again."

"You wouldn't dare," Clarette said, but her voice was groggy.

Savaana slapped her with all the force she could muster.

Clarette came awake with a start, limbs jerking

beneath the waves. "Why do you keep doing that?" She sounded irritable and dangerous, but still muzzy.

"You've got to wake up."

"Why?"

"Because . . ." She searched frantically for a reason. "Because I've got the diamonds."

*"Here?"* Clarette's eyes popped open as Savaana struggled with the bottom of her own gown. Finding the lumpy spot in the hem, she ripped the seam open and dragged out the stones.

They dangled dejectedly between them on the saturated thong.

"Are you insane?" Clarette asked, grabbing them. "Why are they here?"

"What was I supposed to do with them? Give them to your husband for safe keeping?"

Clarette glared as she slipped them around her neck.

"I thought he might be a little peeved when he realized you'd gone to get pregnant by Eduardo whosit."

"I wasn't planning to tell him," Clarette muttered groggily.

Savaana slapped her again, then gripped her arms. Maybe to keep her afloat. Maybe to prevent further violence.

Clarette gritted her teeth. "Why the hell do you keep doing that?"

"Because I've been trying to find you for twenty years

and now that I have I'm not very excited about watching you drown."

"How do you feel about being punched in the eye?"

Savaana almost laughed, but just then her knee slammed into a log and she grimaced, pulling her legs up with painful effort. "Well, I guess that disproves that possibility."

"What are you talking about?" Clarette still sounded irritable, but more alert.

"I used to think Mother kept you because you were the nice sister. But maybe she was worried someone would drown you once they got to know you. She always was kind. I don't think—"

"You remember her?" Clarette's voice was breathy, but whether it was from the cold or some other reason, Savaana couldn't tell.

"Just tiny fragments. Her voice. Her touch. She used to kiss the top of my head and her hair would fall down around my face. She wore it loose and it smelled like—"

"Bellflowers." Clarette's voice was wispy, all but lost in the rush of the waves.

"You remember," Savaana said, but her sister shook her head.

"Sometimes I think I do. But they're really Nina's memories most like."

"Nina?"

"The woman who took me after Mother died."

Savaana's heart contracted. All these years she had hoped her mother still lived, but she refused to focus on death now, when life seemed so utterly fragile. "How old were you?"

"Four. Five, maybe."

"I'm sorry."

"Me, too. Nina smelled like suet. But she was better than the nuns."

"Nuns?"

"The sisters of Wellworth Abby. They kept me for some years."

"Seriously?"

Clarette's scowl darkened. "Extremely seriously. Damn old cows hated me. When I was fourteen I met the butcher's son. Life with him seemed far preferable."

"Was it?"

She shrugged. The movement was stiff. "It was better with the architect, better still with the wine merchant."

"I assume your name hasn't always been Clarette."

"At times it was Abigail, or Milicent. I was a Victoria once, I think." She sounded foggy. "Lord Beuford called me Trixie. His wife *detested* me."

Savaana shook her head. "Surely not," she said, and rubbed her sister's arms in a vain attempt to increase circulation. "You're so sweet."

"I can be sweet."

"Help me with your gown," Savaana said, struggling with the saturated fabric. It was as heavy as mortar against the dragging waves.

"I *can* be sweet, dammit! Ask any man with a hundred pounds in his— Why the hell are we disrobing?"

"Hurry." Savaana glanced up and to the rear. But the bend blocked her view of the cliff from where they'd jumped. "I still have to undress, and they'll be able to see us soon,"

"Good God, even *I'm* not that vain."

Savaana considered that a moment, mind fuzzy with cold and worry, then shook her head. "I don't want them to see us naked, you dolt. I want them to see our gowns floating down the river while we hide on the riverbank."

"Because . . . Oh!" Clarette said. "You're irritating as hell. But you're not completely dense."

"Sometimes I don't know why I've searched for you so long." Clarette's gown drifted between them. "Hurry up. Help me with mine," she said, and shot a glance toward the ridge above.

"Savaana?"

It was the first time her sister had ever addressed her by name. It sounded nice. Soft and almost reverent.

"Yes?"

"How well do you know this river?"

"Not well. Why?"

"I hear something."

Savaana concentrated, listening for the sound of feet. Perhaps the river coursed close to the road here or—

"Waterfall!" she croaked.

"That's what I thought." Clarette was sounding hazy again, but Savaana didn't have time to worry about that. She was frantically trying to drag her sister toward shore. It was like attempting to fall uphill. She scrambled against the current, clawing every inch of the way. Something scraped her leg. She gritted her teeth against the pain and pushed on, struggling for a branch that reached out of the water, but it seemed almost to be moving away. Her foot struck something solid, but instead of drawing away, she kicked hard. Her toes slammed against a rock. They stung like the devil, but she managed to push through the water. Grasping the branch, she dragged them both through the rushing waves.

"Hang on!" she snarled, and yanked Clarette over the top of a fat log. Saturated and slick, it was all but impossible to hold onto, but finally they were wedged between two branches. Stored beneath a sheltering overhang, they seemed safe enough.

"Are you well?" Savaana was gasping for breath, struggling to remain upright, to keep Clarette's head above water, to prevent their garments from floating away.

"Of course I'm well. I'm splendid. Never been—"

"Oh shut up and dress the branch."

"Dress the—"

"Break the branch off, tie your gown to it and set it afloat," Savaana ordered as she began to do the same herself.

Clarette followed suit, fingers fumbling erratically. "Do you think this will work?"

"If they don't kill us we'll know it did," Savaana said, and finishing her task, let the garment set sail. The knobby portion of the branch stuck out of the neck hole.

Clarette glanced up as it rolled downstream. "It looks rather like you."

"Just hurry up!" Savaana said, and Clarette sent her effigy to join her sister's.

They waited as the gowns floated around the bend and out of sight. Still no shouts from up above.

"Maybe they saw us," Clarette whispered, and raised haunted eyes toward the steep bank overhead. "Maybe they're watching us right now."

Savaana controlled a shudder, then dragged her gaze back to the water behind them. "Are you always this pessimistic?"

"Until things go poorly."

"Tell me when that happens," Savaana said, and reaching out, tugged her sister over the log and upstream, keeping carefully beneath the rocky embankment.

"Where the hell are we—" Clarette began, but at that second a dog howled from the hill to their right. A garble of voices was barely discernible from above, and then a shot exploded. The sisters jumped, then crouched in silence, hearts banging like wild drums, but the men above seemed to be hurrying downstream.

Finally, trembling with cold and fear, Savaana caught her sister's wrist and tugged her against the waves, moving as rapidly as she could. Clarette didn't argue, but after a seeming lifetime she stopped, bending over and trying to catch her breath. "Where are we going?" Her words were a harsh whisper, barely heard above the cackle of the water.

Exhaustion threatened. "Can't risk land," Savaana panted. "Not with a tracking dog so close. Have to get as far from the gowns as possible."

Clarette put a hand to her side and scowled at the opposite shore. "Mine was French."

"What?"

"My gown. Designed in France. The lace was brought from Venice."

"So?"

"So you owe me a French gown with Italian lace."

Savaana stared at her a moment, then shook her head and struggled upstream. "How far do you think we've come?"

Grim-faced and silent, Clarette staggered past.

Savaana thrashed after her. Exhaustion dragged at her legs, threatening to pull her under. Raw cold chafed her, slowing her motions, dulling her senses. Something splashed. It took her a moment to realize she had fallen into the water, but she failed to care. It felt heavenly to sit. To give up. To lie back in the waves and let the current—

Clarette turned back with a frown, then stumbled through the water to drag at her arm.

"Just . . . just let me stay," Savaana whimpered, but her sister only pulled harder.

"You can't die until you replace my gown," she snarled, and hauled Savaana to her feet.

After that it was little more than a nightmare of fatigue and fear, of scrapes and curses and near drowning. But finally Clarette staggered to a halt.

"Why are you stopping?" Savaana glanced behind them. "Do you think we've come far enough?"

Clarette didn't bother to turn toward her. Didn't bother to raise her voice or venture a guess. "I think it's a moot point," she said, and dropped like a rock into the churning waters.

# Chapter 28

**S**ounds settled slowly in around Sean. Like sunlight through distant leaves, they trickled in. Voices, anxious, murmured, shifting erratically. Pain, but only in a muffled sort of way.

"I think he's coming to."

"Stand back. Stand back now. Let me in." Light filtered through his eyelids, muted and soft. "Sir, sir can you hear me? What happened? How badly are you hurt?"

Sean opened his eyes slowly. Candlelight flickered across a smooth-featured face. Fair hair, pale skin, long side whiskers. Beyond him, the walls were papered with posies planted in stripes.

"Aren't physicians supposed to be old?" he asked.

Concern chased uncertainty across the man's youthful features. "I fear he may have obtained trauma to the head. Lord Reardon, might you make certain my carriage is brought 'round. I think it best that we transfer him back to the city until we determine all the—"

But suddenly a host of memories swarmed in. Horses, dancing, knives, carnivals, top hats!

"Clarette!" Sean sat up with a jolt. His head spun like a weathervane. A demon stabbed his side. He pressed his hand over his coat, trying to contain the throbbing agony.

"Here now." The physician's hand was on his shoulder. "Don't concern yourself with—"

"Where is she?" Facts swam past, slippery as minnows, merging with memories and half-forgotten dreams.

"Easy now. There's no need to—"

"How long have I been unconscious?" His voice sounded rusty to his own ears.

"There's no need to fret, sir. I can assure you—"

"How long?" he snarled, and caught the physician by his starchy cravat.

"It's difficult to say for certain. Lord Tilmont said you passed out. We brought you inside, hoping you'd come to. We've stanched the loss of blood but . . ."

Sean found himself standing though he wasn't at all sure how it had happened. The room spun in a lazy circle. He searched the vicinity. But faces around him seemed vague and oddly unimportant. A woman in a mint green gown, a young man built like a pugilist. A fair-haired gentleman. A—

He swung his attention back to the gentleman. "Tilmont." The name came with some difficulty, but once he said it, he knew he was right. "Where is she?" His words sounded raspy, but the baron shook his head.

"What do you know of this?" Sean demanded, and stumbled toward him, determined to learn the truth, to set things right, but his feet were strangely uncooperative.

The baron caught him around the middle just before he fell. Something cold and hard was thrust into the waistband beneath his jacket. It almost felt like a pistol.

"Easy now, Gallagher," he said, then quieter. "We don't even know *who* she is, lad, and you've got other things to concern yourself with."

"What do you mean?" Sean asked, and stumbled away. Perhaps he should have noticed the doctor nodding to the pugilist. Perhaps he should have seen that one step forward before he felt a brawny arm lock around his neck from behind.

He struggled weakly.

"Careful now. Careful, Lord Wesman," cautioned the doctor. "We don't know the circumstances for certain. Perhaps he acted in self-defense."

"Or maybe the other chap killed *himself*," suggested the pugilist from behind.

"No need to be facetious," said Reardon, stepping imperially from the midst of the crowd.

"What—" Gallagher began, then remembered the shadowy man bending inside the rented vis-à-vis.

Remembered the thrust of the knife, the sharp report of the gun as the stranger turned it on himself.

"He did. He did kill himself."

"The judge will make that decision," Reardon said. "Let's get him outside."

The pugilist goose-walked him toward the door. Weak and disoriented, Sean shifted desperate eyes toward Tilmont. A terrible silence filled the room.

"Here now, Lord Wesman," the baron said finally.

The pugilist paused, then turned toward Tilmont. There was a moment's delay, a resounding crash, and then the pugilist dropped to his knees. Sean stumbled backward. The shattered remains of a chair lay scattered across the floor.

Sean snapped his gaze to Tilmont's.

"Stay if you like," said the baron, holding a broken chair leg in one hand. "But I thought you were in something of a rush."

Gallagher turned toward the door. The crowd parted before him. The night air felt chill against his face. Rows of carriages lined the curved driveway. He rushed unsteadily between them until he spotted a lone horse.

"Stop him!"

The order was barked from behind, but he had already flung himself into the nearest saddle. The animal reared, pulling at his tether. Sean's head reeled. Dammit, the steed was still tied and men were already racing toward him.

"You're like a bloody child," Tilmont said. Appearing from nowhere, he ripped the tether free and tossed it over the restive animal's withers.

Sean was galloping in less than a heartbeat, fleeing into the night, though God knew where he was going.

# Chapter 29

"**Y**ou should have told me you were injured." Savaana was huddled against a boulder in a washed-out cove etched into the sharp shoreline. Clarette sat up. Newly conscious, she cupped her forehead and steadied herself.

"You take this role of older sister too seriously," she said, and glanced at the bandage now secured around her upper arm.

Savaana knew the wound should be cleaned, but there was little she could do about that just now. Thus she remained as she was, freezing cold and watching.

"So you admit the truth," she said.

"What truth is that?" Clarette wrapped her arms around her lower legs, tucking her knees beneath her chin.

"That we're sisters."

"I didn't say that."

"And I didn't say I was older."

Clarette shrugged. "You don't have enough patience to be younger."

Savaana considered how best to untangle such a statement, but the subject seemed too foolish to pursue. "You have the moon," she said instead.

Clarette gave her a high-browed glance. "And you have the starlit night."

Savaana scowled, wondering if her sister was hallucinating, before remembering her penchant for sarcasm. "Your moon," she said, "where did you get it?"

Clarette only stared, so Savaana lifted her own chemise, baring goose pimpled flesh.

"Attractive as you are," Clarette said, "I'm afraid my interests gravitate toward someone with less bosom and more—"

Savaana turned, showing her back and waiting, breath held. Truth to tell, in all of her years, none but the Irishman had mentioned the crescent on her back. She had only his word to go on, for as she told him, she'd never seen it herself.

Silence echoed between them, and for a moment Savaana thought her sister would say she saw nothing, but when she turned back, Clarette shrugged.

"So?"

She lowered her garment. "Surely you've noticed yours."

No response.

"You've a small moon under your right shoulder blade."

Clarette's expression was bored, but beneath that attitude there seemed to be a layer of uncertainty, of nervous curiosity. "It may have been mentioned a time or two."

Their gazes met.

"What is it?" Savaana asked.

"A birthmark. Nothing more."

"It's blue."

Another shrug, saying volumes with its elitist boredom. But Savaana couldn't be fooled forever, not even by her sister.

"It was two and twenty years ago when I was left with Dook Natsia, the Magic Gypsies. Grandfather said I was not yet four years of age at that time.

"How old were you then?"

"A lady doesn't reveal her true age."

"So you don't know either."

Clarette neither denied nor confirmed it.

"The Beloreich were ousted from power in 1795," Savaana said. "Prince Radu of the Ludricks killed the king, his cousin, shortly after that." Even now it was not a simple task to keep the emotion from her voice, for she had long wondered who she was. Had ruthlessly questioned any who might be able to shed some light on her circumstances. Not until a few years ago had she begun to suspect her heritage. After that, she learned all she could of the tiny Delvanian empire near Romania's border.

"The Beloreich?" Clarette's teeth were clenched against chattering and her lips looked to be an odd shade of lavender.

Shifting her feet beneath her, Savaana reached for her sister's hand. It felt as cold as a gravestone between hers. She rubbed vigorously, trapping her eyes. "Their symbol is a crescent moon."

Clarette scowled. "When I first met you I had no idea you were a student of foreign culture."

"Grandfather's family came from Delvania many years ago."

"Ahh, so he was the one who put these crazy ideas into your head."

"He said that when my mother came to the camp, she spoke a language he could not quite understand. Delvanian, perhaps. Said she wore a necklace of priceless gems. Said she carried a baby in her arms."

"So naturally she was royalty and *I* was that baby."

"Top Hat said her name was Princess Eliane."

"Top Hat."

"The little man in the woods near Reardon's mansion."

"The man who tried to kill us?"

"I don't think . . ." Savaana began, then drew a deep breath and continued where she'd left off. "I believe our mother was being pursued. I think she was desperate to keep us safe." Or did she just *want* to believe that? Had she just dreamt it so often that it now *seemed* to be true?

"So you're sticking with the sister story."

Savaana considered defending her beliefs, clarifying her ideas, but she was so tired. "It's the only one I have," she said.

Clarette snorted. "Well, you don't lack imagination."

That much had always been true. Imagination and resolve. That's what Grandfather said. And she was not about to give up now. She glanced toward the east. Their cover of darkness wouldn't last forever. "Stay here through the daylight hours," she said. "If I'm not back by dusk, head north toward Knollcrest."

"What the devil are you talking about?"

"I think the Ludricks are chasing us, but there may be others who . . ." She scowled, then shook her head, thoughts churning. "Don't trust anyone."

Clarette chortled. Her teeth chattered. "Too late to start now. What others?"

Memories roiled through Savaana's mind like midnight waves. Wisps of scents, fragments of songs, images, so fleeting they were gone before she could visualize them. "The giant . . . I think . . ." He had frightened them, yes. Had caught them. But he had also looked at her with such tenderness, such hopelessness. Hadn't he? "Perhaps they were trying to save us."

Clarette raised her brows. "So you *have* gone mad."

"It's possible."

"Save us from whom?"

"Radu's men. Aren't you listening? The ones who want the Ludricks in power."

Clarette scowled and jerked her hand from Savaana's grasp. "And to think I once pined for a sister?"

"Did you?" Savaana breathed.

"No," she said, and wincing, rose to a crouched position.

"What do you think you're doing?"

"I think I'm not being left behind to freeze to death in this godforsaken wilderness."

Savaana shook her head. "I'll come back for you. Until then—" she began, but Clarette interrupted.

"It's going to be dawn soon. If we're going, we'd best do so now."

"You'll only slow me down."

"Then I guess you'll have to carry me," Clarette said, and grimaced as she stepped away from the river.

"Stay here," Savaana ordered. "I'll return as soon as I can."

"And let you run off with the necklace?"

"What are you talking about? *You* have the necklace."

"Well, maybe you plan to let me freeze to death, then come back and take it from me."

"That's ludicrous."

"Maybe. But you told me to trust no one," Clarette said, and slowly ascended the hill.

Savaana glared after her. "Don't be daft. If all I wanted was the stones, why wouldn't I have taken them and left long ago?"

Clarette shrugged as she stepped over a log and pushed aside a frond of drying thorns. "Maybe you're not very intelligent. Maybe you wanted to make sure I was dead so you'd have the diamonds to yourself. Maybe—"

"You're staying here." Grabbing Clarette's arm, Savaana braced herself for a tempest. Their mother had managed to save them both. Damned if she herself was going to fail them now. But her sister was silent for several seconds before speaking.

"Maybe I don't want to die alone," she said, and something inside Savaana crumbled.

They stared at each other. "Tell me if you're weak or tired," she said, and turned to climb the slope.

Clarette followed in her wake. "I'm weak . . ." she said, "and tired."

"God help me," Savaana rasped, but grinned silently at the tiny flicker of hope in her heart.

It seemed a lifetime before the woods finally thinned. A meadow of sorts lay ahead, dotted with a few lone trees and the jutting corners of rocks. A glimmer of morning was just lightening the eastern sky as they struggled over another log and gazed upon the relatively open moors ahead. It would be easier going now, but caution, or something like it, kept them hidden in the shadow of the old growth. Eyes rimmed with white, they stared out at the retreating darkness.

"What now?"

Savaana shook her head. "There must be a road somewhere up there."

"What if they're waiting for us?" Clarette's voice was no more than a cracked whisper, but her hand felt strong as she steadied herself on her sister's shoulder.

Savaana felt terror tangle with her other senses, but she peeled it away, buried it inside. Just another performance. Reaching up, she covered her sister's hand with her own. "Then they'll have to deal with the Beloreich," she said, and meeting Clarette's eyes, felt a swirl of familial pride unfurl inside her.

"Well, I hope they get here soon," Clarette said. "Because my arm is throbbing like a bridegroom's winkle."

The tender moment was shattered. Savaana tilted her head. "I meant—" she began, then realized she was simply experiencing her sister's dubious sense of humor. "I think I understand why your husband left you," she said, and glanced ahead. "Better to stay to the woods or chance the open?"

They gazed out on the meadow together. Dotted with

sharp boulders and the occasional tree, it looked green and inviting compared to the dark undergrowth through which they'd been struggling.

"We'd make better time in the open."

"And we haven't seen any sign of trouble for some hours."

In the end they stepped tentatively out of the woods, heading north, but the going wasn't as effortless as they had hoped. Half-hidden rocks tried to trip them at every weary step. But finally they came across a trail of sorts. The grasses were worn down, exposing a rough thatch of shale. The path headed uphill in a wending fashion, leading into the trees again.

Their course was easier now, but Clarette's breath was coming hard. The path widened, dividing around an enormous oak.

"Let's stop for—" Savaana began, but suddenly something leapt at them. Clarette gasped. Savaana jumped, but the creature darted past, materializing into a dark stag that disappeared into the underbrush.

"Holy hell!" they said in unison, then laughed together at their odd similarities. Weak with relief and exhaustion, they dropped to the ground behind the oak.

They were silent for several moments, simply resting.

"How are you faring?" Savaana asked finally, then heard a branch snap.

They caught their breath in unison. Savaana leaned sideways to peek past the tree's craggy trunk. A man rode alone through the scattered woods. It was still too dark to make out his face, but the brass buttons of his short jacket gleamed dully, and in his right hand he held a long curved sword. Within minutes he would be upon them.

"What is it?" Clarette breathed.

Savaana drew back into hiding. "A rider. Near the top of the hill."

"Coming this way?"

She nodded, and in that moment they realized they were caught. They couldn't leave their hiding place without darting across the open area of the path. And he was heading toward them, searching. They eased sideways, making certain they were well hidden behind the oak.

Clarette's eyes were wide in her pale face. "Do you think he's a Beloreich coming to save us, or a—"

"Can you ride?" Savaana hissed.

"Isn't this an odd time to inquire about my equestrian skills?"

Savaana drew a deep breath to begin again but there was no time. "You'll have to draw him toward you."

Clarette raised one brow.

Savaana crouched lower, barely breathing. "You're injured."

Still no response.

"I don't know how much farther you can—"

"God dammit, just tell me your idea!" Clarette rasped.

"You're going to be the decoy. I'm going to steal his horse."

Savaana sat in silence, watching her sister's face, waiting for an argument or a question. Neither came. Instead, she finally nodded, her expression stony.

"Very well. But if you botch this up, you'll be an only child again," Clarette hissed.

"Don't you want to know how we're going to do it?"

"I want to know you're not going to get me killed, too, but that's not very likely, is it?" she asked, and gritting her teeth, peeked around the base of the tree.

Savaana remained where she was, back braced against the rough bark. "Is he still coming this way?"

"Have you ever brought me anything but bad luck?" Clarette asked, and dropped her head against the tree's broad trunk. Closing her eyes, she exhaled sharply. "Where do you want me?"

"Can you run?"

She opened her eyes and all but rolled them in exasperation. "Are you asking if I can outdistance a horse? I don't think so, but I'm pretty sure I could do a damn fine job of passing out."

Savaana considered that an instant. "That might actually be better. There's no point in trying to get away."

"I thought we *were* trying to get away."

"Get out onto the trail, then notice him. Act as if you're startled. Scared."

"Will it help if I wet myself?"

Savaana reached for her sister's hand, and for a moment she almost laughed. "Do you think we might have liked each other?"

Clarette met her gaze.

"If we had been together all along. Do you think we would have been friends?"

"I'm told miracles happen sometimes." Clarette's tone was jaded, but her eyes were bright. "What do I do after he sees me?"

"Swoon ten feet in front of this tree."

"Where are you going to be?"

"*In* this tree," she said.

Clarette glanced into the branches overhead and winced, but then pursed her lips, setting her face in that chilly expression that was hers alone. "Swear to God, if you get caught, I'm not coming back for you. Sister or no sister."

Savaana nodded and looked up at the sturdy branch several feet above their heads. "I won't go easily. He'll have to kill me." She frowned, thinking. "Then he'll take time to examine my body. To make sure I have the tattoo. He'll have to dismount to do so. Grab his horse, but don't move too quickly. The best mounts are often skittish. Once you're astride, head north. Eventually you'll find the road that goes west to Knollcrest. Don't stop for anyone until you get there. Gregors is a grouchy old curmudgeon but he'll keep you safe until Lord Tilmont arrives."

She drew a steadying breath. "I don't think your husband's a bad sort, Clarette. Give him a chance. And if you see Gallagher . . ." She swallowed, felt tears well, and willed them back behind the floodgates. "Tell him my name is Savaana. Tell him I never wanted to lie to him." Strengthening her resolve, she rose silently to her feet. "Do you understand?"

"Perfectly. Next time I should get a sister who's not so bloody bossy," Clarette said, and standing, stepped onto the trail.

# Chapter 30

**S**avaana watched her sister stumble onto the path. Then she leapt for the lowest branch and caught it with both hands. Pulling herself up, she eased into the multicolored leaves. To her left, the rider was hidden from view, but from her vantage point she could see Clarette limp uphill, eyes downcast as if too exhausted to look up. The seconds passed like hours, but it was probably only moments before she heard the sound of galloping hooves. Clarette turned as if startled. Her eyes widened. She gasped, frozen in place. The hoofbeats thundered nearer. Clarette shrieked and spun about, but she only made it just past the towering oak before her legs gave way.

Savaana waited, strength coiled. And then he was there, almost upon them.

She leapt. Screaming as she did so, she hit him just as he was turning toward her. He lost his grip on his sword. It spun into the air, and then he was falling, grappling for her as he tumbled to the ground. She landed in the grass and leapt up, ready to spring toward the horse, but as she did so, he snagged her ankle. She shrieked and tried to yank free, but he was pulling her down. She toppled to the earth, fighting like mad.

"Run!" The word was a garbled shriek from her lips as she fought for freedom, but he was a trained warrior and had already recovered from the fall. She struck him in the face with her fists and scrambled to her feet, but suddenly his hands were on her throat. She felt her trachea compress, heard the blood pound desperately in her head, watched the world go black. But in that instant he was torn away. Air pumped into her lungs, and in some vague part of her brain she realized the noise she heard was not her pulse, but the hooves of the horse that had just trampled her attacker.

"Get on!"

She turned in a haze to find Clarette wheeling that same horse toward her.

"For God's sake hurry!" she shrieked as Savaana wobbled to her feet. She reached for the animal's heavy mane with her left hand, grabbed the saddle's high cantle with her right. It was like coming home. Her heel arced across the gelding's croup and then she was up, grabbing her sister's waist as she straightened. The horse reared and leapt forward, racing down the trail. It was then that Clarette cursed.

"The Irishman!"

Savaana leaned to the right, gazing past her sister's

streaming hair. And there in the middle of the path not forty feet ahead was Sean Gallagher. He stood as steady as a stone, a pistol raised in his right hand.

The air left Savaana's lungs in a hiss. She shook her head, unwilling to believe. He wouldn't betray her. Couldn't. But what did she know of him really?

"Dammit!" Clarette swore, and yanked their mount into the ragged underbrush just as a shot rang out.

The women gasped in tandem. Savaana twitched, tensed for the pain, but there was none. Someone screamed in agony behind them. Clarette spun the gelding in a circle just in time to see a man topple onto the trail. Facts jumbled like falling stones in Savaana's scrambling mind. Another shot sounded, and then, like a toppled sycamore, Gallagher dropped to his knees.

"No!" The word was torn from her lips even as a Ludrick stepped from behind a boulder not ten feet from where Gallagher had fallen.

Morning light gleamed off his brass buttons, flickered on the curved sword he carried in his right hand, the sword he pointed at the Irishman's still form.

"Come to me." His voice was heavy with an almost familiar accent. "Come to me and he will live."

Beneath them the gelding half reared with restive energy. Clarette glanced into the woods. So close to safety. Savaana could all but feel her thoughts. But the villain smiled.

"Go and he dies," he warned.

"The trees are our only chance," Clarette hissed.

"How will it be, princesses?" he asked.

"You barely know him," Clarette said, but Savaana was already slipping over the horse's rump. Her legs shook as she landed behind the animal.

"Don't be a fool!" Clarette rasped.

"Disappear," Savaana ordered her, and lifted her hands as she raised her voice. "My life for his," she called.

"Don't do this," Clarette said, circling the gelding.

The Ludrick grinned, a white swath of humor across his dark features. "Yours and your sister's."

Savaana shook her head again. "She's not my sister."

"And you lie like a Beloreich."

"She's my maid. You will let my maid and the Irishman go free."

"Your maid?" he said, and laughed as he glanced at Clarette. "I think not. She's all but identical to you."

"It was planned that way," Savaana said, still advancing. "So that she could take my place if needs be."

He straightened, tall and lean and swarthy. "If such is the case, I would suspect you to be the hireling since you are the one to sacrifice yourself."

Savaana drew herself up to her full height. "Do I look like a commoner to you?"

"You look like a Beloreich!" he said, and spat, but hatred was hardly new to one of Rom blood.

"And hence too good to hand myself over to a Ludrick." She was guessing wildly, hoping desperately. Gallagher remained unmoving on the rocky ground. "Yet I will surrender myself to you if you spare the man and my servant."

He hesitated. She hurried into the breech, trying to appear calm, controlled, though her heart was racing.

"Think what a hero you will seem to the others. There *are* others, I assume, who detest me as much as you."

"More than sands on the beach."

"Yet you are the one who captured me," she said, and raised her chin. "Step away from the Irishman."

"I do not take orders from *gunoaielor.*"

"I remain at your disposal only because he lives."

"I can kill you simply."

"I see you know very little of me," she said, talking slowly, rhythmically, though her hands shook with terror. Had she seen Gallagher move? Did he yet live? "I was raised by the wild Rom, taught to fend for myself." She didn't let her gaze stray from the brigand's eyes, but she was sure now that Gallagher's hand had inched forward, as if searching for a weapon, as if planning a coup. She had little time before he did something foolish, then. And what of Clarette? Savaana dared not turn to see what she was doing. "Step back," she ordered.

"I do *not* take orders from *gunoaielor,*" he snarled, and raising his sword, turned toward Sean.

In that moment, Savaana launched herself toward him, flipping end over end. But he leapt from her reach. She crouched, one hand on the earth, and tried to spin away, but he yelled as he charged. She twisted toward him and covered her face with her arm as his blade sliced downward. But at the last instant he arched his back, hissed, and rose on his toes.

Savaana scrambled backward, and as she did, he toppled forward, his sword clattering to the ground just inches from her feet.

She squeaked in terror and skittered back another few inches.

"What the hell do you think you're doing?"

She yanked her attention from the knife embedded in the brigand's twitching body. Gallagher stood, legs spread, expression thunderous.

"You're alive," she breathed, and felt her heart lurch crazily in her chest.

"A body should never be without a fine blade," he said, but she was already racing toward him.

He braced himself for the impact, and then she was in his arms.

"You're alive," she said again.

"So far," he agreed, and winced as she hugged him.

"I love you," she breathed.

"And I you," he said, and pushed her away a scant inch. "But who are you, lass?"

She laughed, euphoric, terrified, tremulous as she touched his face. "I think I might be a princess."

He scowled, trying to assimilate that. "And her?" He tightened his arm around Savaana's waist, almost oblivious to the pain in his side as Clarette rode near.

"My sister."

He nodded at the woman who rode close. "My brother sends his regards," he said.

"Your brother?"

"Alastar Buckingham."

Clarette's scowl deepened. "You couldn't have fallen for someone whose brother I hadn't slept with?"

"There may not be anyone," Savaana said, and as she did, a half dozen uniformed men stepped from hiding.

Two had guns. All had swords. One was a giant with a scarred lip and ancient eyes.

"I remember—" Savaana began, and stepped forward, but Gallagher snarled a warning and shoved her behind him.

The men came to an abrupt halt. "Your Highness," said the nearest, and dropped to his knees. The others followed suit.

A noise sounded in the woods. They turned as a unit. Three of them disappeared into the trees, silent as wraiths. But the eldest stepped toward her.

"Come now, *cea dulce,* we shall get you to safety," he said, but Gallagher put his arm across her body.

"She goes nowhere until I know far more than I do now."

"We have searched for the princesses for many years. There was a time we thought a woman named Milicent Hennessey might possess the Rough Jewels and therefore must be Her Royal Highness, but when we reached her place of residence, she was gone."

Milicent Hennessey, one of Clarette's many aliases, Savaana thought.

"Our search continued, but when His Majesty died with no heirs to take the throne, our quest became more urgent. We sent agents to scores of London shops in the hopes of finding the jewels and therefore the princesses. But 'twas luck more than anything that brought us to Smith's small shop only a few days past. And therefore to the princess."

"So you had her accosted in an alley?"

"We felt it necessary to make certain she was one of the two for which we searched. To see the moon tattoo for ourselves."

A muscle jumped in Gallagher's jaw. "You sound like little more than thieves and lechers."

The soldier drew himself to his full height. "I am Teodor of Bancastle, master of Delvania's royal guard. My people have protected the Beloreich since the mountains rose from the flatlands."

"Then your people have failed."

"And for that I deserve death," Teodor said, and dropping to his knees, gripped his blade between both palms, extending the grip.

"Holy hell," Savaana said, and stumbled backward. "What kind of place is this Delvania?"

"'Tis a place of honor and fortitude, *cea dulce*. Of courage and endurance, and strength."

"*Cea dulce?*" She tried the words on her tongue. They felt almost familiar.

"It means sweet one in our language. 'Twas what your princess mother called you before your exodus. Dorin traveled with you to this land. He was to keep you safe, but he lost you in a battle with the Ludricks."

The giant nodded, broad face solemn, ancient eyes sad. "For that, I, too, would be happy to die now that I know you are safe," he rumbled.

Savaana winced. "I don't think I like this Delvania," she murmured.

"I do," Clarette said, and Savaana turned toward her, breath held. Their gazes met and melded, sharing a dozen wild thoughts.

"Gentlemen," Savaana said, raising her voice and facing the guards once again. "Meet my older sister, *cea dulce*."

# Epilogue

Janica Ellabeth Beloreich, Queen of Delvania, wore a gown of powder blue to her coronation. Its train, studded with precious stones, was fourteen feet long and carried by five royal bearers. Her chestnut hair was upswept, secured by a dozen golden pins and embellished with a score of glistening diamonds. A thousand excited subjects lined the street down which she rode. Beneath her, an ivory stallion was led by two liveried guards. A cheer like thunder roared through the city as she waved one graceful hand. It was a storybook parade, but for the snarling giant who strode beside the queen's mount. Though Dorin had changed into Delvania's royal colors, he looked incongruous and dangerous as he held back the pressing crowd.

Tears filled Savaana's eyes as she watched from a balcony half a block away. She was dressed in the bright layered gown she had worn while entertaining the crowds only minutes before, and about her neck was a string of rough stones. Beside her, Sean wore a blacksmith's simple garb—leather breeches with a linen tunic. He smelled of wood smoke and freedom.

"She looks like a princess," Savaana said.

"I believe in this case that's actually an insult," Lord Tilmont said. He and Grandfather had accompanied them from England. But while the elderly Rom became reacquainted with relatives, Tilmont watched the festivities, saying a man should really be present at his wife's coronation. Although, in truth, their marriage had been annulled weeks before. Apparently Princess Janica had been promised to another well before her birth, making her union with the baron simply unacceptable.

"She looks like you," Wicklow corrected. But his name wasn't really Wicklow, of course. Or Gallagher. It was Michael Sean Buckingham. And he wasn't a penniless metalsmith. He was a gifted craftsman, a clever businessman, a wealthy merchant. He owned Smith's Ornaments, where Savaana had gone to have the necklace appraised. Indeed, he owned that shop and several others. Not to mention the foundry where the wares were created. Yet he seemed content to dress in worn leather and to shoe weary cart horses while others strutted past like preening peacocks.

"Do you think so?" Savaana asked, and felt her sister's separation with poignant tenderness.

Sean watched her. "Do you regret your decision, then?"

She shook her head. "I couldn't bear confinement," she said. "No matter how beautiful the cage."

But he continued to watch her as if trying to read her mind. Maybe he was jealous. She liked the thought of that, but if such was the case, she couldn't see it in his expression. He made a perfect blacksmith, strong, solid, comfortable with his place in the world. But she suspected he would also make a perfect gentleman. And a perfect father. She felt a bubble of giddy happiness rise inside her. "She has the adoration of thousands," he reminded her.

She watched him, drinking in every arresting feature, every dark, wayward hair. "And I have you."

His emerald eyes sparked with feeling. "That you do, lass. For as long as you'll have me."

She touched his cheek. "Forever, then."

Tilmont cleared his throat, but they barely remembered his presence.

"Forever," he agreed.

"So you'll marry me?" she asked, and leaned toward his roguish lips.

He remained perfectly still. "Do you vow to quit dancing for others?" he asked.

"No," she said, and smiled.

"What of your acrobatics? Will you cease those?"

"I'm an entertainer, Irishman. That you know. But there is one activity I vow to save for you alone," she said, and pressing lightly against him, curled a hand behind his neck. His muscles tightened . . . as well as other things.

"And what if I've no wish to see others ogling my wife?" he asked.

"Then I would suggest you don't look."

"The acrobatics are dangerous," he said. "I—"

"Oh for God's sake, man," Tilmont rasped. "Are you mad? The girl's far too good for you. Marry her before she comes to her senses."

Savaana grinned. "What say you, Wickersham?"

"Will you marry me?" he asked, and lifting his hand, produced an antique ruby set with diamonds.

She flicked her gaze to his mother's ring. "Try to stop me," she said, and kissed the corner of his mouth.

He sighed, then kissed her in return. "I doubt myself able to stop you from anything."

"Because you adore me so?"

"That, too," he said, perhaps remembering the athleticism she'd displayed in the past. "But . . ." He drew back. "You're not already wed, are you?" he asked, and she laughed.

"You're thinking of my sister."

"'Tis unlikely I'll *ever* think of another."

"Please," Tilmont pleaded. "You're going to make me bowke. If you're going to spout such dreamy foolishness, I'll have to find another balcony."

"The baron's uncomfortable," Savaana said, and Sean shrugged.

"He *did* lose two wives in the same week."

"Bloody hell," Tilmont said, and rising to his feet, strode stiffly out of sight.

Sean grinned, but Savaana sighed.

"Perhaps he honestly misses her."

"I thought you met her," he said, and she smiled wistfully.

"*I'll* miss her."

"Well, she is the sweet one," he said, tone dry.

"Perhaps she *will* be," she said, but he shook his head.

"There's only one *cea dolce*."

"I think she'll become what her people expect of her. She's an excellent actress."

"And I think being nice might very well be the death of her."

Savaana laughed. "She *did* return your mother's ring."

"I haven't had it checked yet. Perhaps it's paste," he said, and slipped it onto her finger.

"It's real to me," she said, and kissed him again, but worry still nagged her.

"What is it, luv?" he asked.

She fiddled with his collar. "It hardly seems fair. I have you and freedom and Grandfather. What does she have?"

"An immeasurable fortune and the fealty of a million enthralled subjects?"

"Maybe. But do you think she might have feelings for Tilmont?" She glanced toward the approaching procession.

"I think she'd eat Tilmont alive. Although, I'll admit, I've an idea he may be more than he appears."

She nodded, thinking the same. Apparently the baron had given Gallagher a pistol, so the Irishman could defend her. Where would Tilmont have come by a pistol? "It'll be interesting to see what he does next," she said.

"I'm more interested in what he did before."

"When he last spoke to Clarette before the coronation?"

"When he was in your bed."

She smiled and kissed his jaw. "Are you always so jealous?"

"Jealous, am I, lass?" he asked, and slipped his arms around her.

"It sounds like it."

"God help me."

"I think he already has. How are you feeling? Are you well? Are you mended?" she asked, and smoothed a palm over the bandage that still bound the wound in his side.

"Move your hand any lower and I'll be feeling a good deal more, regardless of the crowd."

She glanced up through her lashes at him. "Is that a threat, Wicklow?"

"'Tis a promise, lass," he said, and lifting her into his arms, carried her into their life together.

*At Avon Books, we know your passion for romance—once you finish one of our novels, you find yourself wanting more.*

May we tempt you with . . .

- **Excerpts** from our upcoming releases.

- Entertaining **extras**, including authors' personal photo albums and book lists.

- Behind-the-scenes **scoop** on your favorite characters and series.

- **Sweepstakes** for the chance to win free books, romantic getaways, and other fun prizes.

- Writing **tips** from our authors and editors.

- **Blog** with our authors and find out why they love to write romance.

- **Exclusive content** that's not contained within the pages of our novels.

Join us at
**www.avonbooks.com**

**AVON**

*An Imprint of* HarperCollins*Publishers*
www.avonromance.com

FTH 0708